CW00434969

SISYPHUS
UNLEASHED

SISYPHUS UNLEASHED

MICK MITCHELL

PUBLISHING

ABOUT THE AUTHOR

Mick Mitchell has completed an Open University Degree, gaining 2.1BSc (hons) in Arts and Humanities with English Literature. He has always read widely but never mixed in circles where knowledge or erudition was encouraged.

He has an interest in exploring the social history of ordinary working class people, and presenting it in his fiction work. This is a subject he knows well, having been born and bred in a mining community.

He now lives with his wife in South Nottinghamshire and is currently working on his second novel.

First Published in Great Britain in 2018 by DB Publishing,
an imprint of JMD Media Ltd

© Mick Mitchell, 2018

All Rights Reserved. No part of this publication may be reproduced, stored in a retrieval system, or transmitted in any form, or by any means, electronic, mechanical, photocopying, recording or otherwise without the prior permission in writing of the copyright holders, nor be otherwise circulated in any form or binding or cover other than in which it is published and without a similar condition being imposed on the subsequent publisher.

ISBN 978-1-78091-569-2

Printed and bound in the UK

Dedicated to Margaret May Mitchell
from whom I inherited a love of literature

CHAPTER ONE

The crowd assembled in the market square is enormous, even reaching as far as the top of Leeming Street. Several members of the crowd have climbed onto the Bentinck Memorial in the centre of the square to gain a better vantage point. The set is reaching its climax; a free homecoming gig for the people of Mansfield, performed by their very own working-class hero. One moment I'm blending flamenco-influenced fingerstyle playing with traditional blues; the next, I am hammering out power chords that shake the surrounding buildings like the thunderbolts of Zeus. The extended version of 'My Generation' reaches its crescendo. Banging my Gibson SG on the stage then waving it in the air, I create harrowing feedback noise which ends with my ritual sacrifice of the instrument, throwing it into the ecstatic crowd.

The trouble with this job is that you can end up a Walter Mitty type character. I turn off the portable cassette player; *Live at Leeds* is surely the best live album of all time. The big clock at the end of the shop floor tells me it's a quarter to three and the last shift is nearly done. I love Friday night shifts, starting at eight and finishing at three on Saturday morning; one small mercy on this unnatural shift. I prefer finishing at eight on Afters on a Friday evening and going straight into town, or even better, finishing at one on Earlies and taking the pay packet on the town. Working just seven hours instead of eight on a Friday means that something of the weekend can still be salvaged.

Of course, I shouldn't even be doing night shifts yet, at the age of sixteen. They couldn't get anyone to fill the vacancies for my job. I was hanging out with a group of scooterists who gathered upstairs at the White Hart when a woman came in asking if anyone wanted work. I liked going up to this scooter club meeting each week, mainly because I liked the music they played, mostly Northern Soul. Here they played records like 'Interplay' by Derek and Ray and 'Fortune Teller' by Benny Spellman. A friend of mine was seeing a girl from this club. Her mum

7

was personnel manager at one of Mansfield's hosiery factories and had come on a covert recruitment drive. I wasn't actually asked myself, but one of my friends dropped out and asked me if I wanted to go instead; anything to get my dad off my back. I had only been out of school a few days when he started complaining as I enjoyed a leisurely breakfast: 'You can't spend your whole life reading the paper and listening to Radio 1,' was his churlish advice. He'd tried to get me pressed into service at the pit, but I had defiantly refused. *The Black and White Minstrel Show* had been cancelled in 1978 and I had no intention of reviving the old blackface routine. A further opportunity to work at a video rental shop on the YTS had also resulted in failure, after my interview performance had proved anything but a triumph.

So here I am, a few weeks later, earning the princely sum of ninety pounds a week; twenty pounds for Mum and the rest for me to spend at the weekend. I had a feeling that today would be a memorable one. My best friend Myfanwy would be coming out of the gates of Lincoln prison in just a few hours' time. This coming evening would be a bacchanalian celebration of his freedom. You could say we had a kind of fucked up, Huckleberry Finn and Tom Sawyer relationship.

Derek, the knitter who I assisted, told me to get a last smoke while he reckoned up his production for the night. I sat in the smoke pen contemplating its yellow complexion. Oz and Harry were in there discussing the merits of an American porn film called *Taboo II*, comparing and contrasting it with its predecessor, *Taboo I*. I hadn't heard of this film, nor was I aware of its content, and asked if it was anything like *Porky's* or *Animal House*.

'No, bummer,' Harry replied somewhat pityingly. 'Bummer' was a standard term for a work colleague in that part of the factory. To be referred to as 'My old knacker' was an honour bestowed on only the most exalted workmate.

We were joined by a mechanic called Pappy, who pushed himself against me and began giving me lascivious looks. It was Pappy who would approach all the new youngsters and try to make them feel uncomfortable with his gay routine. Oz and Harry sat smirking as Pappy produced a pornographic magazine which contained photos of naked men whose appendages were of the proportion of stallions. I nodded and said, 'Yes very nice,' as he tried to gain my attention. I felt more embarrassed for him than myself: his camp routine was more like Dick Emery than anything rooted in reality. I had recently discovered that my brother Ian was gay, after our father caught him *in flagrante* with another young man. Ian was certainly nothing like the cretin who was sat next to me. I gave Pappy a big kiss on his cheek, which was the last thing he had been expecting. Oz and Harry cracked up laughing as Pappy walked away feeling somewhat embarrassed.

An old knitter known as Stubby came over for a quick drag. He was dressed in the standard uniform of the old men: denim bib and brace overalls, and a plaid shirt. Stubby took a couple of puffs on his Players Navy Cut and then snipped the cigarette with a pair of scissors. He contemplated my torn jeans with the epigram 'Oh to be a piss artist' written in biro above the knee. I had on my stripy green shirt, which was alternately referred to by my work colleagues as my pyjama top or a deck chair. My self-styled 'bastard child of the Beat Generation' image wasn't to everyone's taste, least of all my dad.

Replacing the remainder of his cigarette in his shirt pocket, Stubby scurried back to his machine to squeeze the last drops of production. He had earned the cognomen of 'Stubby' for his habit of stepping over to the smoke pen for a quick fix of nicotine and swiftly returning to his work. Time was money for people like him. Only break times were sacred, as the union had forbidden working during breaks that had been fought for over many decades.

I headed down the long corridor to the toilet to wash my hands. I contemplated the question of which was the best live album. Maybe *Kiss Alive II* is as good as *Live at Leeds*; I needed to consider the merits of each album. At the washbasins I joined Stewart Hopkins, who was telling Mahmoud from the yarn cellar about a man who worked at Clipstone Colliery who had an enormous cock. 'It was a beaut!' he exclaimed excitedly. Hopkins was a jovial old character who had warmed to me from my first day at the factory. With his thick-lensed spectacles and missing teeth, he reminded me of Cosmo Smallpiece.

'I fucking hate Cockneys!' he had explained on my first day. His aversion to what he referred to as 'Cockneys' dated back to an incident at a football match. He had been hit on the back of the head by a brick, thrown by a Spurs fan at Field Mill; back in the glory days when Mansfield Town were playing in League Division Two. Spurs fan would remember the period as a nadir in the history of Tottenham Hotspur. Stewart's favourite story was the one about West Ham United being beaten by Mansfield Town in the 1960s.

'Where the fackin' hell is Maaansfield?' Bobby Moore asked, according to Stewart. 'Well he found out that day, dint 'ee!' the old loon would announce triumphantly.

I began to put my copy of *Observations on the Feeling of the Beautiful and the Sublime* in my bag stashed behind the giant Bentley & Cotton knitting machine. There was always time to read once you'd got up to speed with the repetitive tasks involved in the production of men's knitwear. The only benefit of working nights was that the prying eyes of the management were all tightly closed.

'Ayup youth, is that a dirty book?' shouted Derek, with a cheeky wink.

'Kant,' I replied.

'Brian Cant,' said Derek, giving me a thumbs-up sign. 'Play Awaaay!'

'No, Immanuel,' I said, holding the book up for him to inspect.

'Emmanuelle, I knew it was a dirty book,' said Derek, then added, 'Lend us it when you've done with it.'

I said my farewells to Derek and hurried away to clock out. When the clock struck three, the assembled workers jostled for position at the clock machine. I collected my clocking-in card in readiness and joined some of the shift's colourful characters. Young Mo, who always reminded me of Keith Moon, would spend the shift trying to evade any kind of labour. He would shake his head as he passed by as if he had the weight of the world on his shoulders. 'It's all go, bummer,' he would say, 'I haven't had time to have a minute.'

Mo had been in the doldrums all week because his girlfriend had dumped him.

'How's it going, my old?' asked Old Tom, the nearest thing we had to a patriarchal figure.

'Terrible, mate, terrible!' Mo complained.

'What's up, my old knacker?' continued Tom with exaggerated concern.

'Not getting me hole, mate,' Mo replied remorsefully, slowly shaking his head from side to side. Tom turned round to me and gave me a sly wink.

He lit his pipe and then, pointing its tip at me, said, 'You're Norman Swift's lad, aren't you?'

'Yeah, 'fraid so. I'm Dean.'

'You take after him. I used to work with your dad at Grassmoor many years ago; tell him Tom Walker said hello.'

I had noticed the formidable-looking figure of Tom looking at me several times with what I assumed was an expression of disapproval. It was now evident that he had merely been trying to establish whether I was related to his old work colleague.

Zoot and Harry were two inseparable stoners who would sneak outside on nights to smoke a cannabis mix, equipped with their *Blue Peter*-style bong, made from a plastic bottle. When they went out on the town in their matching Hawaiian shirts they looked like Cheech and Chong doing a stint in the Beach Boys.

Spaceman Pete was a character most people gave a wide berth. Pete was a Christian of the happy-clappy variety, obsessed with Americana and harbouring a pathological hatred of socialism. He would race young workers at their tasks, laughing maniacally, regardless of his opponent's lack of interest. He mumbled something to me about Kinnock and evil men, before I managed to get out of his way. 'Sing us an Elvis song, Pete!' someone called to him, and he eagerly obliged. He began to sing some nonsense about Hawaii, dementedly gyrating his hips in a hopeless parody of the King.

I was occupied talking to Steve Nuttall, a tall and bespectacled rock 'n' roller with a blond, flattop haircut. He wore a King Kurt T-shirt with a picture of a drunken rat on it. He was in a band called The Queercats. He was telling me all about his Fender Telecaster guitar. He said they were doing a gig up in my neck of the woods in a couple of weeks' time. 'Great, I'm actually on days that week,' I said with one eye on the machine.

At last, the cards started being fed into the machine that documented the wasted hours of working-class purgatory. *Kerchunk!* it went, like a guillotine chopping off another head. Up the yard to the car park I scurried to fetch my pushbike, not daring to look back as I heard Pete cackling and running behind me, egged on by our colleagues. No doubt he wanted to denounce me as a Soviet spy. I was bound for freedom, at least until two o'clock on Monday afternoon.

I freewheeled down Sutton Road, passing the ghostly bus garage where a lonely radio blasted out music to the dozing buses. Tony Birch flew passed me on his racing bike, bidding me goodnight. Riding into the concrete world of Stockwell Gate, I admired the uninspiring Soviet-style architecture of the bus station and multistorey car park. The walkway that joined the big department store to the shopping centre was like a concrete Bridge of Sighs. Further on, two pubs faced each other, each the antithesis of the other. On one side stood the King's Head, the place to be at the weekend. Its ultraviolet entrance lit up the underwear of Mansfield's material girls and led to fun pub paradise. Across the road was the Blue Boar, with its fat old whores and their geriatric clientele. In the Blue Boar, ladies and gentlemen and children of all ages could enjoy the time of their lives. Ales spicier than any Flemish brew, flavoured with washing-up liquid, were served up. The back room was the whore's headquarters and the taproom entertained the old men. The jukebox endlessly played Ned Miller's 'From a Jack to a King' and 'Lightin' Strikes' by Lou Christie. The pool room was basically where anyone tall enough to reach the bar could play pool and carve graffiti on the benches, while sipping lager snakebite. I was still very much a fresher in drinking terms, and the King's Head was still out of bounds for my clearly underage face. In the Blue Boar I was already viewed as a man of the world, and it was here that I normally took luncheon.

I rode on through the almost deserted market square. A few pairs of lovers kissed and caressed on market stalls; all refugees of nightclubs, thrown together by drink and Phyllis Nelson. In this theatre-in-the-round, real-life tragedies and comedies were performed daily. Lawrence had experienced and captured the Dionysian spirit of the people of Notts in his books. A whole universe of characters that Shakespeare himself could not make up. These pubs and market stalls were the beating heart at the centre of the modest body of Mansfield. In another couple of hours, the fruit and veg stalls would be setting up, hours before their customers would emerge.

My freewheeling reverie ended as I began to pedal up Leeming Street, beginning the steep incline that would take me as far as the Queen Elizabeth Girls School and the downhill descent through Mansfield Woodhouse. Up the boulevard of enchantment I went, passed Chan's Garden, Brigadoon and Sally Twinkle's. I passed the cinema, which was dark and deserted. A week earlier I had spent the night there in an all-night orgy of horror films. I had spent much of the night in a drunken stupor, apart from an entertaining interval, spent watching a film about a psychopathic car; basically *Herbie* for grown-ups.

A young black lad was chatting with a girl next to the flower bed at the side of the Eagle Tavern. How strange it seemed, how these different worlds existed together: the industrial factory world that I was now desperately trying to pedal away from, and the adolescent romantic pleasure world that this couple were still occupying.

Onwards and upwards I pushed. My faithful old bike was a reminder of childhood Christmases. I remember my dad choosing it for me.

'You want a proper bike, with proper mudguards and Sturmey-Archer gears,' he had said; with its straight handlebars and quaint rubber horn, it was worlds away from the Grifters and racers which other boys owned. Maybe in Bruges or Amsterdam I would have looked the part, but not in a Notts mining village. Nevertheless, the old bike had been a useful mode of work transport at times when it was too early or late for buses. It would take me another half hour to get from Mansfield to Meden Vale, mercifully, mostly downhill.

The journey to work was always harder. I would always walk up the bigger hills; taking my time and catching my breath from the incessant wind which relentlessly pushed me back. Sometimes I would quench my thirst with a stolen bottle of milk. Riding to work on the day shift would begin after getting up at four thirty, to get to the Hosiery Mills just before the six o'clock shift. No bus services operated till it was tantalisingly too late. The whole ordeal of getting up in the middle of the night and cycling in all weathers was part of the endless treadmill that conversely eased off on the journey home.

I serenely freewheeled down the big hill that ended at the bridge which used to advertise Landers bread. Near the Black Bull pub, the Landers bakery had prepared bread for the populace of Mansfield till it had closed in 1981. As I turned and glanced down York Street, I wondered whether this was where the pianist John Ogden had been born. The concert piano player and composer, whose life had been marked by mental illness, was one of Mansfield's most famous sons.

There must have been something about the area that drew literary figures such as D.H. Lawrence and Lord Byron here. Byron himself had lived down the road at Newstead Abbey. I could imagine Byron being driven into Mansfield in his equipage to enjoy some convivial company. He would be sat by a fire in a tavern with his feet up, a fiddler playing 'The Black Nag' in the background. Accompanied by some new-found drinking buddies, he would rant a polemic on Peterloo.

'Are you supping that ale or what, M'lord, it's your round youth!' a veteran of the Peninsular War would interject.

'Tell us that cheeky one about Don and June!' requested an unemployed weaver called Ned.

The streets were empty as I approached the boundary of Mansfield Woodhouse. I was leaving the glamour of the big city now for a more pastoral setting. Past the golf course I rode. A week earlier, a group of us had walked home from town at this same hour, successfully attempting the Madness walk in this exact spot; half a dozen of us replicating the trademarked Nutty Boys walk with perfect synchronicity. Feggy Edwards had taken a golf flag from one of the holes and was running around the course, hollering some football nonsense. It seemed strange that someone like Feggy, who just a year earlier was still considered a bully, was now on the fringe of our circle of drinkers.

It was quite common for us to walk the seven miles from Mansfield to Meden Vale, back then. Drinking at the Sherwood Rooms, we would emerge long after the buses stopped running. Sometimes queuing for a taxi was too much hassle and it frequently degenerated into violence. Police would often stop and question us on these early morning rambles. Answering a question incorrectly to one of the officers might result in a reply of, 'Don't be fuckin' cheeky with me, you little bastard!' In the wake of the pit strike the police had often become easily confrontational, wound up by their Metropolitan cousins. I had recently attended a football match at Field Mill when one of my friends was randomly picked from the crowd and taken away with assorted others in a Black Maria; quotas needed to be achieved.

I pedalled past the fragrant yellow rape fields which would soon be deflowered for their oil. It would soon be daylight. Only working on shifts like these could you truly see the passage of the year. The brutal cold and dark mornings would be replaced by the miracle of early daylight that the majority of people slept through. The early morning summer air was moist and refreshing. Nature was becoming rich and overripe before it rotted away in the autumnal demise of the year. The road belonged to me, and the trees rustled gently, like a modest round of applause.

I arrived at the small hamlet of Spion Kop, which was named after a battle fought during the Boer War. This small settlement signalled the prelude to my arrival in Warsop. This small market town was bigger brother to the village of Meden Vale, where I lived.

Passing under the railway bridge that served as the gateway to Warsop, I was soon parallel with the high street that brought back so many early memories; the club where I had got my first job, collecting glasses. I had recently witnessed a gay man have a glass smashed in his face here for making too much fuss after a bingo win. Further on, the hairdresser's where my mother sat under a drier that looked like the papal tiara. In the library, with its shiny floor, the children's section beckoned me to sagas of Asterix and Noggin the Nog. Across the road from the library was a furniture shop which was always empty, and where a sinister mirror stared back at you. Further on was the butcher's, with dead rabbits hanging in its window. In the indoor market my dad would take me on a ride on a little orange speedboat.

I was now approaching my old comprehensive school, which I had walked away from in May for the very last time. It already seemed like another lifetime. Seeing the garage on one side of the road and the park on the opposite side brought back a memory of recent warfare. A group of bellicose fifth year boys had been challenged to fight, by a group of upstart fourth year pups. For three successive Fridays after school, one of each group was chosen to represent his year in single combat. This Homeric struggle had attracted massive attention from the student population. On the final Friday, the scheduled fight had begun early. Dozens of excited kids dashed across the road, stopping traffic in their haste. These gladiatorial contests were of special interest. What made these spectacles all the more attractive was the nature of the fighting. This was not the half-hearted wrestling of the playground, but bare-knuckled, no holds barred violence. All was peace and quiet now as the River Meden meandered alongside me.

The Meden Comprehensive School churned out foot soldiers for the local mines and factories. Parents who had ambitions for their children would send them to schools which statistically yielded higher academic success rates. Supercilious pedants complain about the use of incorrect grammar, but I don't remember ever being taught any. The only grammar I ever remembered learning was French past participles; some good they would do you when buying an ice cream in Boulogne. The only thing I could clearly remember was the checklist for the metalwork tools: rule, scriber, centre punch, one small smooth file, two large rough files, engineer's try square, hammer.

My one ambition in life was to write epic poetry, just like Homer or Milton. Canonical literature was another aspect of the arts we were denied at school. The fact that I wasn't put off by any adequate learning of literature at school made it something special just for me, like rock music; this, combined with the fact that it was above my dad's level of comprehension, made literature and poetry even more attractive. I was going to write an epic poem on the history of Britain in Spenserian stanzas:

Welcome to my history of Britain,
In the stanza style of the *Faerie Queene*.
Although at times somewhat crudely written
Neither Spencer, Byron or in-between.
A little rude and base but not obscene,
A product of my whimsical foibles
Each age and event, I shall paint a scene,
From the Stonehenge circle to The Beatles,
Chaucer and Wellington and other notables.

I passed the old water mill and checked the time on the church clock, which said 3.35. Warsop had a church and mill here since the eleventh century, according to the Norman Domesday Book. The road here would continue passed the church, up the big hill into the rural world of Cuckney and Norton. I turned right before the church through Old Church Warsop. This area was a middle-class enclave sandwiched between the mining communities of Meden Vale and the rest of Warsop. People here owned big gardens with fruit trees laden with rich pickings for scrumping enthusiasts. I was just a few minutes away from home now.

As I cycled quickly up the last stretch of road towards the village, I noticed a light shining briefly. In the woods at the end of a field on my right I could clearly see the beam of a torch intermittently shining. Someone would be in the woods, lamping for rabbits. The idea was to shine a torch or lamp onto a nearby rabbit, which would become mesmerised by the light, making it an easy target for a pellet gun. During the strike, such pastimes had risen in popularity as hungry strikers in the area had sought food for their families. Poaching on the whole had a rich tradition in the area, with the forests, rivers and parks of the Dukeries providing fish and fowl aplenty for both gentry and peasantry.

I heard the distant sound of continuous gunfire, which meant that the army must be training on Budby Common. The common, which we always referred to as the army grounds, was situated at the far end of the woods between Meden Vale and Edwinstowe. Budby Common belonged to the Ministry of Defence, and entry to the public was prohibited. Despite the restrictions, boys would make expeditions to the army grounds, where it was possible to climb into several disused tanks. In the age of the cruise missile, the sounds of the military manoeuvres were a chilling reminder of the Cold War that threatened to annihilate humanity.

I turned through the alley that led up to my home. I lived in the new estate nicknamed 'the reservation', so called for its population of migrant colliers from the north-east. When County Durham's mining industry had the heart ripped out of it, many had migrated to pits like Welbeck. The village had not even had a proper name until a decade ago, when it had officially been renamed Meden Vale. Until then, it had been simply called Welbeck Colliery Village; a name that did not inspire visions of the utopian socialism of Robert Owen and New Lanark. I looked up at the mountainous lunar landscape of the pit tip, noticing the lights of a vehicle up there like some kind of moon buggy. Someone was still up there working, but for me it was the weekend: I was free.

CHAPTER TWO

The man in the moon buggy was lord of all he surveyed; a huge pile of shale and other by-products of the coal industry, dug from the underworld. Daylight was descending on the valley as far as he could see, to the forest and beyond, where Edwinstowe nestled. It was the weekend, and he hated weekends. Alex had once loved weekends, coming home to his beloved Maggie and the boys. She had left him for another man, and his son John had packed and left a year ago, growing tired of his father's drinking and depression. Bouts of self-loathing had ultimately turned into rage, and he had turned his anger on his son one night and knocked him into a glass-fronted cabinet. A night in the casualty ward at King's Mill gave John enough thinking time to decide to move on quickly. The following day, when Alex returned from his shift driving the tip lorry, he learned that John had gone. *FUCK YOU!* was the message painted across the living room wall in red paint. He had helped himself to a few quid before taking off. It wouldn't be enough to get very far, and Alex wished he could have at least given him more to get by on.

Alex hadn't touched another drop of alcohol since that night. He spent as much time as possible at work, and then slept as much as possible, with the help of the tablets he had got from the doctor. His interest in football had completely dried up. He used to love his trips to watch Forest with John, until the boy had got old enough to prefer the company of his friends. He could no longer even concentrate on the TV to watch a game any more. His wife had phoned him after John had left, saying he was okay, but she wouldn't say where he had gone. Bridges had been burned completely in that department. He had hoped at one stage that her new relationship might just be an infatuation and she would return. She had filed a petition for divorce now, and he had received the papers on Monday morning.

Everything had rapidly gone out of control after Kevin had died. Their eldest son had died during the Falklands War, three years earlier; killed during the bloody Battle of Mount Longdon. It had been no consolation for the family when they were told that the battle had been an important, strategic victory for the British troops. It seemed like he had hardly even got off his mum's tit before he had signed up for the army, and then been killed nine months later. Nine months he had lasted, like an inverted gestation period which ended his life.

Alex and Maggie had retreated into their own personal world of grief. They had not shared their feelings, but instead built a wall of sorrow around themselves. John had lost a brother whom he hero-worshipped, but he had somehow been isolated from his parents' spiral into inward despair. Maggie had found solace in the arms of another man. Alex had found no such escape from the demons which had found a home in his head.

Maggie had left around the time that the pit strike started. Alex had driven past the picket lines each day, oblivious to their animosity and ambivalent to their cause. He had no intention of staying away from work, it was all he had. When Kevin had died he had felt sorry for himself, as he did when Maggie left him. Even when he had laid out John and put him in hospital, he had wallowed in self-pity. But now he had gone through the pitying stage. He felt self-loathing, and hatred for the world he had to inhabit each day. His self was just a burden to him now. His body was just a slave that went through the motions, controlled by the negative energy that ruled him and forced him to go on each day.

He climbed out of the lorry to go for a piss. When he had finished, he stood still for a moment to take in the fresh air and find solace in the silence. After a moment of quiet, Alex recognised the familiar sound of guns firing on Budby Common. He immediately imagined his son, alone and afraid in the dark, on a cold and distant island. He got back inside the lorry and hurriedly turned the ignition key; anything to drown out the sound of the guns. It was getting light, but this hour of the morning had never felt darker for Alex. Something snapped at that moment inside Alex's mind, and he decided it was time to prepare to escape this infernal world.

★ ★ ★ ★ ★

In London, frantic preparation was already underway for the concert at Wembley Stadium. In less than six hours' time the gates would be opening to let in the eager fans who had queued up early to get to the front of the stage. Engineers were still working on the revolving stage to ensure its smooth operation. It was crucial that the stage would revolve, so that each act could have its own equipment ready to perform. Time was at a premium, and to get each act on at the appointed time meant organisation of military precision. The first act was scheduled to go on stage at twelve noon.

John had been part of a team that erected the safety barriers in front of the stage area. He had volunteered his services for free, in the spirit of the entire Live Aid endeavour. Although he could have done with the cash, he felt excited to be part of the historic event. He also believed his efforts might hold him in good stead for any future work. The whole affair had been organised in such a brief period that everything was being put together on the hop. The pitch area had to be covered to protect the turf from damage. Meanwhile, the lighting and sound equipment was still being tested before the show. John had been there since five o'clock on the previous afternoon. Al Wilson had brought them up in his van from the digs in Kilburn. They had done all this a week earlier at Wembley, for a Bruce Springsteen concert. John remembered his dad bringing him to see Forest play Wolves in the League Cup Final once. Now it was a concert venue as well as a cathedral of football. Thinking back, he wished he'd been watching Bruce Springsteen that day, instead of Forest losing to Wolves. When Al picked them up, John got in the front with him.

'Kilburn and The Highroads, eh! Ian Dury!' said Al.

'Yeah,' replied John with a wry smile, wondering what the fuck the old hippy was wittering on about. Too many drugs that lad, he concluded. John had heard Al saying the same thing a week ago to Jean Louis when they had been picked up on Kilburn's main street. Maybe it was a song or album by Dury.

It was shaping up to be a beautiful day and John would spend half of it in bed. He was just glad to finally have a place to stay. Things were finally starting to settle down now. It had been hard since that first day, coming down on the National Express coach. John had only managed to get together a couple of hundred quid, which he knew wouldn't last long. His funds had quickly run out after a couple of weeks in a cheap bed and breakfast. He had ended up sleeping rough for a while, until he had found himself in the company of a group of punks who invited him to stay in their squat. His guitar had been the first thing to go when funds had run out.

His attempt at busking had yielded enough for a couple of cups of tea. He knew he should've learned at least another song before he left home. His entire repertoire had consisted of 'The Boxer' by Simon and Garfunkel. He didn't think he had been all that bad. Paul Simon wasn't so great without Art Garfunkel's harmonies.

A punk band he had seen a few times came down to stay at the squat and organised a gig there. Bostik Tea Party were a hardcore punk band from Leeds, who had played regularly in Mansfield with local bands. It was during the band's stay that John met Al. This thirty-seven-year-old hippy had been around the scene since the days of the UFO Club, where he claimed he had met Jimi Hendrix and Syd Barrett. He had spent a couple of years living in a bus in a layby in Pembrokeshire with a group of travellers. Too many confrontations with the police had convinced him that it was time to settle down and lay down some roots. He wore his long black hair in a pigtail; the top of his head was now completely bald. Hailing from Washington in Durham, his accent was more *Auf Wiedersehen Pet* than Haight-Ashbury. It was this lank and bony hippy who had found John somewhere to live, and the occasional work setting up various live events over the summer.

Al was talking to some guy who seemed to be in charge. They shook hands and then he came jogging over to where John and his colleagues had finished their final task.

'They think it's all over – it is now!' he cried out with his hands in the air.

John had no trouble recognising Al's latest reference. He had seen the archive footage on TV of England winning the World Cup, and recognised Kenneth Wolstenholme's famous words. It was time to knock off. Twelve hours had flown by since they had arrived. Queen had been doing a soundcheck when John had first started work the previous evening.

'Get some sleep, lads, we're back again to clear up at eleven tonight,' said Al, looking through his rear-view mirror as they left behind the view of the famous twin towers. Al turned over the cassette of *Revolver* that was sticking out of the tape player, and after a few seconds 'Good Day Sunshine' began to play. No doubt 'Tomorrow Never Knows' would call time before the day was out.

* * * * *

Spike, Dog and Sammy all crossed the black pipe one by one. First Spike, who expertly walked across the metal pipe, which was just wide enough for someone without circus training to traverse. Dog and Sammy both straddled the pipe for their crossing, afraid of falling into the shallow waters of the River Meden. The famous black pipe had provided a shortcut to and from the Meden School for many years. It was some kind of water pipe or sewage pipe crossing the river; considered too hazardous and narrow for many, a source of boisterous adventure for others.

They had shot a couple of rabbits but had soon become bored and weary of their sport. Earlier in the night, they had surreptitiously sneaked onto the pit yard and stolen some bricks for Sammy's dad. They walked up the field from the river up to the village. All three wore black, fourteen-hole Dr Martens boots. Spike's had red laces in his, which might suggest National Front affinities to some, but he didn't care for any of that. Sammy had brought red laces for his pair and had been confronted by a large black man with dreadlocks, who ordered him to take them out in front of him. Spike had on his donkey jacket that he used for these outings. The other two wore black shiny pilot jackets that could be bought cheaply at the army surplus shop. Each wore a woollen hat on the back of their head like a Jewish Kippah. Spike removed his hat, revealing his lank Mohican that hung limply down the left side of his head, leaving the tattoos on the right side exposed. He couldn't be arsed to keep getting it spiked in the fashion that had given him his nickname. He was still a punk and an anarchist at heart, but he was beginning to realise that he didn't need to wear a uniform to identify himself.

Daylight was emerging quickly, revealing the prospect of a fine morning. He thought about meeting up with Mel again later that day. They had been spending a lot of time with Mel's mate Kaz and her boyfriend Danny. Danny owned an old Datsun car and they'd had several outings. They had driven to Clumber on Tuesday night, Danny and Kaz fucking in the front while Mel and himself got down to business in the back. It had been okay; Mel obviously enjoyed it more than he did. He had noticed her frequently looking over at the other pair which evidently was getting her warmed up. He should have been at work on Friday night but he couldn't be arsed. In fact, he hadn't been in all week; he hated nights, in fact he hated the pit altogether. He would prefer to be on the dole like most of his other friends, sharing a bumper bottle of cheap cider under a tree somewhere.

They walked along the hedge of a field which ran parallel with the road, which led them to the rear of the old concrete bus stop. They crossed the road and climbed over the fence at the back of Sammy's. The bricks were stacked behind the shed in the gap next to the fence. Sammy's dad was planning to build something or other which would never materialise; his big ideas never did. He had always promised to do this and that for Sammy and the other kids, but they were lucky if he even remembered them at Christmas and birthdays. Spike noticed that Sammy was wearing the Exploited 'Fuck the USA' T-shirt he had given him. He had been so pleased to have received this old black T-shirt that it was now practically in tatters from so much wear and tear.

In the house, Lupo the dog was waiting to welcome them. Lupo was some kind of greyhound crossbreed. Sammy's dad said it was a Heinz 57 varieties dog. Spike didn't know what that meant. They all loved Lupo, who had to stay home when they went out lamping. The sound of a gun going off nearby would send him running in panic. Lupo had no road sense at all, and if left out in the garden would crawl through the hedge and a search party would have to follow. After receiving the mandatory fussing, he returned to his hiding place under the kitchen table accompanied by a pork bone with fluff on it.

Spike crashed out in an old armchair, and Dog and Sammy sat on the two kitchen chairs around the table. There was no covering on the bare floorboards apart from a few sheets of cardboard. Spike didn't bother asking for a cup of tea as there wouldn't be any milk, let alone tea, and he was too tired to bother stealing a bottle from a doorstep. He stretched and then got up to go, noticing the old record player in a corner. 'Headbutts' by John Otway and Wild Willy Barrett was still sat on the turntable. That had been John's record, it hadn't moved off that turntable since he had done a runner. Maybe Sammy's dad would make the effort to change the plug on the record player one day, so they could listen to it again. There was more likelihood that the old rogue would get Sammy to steal another one from school. Spike muttered a weary farewell and headed home.

Seeing that record of John's had brought memories flooding back. The two friends had been inseparable before John had headed off to London. Things weren't the same without him. It was okay hanging around with Dog and Sammy, but the two weren't even out of school yet. Both clung to him and seemed to view him as some kind of hero. He missed the conversations he and John had when they had a smoke. He fondly remembered the trips to the Porterhouse at Retford to see bands. He remembered how they had ended up spending the night with two girls in a bus, in a bus garage in Langley Mill.

It was too much of a nice morning to be indoors, so instead of going home to his grandad's house, he decided to crash in the field behind the bus shelter. After crossing back over the road to the field they had recently emerged from, he made himself comfortable by the hedge. He took out the half bottle of vodka from his coat and drank.

John had sent him a postcard from London recently. He'd basically said he was okay, and had written an address down in the hope that Spike would visit. He was resolved that he would go and join his friend. He would probably hitch there if he couldn't get the money together for the coach fare. He mused on this while he polished off the vodka, then settled down to sleep like a faun in Arcadia.

★ ★ ★ ★ ★

Tony had gone like the clappers to get to Dawn's on Blake Street. He knew that Dean, the new youth he had passed earlier, came the same way and would know that this wasn't Tony's normal direction home. Lying in bed with Dawn after an hour of passion, he lay exhausted while Dawn seemed to have dozed off. The alarm clock on the bedside table said 4.45 and he knew it was time to roll a last cigarette and make a move. Dawn's husband would be coming home from his shift at Mandora soon. It seemed as though everyone had been on nights.

He stroked the little tuft of hair on the small of her back. She had some hair on her buttocks as well. He found these hairy regions strangely attractive. He loved her wide hips and large, pendulous breasts with their big and dark nipples. Mandy's nipples were small and pink. She was slim and there was not a trace of hair on her back and bottom. Paradoxically, he found something far more womanly in the slightly masculine features that distinguished Dawn.

He put his right arm around Dawn's waist, his hand wandering down to explore her most private parts again. She snatched his hand away with a giggle.

'You dirty bastard, isn't twice enough?' she whispered.

'I've got to crack on, he'll be back soon,' he replied.

'Shit, what time is it?' She leapt up to look at the time.

He jumped out of bed and hastily pulled on his jeans and black T-shirt.

'If he would just fuck off, everything would be fine!' Dawn considered, with a distant look in her eye.

'Yeah, well let me know and I'll walk out and come running straight away,' Tony replied.

Dawn looked at him, knowing full well that he would never leave Mandy and the kids.

'Aww, do you love me, duck?' she said, knowing he would say anything for sex. She had heard it all before with her cheating husband.

'Course I do, duck. You know I would,' he replied, like a fifteen-year-old with his first crush.

'Yeah righto, tell me owt,' she replied, pushing him towards the door with a squeeze and a slap of a buttock.

Cycling away he suddenly felt weary, and his former euphoria was subsiding into doubt and guilt. Was she just using him? What if her husband found out? Would he give her a good hiding? Would he give him a good hiding? No, it was time to stop this. It wasn't as though he had been in an unhappy relationship. Mandy was great, and he would do anything for his kids. It had all just seemed to have come out of nowhere. Dawn worked in the canteen at the hosiery mills and they had flirted for several years, each time he paid for his full English on the day shift. Last Christmas they had got talking, down in a pub during the annual work's piss up. One thing had led to another. Now, six months later, things seemed to be getting more intense.

He headed down Bath Lane and was feeling weary now. Mandy had got him up at eleven on the previous morning. They had caught the bus into town then walked up Sutton Road to get his wage packet. They had a quick half in the William IV, then headed back into town for the shopping and paid the TV rental at Wigfalls. They fetched the kids from school, then headed home. He had just nodded off in front of *Blockbusters* when Mandy's mum had come around to make a fuss of the kids.

It had certainly been an eventful day, what with one thing and another. The bike picked up speed as it headed towards the bottom of the hill. He had begun to relax as he freewheeled down the hill, enjoying the early morning sun. Suddenly, his head nodded and he momentarily dropped asleep; just a second, long enough to veer into a parked car. He awoke as the bike hit the rear of the green Ford Escort and he was catapulted face first into the rear windscreen. The green transparent windscreen sticker at the front of the car had the name Colin on the right side. On the passenger side of the sticker was the name Dawn.

CHAPTER THREE

Hawkeye and B.J. were in the Swamp, enjoying the fruits of the gin still. Hawkeye was wearing a straw Stetson while B.J. was sporting a fez. Both are singing 'By the Light of the Silvery Moon' to the accompaniment of B.J.'s ukulele. Winchester is futilely trying to concentrate on *Prufrock and Other Observations* amidst the racket. Meanwhile, Clinger is trying to get his discharge by pretending to be Whistler's mother, complete with frame. Hot Lips has fallen in love with an injured officer who turns out to be a serial bigamist. I always think the blond woman in *Cagney and Lacey* looks like Hot Lips. The programme is set during the Korean War, but I always think it's the Vietnam War because people are always dressed in Hawaiian shirts and funny hats. I decided that I needed find out more about the Korean War in the encyclopaedia.

I'd spent the last hour catching up on TV that I'd taped from earlier in the week. I crumbled the last smidgeon of Lebanese Black into a Pot Noodle when I got in and it was finally starting to kick in. Andy Kershaw's face appeared on *Whistle Test* like a rock music sphinx talking in riddles. All of a sudden, Kershaw transformed into Sade, shrouded in purple light, and began singing 'Is it a Crime'.

Like a vision of Lady Day painted by Gaugin she sang to the accompaniment of that busted old tenor saxophone. His best years were over, playing at Ronnie Scott's with the likes of Tubby Hayes and Joe Harriott. Then he'd got a reputation doing session work for some of the cats on the pop scene. That was where he'd met her. The other guys in the band didn't have a clue about her relationship with this older man. They laughed when they saw him looking at her, he didn't stand a chance.

I float down a stream of musicality that seems to last an eternity before my reverie is disturbed by the sight of Ivor Cutler, dressed like Great Uncle Bulgaria and singing a song about a dead mouse. Maggie the budgie is also evidently disturbed by this abrupt change of ambience. I uncover the blue budgerigar, who stretches and stands on one leg and then the other, in anticipation of another exciting day. The old bird was getting on a bit now. We had inherited her when Grandad had come to live with us a few years ago. He had died the previous Christmas, leaving this orphaned avian pet.

Grandad had come to live with us after Grandma died. After the death of his beloved, his mental health had declined rapidly. We'd first been alerted to this when we paid him a visit one day and he refused us entry. He claimed that my parents were stealing from him, uttering a string of expletives that left my parents in tears. I had never once heard him use swearwords before. Once installed with us, he would often wander off back to his home in Chesterfield. He would turn up some hours later accompanied by a police officer. His trousers were caked in mud from his peregrinations through ploughed fields. His pockets contained cream crackers that he had stored for sustenance.

Grandad was born under the warped, green and twisted timbers of the Crooked Spire. Most spires pointed straight to Heaven like an arrow. The spire of the Church of Saint Mary and All Saints was suggestive of a more tortuous route, more suited to *The Divine Comedy*. Grandad had been too young to fight in the First World War and too old when the next war came along. He was a veteran regular of the King Coal Regiment when the Bevin boys came volunteering. He lived to be the last survivor of the Grassmoor Colliery explosion of 1933, that took fourteen lives and left eight injured.

I opened the curtains and looked out at the perfect July morning. The village often seemed to be in sepia, but it was one of those *Wizard of Oz* days where everything was magically transformed into Technicolor. The hydrangeas were blooming in the garden and would be getting thirsty. Cabbage White butterflies were already doing their rounds. I liked the Cabbage Whites best of all the butterflies. They didn't have the Zen pretensions of the Orange Tips, or the martial self-importance of the Red Admirals. They were just like average people, trying to navigate their way through the mysteries of life.

The huge figure of Raf Chlipala lumbered up the street with his two dogs. The old Pole would always be out early with his two old dogs. The old German Shepherd was blind, and the black Labrador deaf. When the German Shepherd stopped, the Labrador would always turn round and guide its companion onwards. Raf had been in England since he had served with the Polish Volunteer Air Force in World War Two. It suddenly occurred to me that the man called Raf had served in a squadron of the RAF. This giant of a man was a keen gardener, and would no doubt have some of his tomatoes ready for us.

Raf's walk would take him past the pine trees and up the hilly field with the pit tip at the top, extending its height. Around the perimeter of the tip was a modest woodland area. Chestnuts could be picked here each autumn and fragments of discarded erotica could be found anytime. Old ruins of bunkers and buildings from World War Two were hidden amongst the woods like a poor man's Pompeii. Nobody seemed to know what had gone on here during the war. Several of the ruins had filled with water that became a regular settlement for frogs. I once took home some tadpoles in a jar. Maybe four or five lived long enough to grow legs and hop to freedom. You could learn a lot about nature, growing up amongst the woods and parks of Nottinghamshire.

I was beginning to feel weary. The effects of the hash were wearing off and were being replaced by the natural trippy sensation induced by lack of sleep. I was wrestling with Morpheus, who was dragging me and my outstretched fingers from those rosy digits proffered by Aurora. I desperately wanted to begin the weekend and forfeit sleep in favour of consciousness.

I returned to the images and sounds of the television set. Some remnant of the Sixties was making a comeback with a new album. His long spiky hair was dyed blond. He wore a jacket with the sleeves rolled up and a T-shirt with some kind of Soviet artwork on it. He was raving about this new project which he had recorded in Antigua, with the hip producer who was making a name for himself by recycling the careers of rock dinosaurs.

I focused my attention on the Alpine scene above the television. This picture had always fascinated me since I was a small boy. If I studied the range of peaks horizontally, they would form a face; a pointed nose here, a chin or eyelid there. I would often play this game with the flowery patterns of wallpaper and curtains, finding strange creatures hidden within.

I heard my father creeping slowly down the stairs; the joints still stiff after a troubled night's sleep. Each time he went down that black hole it would chew him up and spit him out more broken each day. He would be going out to work soon to reap the rewards of the overtime that would purchase a week's holiday in Wales in September. I listened to him shuffle into the kitchen and fill the kettle. We would respectfully avoid each other, conversation for us was mutually discomfiting. The last time we had exchanged words was when he had returned one night from the club and announced, 'You can smoke yourself to death, you can drink yourself to death, fuck you!' He had followed this with a two-fingered benediction of contempt; all this because he saw me rolling a cigarette during the brief interlude between school and work. He had already written me off as a bad job. I think he had been hoping for a girl before my mother had given birth to me. Since discovering that Ian was gay, he only had me to project his anger and disappointment towards.

The only time me and my father had really found any common ground was on our visits to watch football matches at Chesterfield. For several years we'd spend Saturday afternoons at Saltergate, with its medieval toilets and tinderbox of a grandstand. The smell of cigarette smoke and Bovril was tempered with the odour of drunken flatulence. Players with names like Tingay and Tartt played their hearts out in the hope of a place in the Second Division of the Football League. Decked out in my blue and white scarf and hat, my proudest moment was catching a ball signed by the team. One day I grew tired of spending my time watching football with him; he never truly forgave me for this betrayal.

The bitterness and resentment that had festered since the strike, in men on both sides of the dispute, was hard for me to comprehend in my juvenile naivety. Dad had worked throughout the dispute like most of the miners in the village, but I could see that since the conflict, something had changed in him. There had been an altercation with someone in a club car park and another incident where he'd found his car with a smashed window. He showed no outward signs of any of this affecting him, but I could tell the whole thing had taken its toll on him. He had supported earlier strikes, but like many of his colleagues he had voted against the recent strike, which had proceeded regardless of opposition. Arthur Scargill, the leader of the NUM, had vetoed taking a national ballot on taking industrial action and the strike had gone ahead regardless.

Scargill had visited the village one evening to deliver a speech at the old junior school I'd once attended. When he arrived, he was mobbed by cameramen and photographers from the national media. He strode through them into the same school hall where I had said prayers and played the part of a nativity shepherd. Rows of his supporters awaited him. With their arms folded, they earnestly listened to the rhetorical oration of a man more like Zeppo Marx than Karl. As we watched through the window, growing increasingly bored, a friend suggested we should 'moon' at Scargill.

Little of this had meant anything to me during the conflict. Dad had actually asked me if everything was okay at school, in an uncharacteristic display of concern. I couldn't remember anyone mentioning the strike at school throughout the whole affair. Occasionally, pairs of policemen would patrol the streets where people were more accustomed to seeing the village bobby on his bicycle. Once I saw a policeman in riot gear riding past to give his horse some exercise. The only evidence of schism in the community was when the kazoo-blowing, juvenile jazz band was disbanded.

I decided to creep away to my bedroom to avoid any possibility of an encounter with pater. I could hear him preparing his flask for work, and I quickly crossed from living room to stairs while he was occupied in the kitchen. Up the stairs I fleet-footedly climbed and crossed the landing, to the seclusion of my secular hermitage.

Once inside, I walked over to open a window. Pushing the curtain out of the way, I opened the latch and pushed it open, sticking my head out to survey the summer scene. I breathed in deeply the scent of dew-fresh grass. I looked at the clear sky over the pit tip. I remembered looking at the sky like this when I was very small. I had no concept of the size of the Earth then, and imagined the endless lands that stretched forever for countless explorations and adventures. How small my world seemed now, compared with the possibilities of my infant imagination.

I closed the window and retreated behind the curtain, surreptitiously watching another dog walker passing. It was Mr Wright with his Border Collie, which was fouling the pavement in front of nosey old Mr Fleet. That would serve him right for spying on me when I was trying to watch a dirty video.

I lay on the creaky old bed and looked at the posters on the wall. Mostly they were posters advertising gigs that I had taken down from various locations after they had been hastily fly-posted. They were mostly written in marker pen, and advertised bands with names like The Scum Dribblers, Greetings From Moscow and Concrete Sox. Hardcore punk bands would play regularly at venues such as the Folkhouse, The Malthouse and the Beer Cellar. It had been at one such event that I had first met Heidi.

Just over a week ago, I had headed into town to see the Scum Dribblers play a Thursday night session at the Beer Cellar. I'd already drunk slightly too much before arriving and found myself slipping on the narrow staircase that led to this subterranean bolthole. On my arse I slid down this cubist helter-skelter, and came out in the corridor where a plaster knight in armour guarded the entrance. It was here that I collided with a group of girls. One of the group began to berate me for spilling her drink and demanded that I buy her another.

After buying her another glass of Woodpecker, we began to get acquainted. They had dropped into the Beer Cellar on their way up to the cinema. They were all celebrating completing their O level exams. While we were talking, Spike and his little entourage came in. While Spike got the drinks in, his underage buddy Sammy waited in the corridor. A huge skinhead known as Gunther had come over and pinned Sammy against the wall with his hand around his neck. Spike quickly came out and grabbed Gunther, spinning him round and headbutting him repeatedly until he crumpled to the ground. The girls had quickly fled from the carnage and the sweet cacophony began.

I had seen her again the following Saturday afternoon, sat in the Four Seasons shopping centre with her friends. She had been very friendly and said she would be out next Saturday, and would I try not to spill her drink if I saw her. I said I couldn't promise anything but would try not to make any grand entrances. I had been thinking about this all week, analysing every nuance of my performance and her reaction. I would have to try and play it cool if I met her again. Descending into some kind of demented version of Jerry Lewis doing an impression of Woody Allen was not the way to win a girl.

I continued to study the pictures that adorned my bedroom. My favourite posters were prints of Salvador Dali paintings which my brother had left behind. One was entitled *Metamorphosis of Narcissus* and the other *Swans Reflecting Elephants*. I always preferred *Swans Reflecting Elephants* to the other poster. Something about the clouds and the man in the background reminded me of the Terry Gilliam cartoons I'd seen on *Monty Python's Flying Circus*. The swans and trees in the centre of the picture cast reflections on a lake which looked like elephants. This image always reminded me of the time I'd walked in the woods and thought that I'd seen elephants grazing in a nearby field. The elephants had been bales of hay which for a moment had flashed by my peripheral vision. I had been enchanted by the notion of elephants grazing peacefully in a field in Nottinghamshire. The Dali poster always reminded me how the senses cannot always be trusted. I was sceptical of the ideas of philosophers like Locke and Descartes about the mind. I regarded the mind to be as untrustworthy as the senses; *ergo* I might be.

I began to drift off into a sleep filled with pleasant dreams. I dreamt I was watching a situation comedy about an agency for strippers. In this episode, the strippers were accidently booked to perform at a Women's Institute meeting. I then dreamed that the Joker was chasing me through the village in a huge purple airship.

What a wonderful adventure playground sleep is for the unconscious mind. The Id spends all its waking hours in a straitjacket, waiting for freedom. Whether mundane, erotic or nightmarish, every dream alleviates to some degree the anxieties that build up during the hours when we are conscious; a secret labyrinthine world of riddles, endlessly spiralling from one rabbit hole of adventure to another.

★ ★ ★ ★ ★

In the kitchen, Norman prepared a mug of Camp Coffee and turned on the radio. He flexed his hands, which were already starting to awaken with the pain of arthritis. The copper bracelet the doctor suggested he wore to alleviate the pain had been useless.

Matt Monro was singing 'Born Free' on the radio, providing a soothing early morning accompaniment. He could hear the faint dirge of pop music coming from the front room when he had come downstairs. What a load of rubbish Dean listened to, the whole lot of them were drugged up to the eyeballs. It sounded just like something from a lunatic asylum, the noise that constantly came from Dean's bedroom. Now he had plastered those posters all over his room after it had been decorated. The lad didn't know how lucky he was to even have a room of his own. Memories of sharing a bed with his two brothers and the strong smell of piss from the pot that lay beneath still haunted Norman.

Well, at least Dean hadn't turned out a poof like his brother Ian. At least there was still the faint hope of his younger son providing him with grandchildren. Yes, there was definitely nothing wrong with Dean in that department. Ann had been so shocked when she found the 'very explicit' magazines hidden in his wardrobe. Nothing worse than the stuff people left lying around at work.

He wondered how Ian was getting on now. He shuddered to be reminded of what he had witnessed when he opened that bedroom door to find Ian and his disgusting pal on the bed. Both sat there with their trousers round their ankles, holding each other's cocks. He didn't regret giving him a good hiding; he wouldn't have any perverts under his roof. Dean was still sulking about it; the two had been very close. He said Ian was doing fine in his flat on Bellamy Road. He was a man now and old enough to fend for himself.

He inspected the tomatoes that were ripening in the window sill and chose one to take with his snap. Saturday morning overtime usually consisted of pretty steady maintenance work; staying awake would be the hardest part of the job. Fish and chips for dinner from the Clumber Street chippy; always Clumber Street now, Tonk's didn't make them like they used to. After his lunch he would spend the afternoon dozing off in front of the test match. This match looked like it was going to end up a draw, if England carried on accumulating runs like Australia had on such a lifeless pitch.

He was looking forward to hearing the tenor perform at the club that evening. He hoped he would sing some Mario Lanza songs. He secretly wished he could have been a great singer like Lanza; proper music, not like the racket that Dean listened to. When Dean had asked if he could buy an electric guitar from the catalogue, both he and Ann had said no. He wouldn't keep up the payments and they would have the neighbours complaining about the noise anyway. What was the point him having a guitar if he couldn't learn to play it?

He collected his things together to take to work, headed out through the front door and walked down the drive to his car. He looked at the garage door that Dean had painted for him. He remembered when he used to enjoy gardening so much and Dean would reckon to help him. They would take the garden waste down to a patch of waste ground near the house and Dean would ride inside the barrow. On other occasions they would go up the woods together, gathering leaf mould for the garden. They had always enjoyed the chestnut season.

He didn't want to be a bastard like his dad had been with him. He remembered the funeral when everyone thought that he was crying. He had hidden his face behind a handkerchief because he was laughing with joy. Yes, he had been glad to see the old bastard six feet under. His relationship with his mother hadn't been much better either. He tried to recollect how long it had been since he had last visited his mother. The boys had only ever seen her a handful of times during their lives, and she had shown little interest in them when they had. Neither had they seen any of their uncles. A fine bunch they were, one in Mickelover Lunatic Asylum and the other one in and out of jail.

He reversed the car up the drive onto the street and began his journey round the estate to work. He waved to Raf Chlipala, who acknowledged the greeting with a wave of his stick. The Pole had been one of the few neighbours on the street who Norman had taken to. Since moving to the village, he had made few lasting acquaintances with any of the neighbours. His irascibility and lack of tolerance with local tearaways had not endeared him to some residents. He passed the house of Councillor Lester Davis, a man for whom Norman reserved much of his contempt; such an arrogant bastard, feathering his own nest and swanning about in his big car and his chains of office.

He thought how he could have got on better if only he had done better with his writing and arithmetic at school; that's what you needed to get on, he thought. That was why he hadn't been confident enough to get on as a gaffer at work; you needed to be good at maths and English to get anywhere. That was why Dean wouldn't amount to anything: he didn't have the brains he was born with. Of course, that was how Davis had worked his way up, by being a gaffer's man; always having a mug of tea waiting when anyone important came round. Nobody took any notice of you if you just kept your head down and grafted. Keep up the good work and bend over and take another shafting.

He turned down the sunshade as the bright eastern sunshine began to dazzle his eyes. It was going to be a glorious day and he would be stuck underground. He was glad he had an easy job instead of one where he would have to drink umpteen litres of water to replace lost fluids. It would be a great day to be at Trent Bridge, watching the cricket and supping ale.

The memories of his last visit to Trent Bridge came flooding back to him. The hot, sweltering summer of 1976, when smoke from forest fires could be seen from the village and everywhere was snided with ladybirds. Tony Grieg had taunted the West Indians, saying he was going to make them grovel. Michael Holding and Andy Roberts had left some sore ribs with their aggressive pace bowling. Viv Richards and Gordon Greenidge had batted in such a cavalier fashion; it had been marvellous to see. John Arlott's commentary on the radio had been the nearest Norman had ever got to poetry. He and his pal Alex had supped a crate of ale that day at Trent Bridge, while ecstatic West Indian fans had done cartwheels across the field.

He could just as easily have walked the half mile through the village to the pit, but he preferred to save his energies for the pit face. It was such a short distance to work every day, yet once underground he would travel three or four miles on the man-rider train to his destination. He would probably travel vertically down the pit shaft as far as he drove to work each day; descending into the compressed, prehistoric world of darkness.

He ascended a big hill, which obscured the colliery for a moment before descending the opposite side of the hill. The towering headstocks, with their spinning wheels, came into view like a fairground ride into the infernal regions. As he parked up in the colliery car park he wondered how his old pal Alex was. Since Alex had started working on the pit top, Norman hadn't seen him for several years. There had been some rumours about him going crackers since his wife had left him. Alex had been a close friend since before moving to the village. It had been him that had suggested moving from Derbyshire to the more productive coal seams of Nottinghamshire. They had both moved to the village at roughly the same time.

As he walked into the locker room, he nodded to Bob Mitchell, who was getting changed ready to go home.

'Eh Norm, you're big buddies with Alex Freeman aren't you?' Mitchell asked, while combing his damp hair before a mirror like a jaded Teddy boy. The stubborn coal dust around his eyes gave him the look of a faded glam rock star.

'Completely lost it last night apparently; backed his lorry into Cooper's Jag and just fucked off.'

Norman sat on a bench, shocked at hearing this news, minutes after he had been reflecting on the good times he and Alex had shared all those years ago. Mick Cooper was a vindictive colliery overman who had the power to arbitrarily deny overtime to anyone he didn't like. He liked to park his flashy Jaguar XJ-S HE next to the manager's Skoda Estelle to demonstrate who was on the highest pay.

'I reckon he'll top himself he will,' Mitchell continued, trying to squeeze all the goodness out of this juicy piece of gossip.

'Yeah well, he's had it rough lately; he probably just needed to let off some steam,' Norman retorted in defence of his friend. 'You're a cheerful fucker aren't you!'

Mitchell, who had not anticipated this conversation becoming confrontational, shrugged his shoulders and skulked away to see if there was anyone in the canteen to share this latest nugget of news.

Norman sat staring ahead at the lockers; several still sporting 'Coal Not Dole' stickers, which still defiantly resisted being scratched off the doors. He was concerned for his friend. He was normally intolerant of such self-indulgence; even Dean's little depressions just irritated him.

'If you're going to have a nervous breakdown, go and have it somewhere else!' had been the advice he'd given his son. He just didn't know how to react in these situations. Norman remembered the embarrassment he felt when his brother was sent to Mickleover, and the gossip about the basket case. He wondered whether deep down he was just turning into everything he had detested about his own father.

Enough is enough, he thought. He would go round to Alex's and check whether he was alright. Alex had stuck by him and seen him and his family right during the bitter struggles of the early 1970s strikes. He would say he felt ill; it would be the first time in years since he had had time off. He was normally sceptical of others who regularly went on the club.

He walked out of the locker room into the yard, to be confronted once again by the emergence of such a fine day. He remembered the cricket. They could go to Trent Bridge and watch the test match, just like they had done nearly a decade ago. He suddenly wondered whether Dean would want to come with them as well. Normally, he left the room when the cricket was on the television. Dean would surely love the atmosphere at Trent Bridge and he wouldn't turn down a day on the ale. This could be the chance to spend some time with his son and repair a few bridges. But what was he going to say to Ann?

CHAPTER FOUR

Heidi sat at the dressing table, applying make-up and gravity-defying hair gel. She had decided to wear her 'Frankie Says Relax' T-shirt, tight faded jeans and her black suede pixie boots. She had been far too excited to feel hungry, but her mum had insisted on her eating a good breakfast and had made enough sandwiches to end the Ethiopian famine.

Tom, the Baptist youth group leader, had spent an entire morning trying to get through to the hotline responsible for selling tickets for the Live Aid show, eventually paying for them with his credit card. He had been fortunate to acquire the tickets, which had sold out on the same day. Tom had fervently raised money for the cause since Michael Buerk's horrific news report on the Ethiopian famine had first raised awareness of the catastrophe. Heidi and the rest of the group had been mainly motivated by the list of stars who had finally agreed to take part in the concert, rather than any altruistic instincts.

Her dad was worried she would end up a drug addict and run away with a group of hippies to a commune. He thought Live Aid would be another Woodstock. When he had heard the news that Prince Charles and Princess Diana would be attending, he seemed to calm down.

Heidi looked at the Spandau Ballet posters on the wall. She was so excited about seeing them, especially her beloved Tony. The boy she had been getting to know reminded her so much of Tony Hadley. She was looking forward to seeing him again today, he was so funny.

Moving to Mansfield hadn't been such a bad thing after all. She had been heartbroken when she'd had to leave all her friends behind at Chelmsford Girls School. She hadn't even been interested in making friends for a long time, and when she finally made the effort to fit in they had moved away. That was two years ago now, and she had settled down and quickly made new friends. She was quietly confident that she had excelled in her exams and was looking forward to being a sixth former. Then she would follow in her brother Andrew's footsteps and go to university; maybe she would get to see a bit of the world like he was currently doing as well. Andrew was spending the summer shagging round Europe, equipped with only a rucksack and an Interrail rail ticket. Mother seemed to think that he was on some kind of Romantic Grand Tour, like a latter-day Childe Harold. Heidi's dad wasn't so naïve, and told him ambiguously to 'Remember to pack the necessaries; I learned never to go out unprotected when I did my National Service in Malaysia.'

She opened the curtains, revealing a beautiful sunny morning. Dad had worked hard to get the garden looking like a Monet painting. There he was now, watering the petunias and begonias that spilled out of a big terracotta pot, like Bill and Ben. The garden was where he always retreated to in pursuit of personal space. Heidi knew they only stayed together while she and Andrew were still studying. They always seemed blissfully unaware that she could hear them arguing while she lay in bed at night.

She was certain that something major had happened for them to move away from Essex all of a sudden. Dad would never cheat with another woman. Mum had been raving on one night, about how she had settled for him when she could have had her pick of the men, and how she could have made something of her life if it hadn't been for him getting her in the family way as soon as he'd dragged her down the aisle. She was always flirting with other men whenever she had the chance; all those times when she was supposed to be organising some event or other. Heidi imagined that the two of them would divorce as soon as she and Andrew had flown the nest. If it came to making a choice between them, Heidi was resolute that she would stay with her father.

Heidi felt her resentment getting the better of her and refocused on looking forward to the day ahead. She looked up at the framed Bible quotation on the wall which always gave her succour, which said, 'For I know the plans I have for you, declares the LORD, plans for welfare and not for evil, to give you a future and a hope.' She looked at the time on the digital alarm clock and realised that the minibus would be coming to pick her up shortly.

She looked at herself in the mirror one more time to check she looked okay. Grabbing her Sony Walkman, she chose a C90 cassette with *Lexicon of Love* on one side and *Gentlemen Take Polaroids* on the other side. Now she could look out the window all the way to London and shut out the sound of Jeanette's voice.

Heidi hurried down the stairs in response to the ringing phone. *Please don't ring to say the transport has broken down and it's been cancelled.* She grabbed the cordless phone a moment before her mother got to it. It was Kirstie, who was also waiting and getting anxious about the time.

'It's not even seven yet, Tom said seven!' said Heidi, hoping she had remembered correctly.

'Oh shit, yeah, I was sure he said quarter to!' answered Kirstie, getting her knickers in a twist as usual.

'You wally!' giggled Heidi, feeling a little bit more relaxed after hearing her best friend's voice. 'I had this dream last night that me and you were at Live Aid and we had to get up and sing and then my mum came out and started berating Bob Geldof that I couldn't sing because I had to do my A levels instead.'

'Wow, I slept like a log, can't remember any dreams.' Kirstie thought for a moment, then added, 'Hey, maybe Jeanette is just a bad dream and we'll go out today and she'll never have existed.'

'We can always live in hope.' Heidi decided she needed to get a move on. 'Anyway, I'll see you shortly, byee!'

Heidi had been introduced to Kirstie when she had first got involved with the Baptist youth group and the two had become inseparable, both at school and elsewhere. Kirstie had moved up from Milton Keynes, and had been one of the few people that Heidi spoke to who didn't speak in the strange Nottinghamshire dialect. At school recently, Heidi had laboriously studied *The Canterbury Tales.* It came as no surprise to her to find that Chaucer's style of Middle English was known as East Midlands dialect. Kirstie was pretty much the only other person Heidi knew who actually enjoyed school and seemed to want to succeed in life. Kirstie also seemed to be the only girl she knew who wasn't obsessed with losing their virginity; a total contrast to Jeanette, who had been deflowered at the previous year's summer Baptist camp. It must run in the family, because when they had gone round to Jeanette's house one afternoon, they'd had to listen to her mother upstairs having sex with her latest boyfriend. They had gone round there to listen to the new Frankie Goes to Hollywood album, which Jeannette had on tape. It had been so embarrassing listening to the suggestive lyrics to 'Relax', with the erotic sound effects in the background; yet Jeanette didn't seem concerned, she was probably used to it.

Heidi's mother was doing some ironing in the kitchen. Outside, her father was pruning back the climbing pink roses. The breakfast news was on the portable colour television. They were doing a report from Wembley Stadium on the preparations for Live Aid. An overexcited presenter, in a way-too-loud shirt, was stood on the Wembley stage as people furiously worked on stage lighting and other last-minute technical problems. He was joined by Harvey Goldsmith, who along with Bob Geldof had organised what was being described as a 'Global Jukebox'. Goldsmith began discussing the anxieties caused by the rotating stage, which was crucial to the smooth running of the concert. He mentioned that at one point, using horses to operate the rotating stage had been an option. Heidi clapped her hands and pointed at the screen.

'Look Mum, that's where I'll be in a few hours!'

'You ought to become one of them presenters, you're bubbly enough first thing in the morning when everyone else is still waking up.'

'Normally you complain that I'm a misery!'

Heidi's mother simply rolled her eyes and shook her head in exasperation. Not wishing to concede that her daughter had correctly detected her hypocrisy, she counter-attacked.

'Well, you are a misery, except when it suits you; you'll never meet a nice boyfriend with your attitude.'

'I don't want a boyfriend!' Heidi fired back. 'It's always been the same, even when I dressed as Queen Victoria for the Jubilee street party you complained that I never smiled.'

'Well, you didn't.'

'But I was meant to be Queen Victoria, for goodness sake! And I won the best fancy dress contest and all you could do was complain that I never smiled.'

'You're giving me a headache now Heidi, go and make sure you've got everything, Tom will be coming for you any time now.'

Heidi turned her back on her mother; another pyrrhic victory in a war she knew she couldn't win as long as she was under the same roof as her parents. She decided to go out and quickly say goodbye to her father before she went out. She found him in the greenhouse, tending his tomato plants. He was contemplatively pinching out unwanted side shoots. He was thinking that they were just like children, and no matter how much you tried to curtail their growth, they carried on growing up regardless. As if to prove the point, his daughter appeared, looking very grown up. She gave him a big hug, which reassured him that she was still his little girl. He put his hand in his pocket and produced a twenty-pound note.

'Here, buy yourself a programme or whatever you buy at these pop concerts,' he said with a wink.

'Thanks Dad, I'll buy some heroin with it,' Heidi replied with a cheeky expression.

'Okay, but just make sure you share it with your friends and don't make yourself sick.'

'Love you Dad!' She gave him a kiss and hurried back inside.

As he watched her walk away without a care in the world, he hoped she would do a better job than he had done at settling down in a relationship; no, she was too smart for that, he concluded. Andrew, on the other hand, was a chip off the old block. He had already nearly thrown away his chance of a degree when he had fallen for some girl. A hopeless romantic like his father, who would probably make all the same rash mistakes that would cost him dearly.

He thought about his affair with Linda and the anxiety and upheaval that had unfolded in its wake. The transfer to Mansfield had been a result of this secret romance, that had nearly ended his marriage when it had been exposed. After the whole thing had come out in the open, it had been his boss who had suggested the transfer, to clear the air and make a fresh start. What had ostensibly been a promotion and an offer too good to refuse had in fact turned out to be a poisoned chalice. His management of the knitwear factory was solely to oversee the gradual winding down of the site and the selling of its machinery to a company in Turkey. The knitwear could be produced for a third of the cost at the Turkish factory.

Ian MacGregor had recently gained notoriety as the architect of the dismantling of the coal mining industry. It chilled him to think that he had now become a creature of ruthless industrialists like MacGregor. The Industrial Revolution had created communities like those around Mansfield for two centuries. That great era was now on the cusp of extinction. The miners had recently seen the way the wind was blowing, and had fought a desperate battle against the irrepressible tide of progress.

He remembered his time in Mansfield as an evacuee when he was a small boy. He remembered the kindness of the couple he had been billeted with in Skegby. He was cared for by a miner and his wife, who shared what little they had with him and showed him more love and affection than his own parents had ever done. He wondered whether they might still be alive now, and tried to remember the names of some of the children he had made friends with back then.

While Heidi continued watching the latest news from Wembley Stadium, her mother continued to meticulously do the ironing. The task had a meditative quality about it that strangely brought her calmness amidst all her anxieties. She had noticed Heidi's demonstrative display of affection for her father in the garden.

Neither had it gone unnoticed that since the move and the evident estrangement in their marriage, Heidi clearly despised her mother. The strain of keeping up appearances after her husband's adultery had almost driven her to the point of nervous breakdown. They had done their utmost to keep the truth from Heidi and Andrew, but she sensed that Heidi blamed her for the deterioration in the relationship. Since moving to Mansfield, it had only been her involvement with the Baptist church that had given her spiritual relief from the whole debacle. She knew that Heidi would one day find out the truth about the disintegration of the marriage. Her daughter would no doubt find a way to level the blame at her for the marriage's failure.

A horn sounded outside. It was probably the minibus for Heidi. Her father jogged up the garden path and headed through the conservatory into the house, to wave goodbye to his daughter. He pretended to ignore his wife's disapproving expression as he passed her without having taken off his gardening shoes. Heidi was heading out of the front door as he followed along the hall, calling out, 'Have a great time!'

He stood in the doorway waving as she walked up the drive to where the minibus waited on the tree-lined road. Heidi looked expectantly to see if Gareth was there. Her heart raced as she spotted him, sat at the front. Her spirits swiftly sank when she saw that he was sharing the front passenger seat with Jeanette.

Tom opened the side door to allow her entrance. Near the back sat Kirstie, waving and beaming with delight.

'Here, I've saved you a seat, partners in crime eh?'

'Too right,' answered Heidi, feeling much better now she was with her friend. *Who needs boys anyway*, she thought. Kirstie proffered a bag of cola bottles and Heidi stuffed a couple in her mouth. There was definitely more to life than boys.

Heidi couldn't help noticing Jeanette giggling and whispering to Gareth, who she seemed to have interrupted whilst trying to make conversation with Tom.

'Hey Heidi, I've been telling Gareth about your scarecrow friend who bumped into you in the Beer Cellar!' Jeanette shouted out, without even attempting to turn round to look at Heidi while she spoke.

'Oh right, this again,' replied Heidi, looking at Kirstie and rolling her eyes.

'So when are you seeing him again, then?' continued Jeanette, like a dog not willing to let go of someone's leg.

'Oh, didn't anyone tell you, we got married last week. Sorry I forgot to invite you, it was friends only,' Heidi replied, making Kirstie cover her face up while she giggled.

Since Dean Swift had unexpectedly dropped into Heidi's life, Jeanette had taken every opportunity to tease her about it. Jeanette was far too immature to be able to grasp that Heidi might just want to be friends with a boy. Heidi had found Dean quite charming in his own odd way. She found it amusing when he tried to speak without his Mansfield accent, but would forget himself and drop in words like 'norrit' instead of saying 'won't it'. She had found him a quite interesting, bohemian-type character, with his poetry and his artistic brother. Whatever Jeanette believed, there was no question of Heidi having a relationship with Dean. She hoped to one day marry a man like Gareth, who was well turned-out, athletic and ambitious.

Gareth was already resuming his conversation with Tom. Noticing that she wasn't getting the attention she had anticipated, Jeanette dived into her handbag and began rummaging round for a cassette.

'Hey, let's get some sounds on in here!' she shouted, trying to regain everyone's attention.

She stuffed a tape into the cassette player and Bananarama began singing 'Cruel Summer'. She turned up the volume, and then a moment later Gareth turned it down again as he tried to listen to something that Tom was saying to him. Heidi studied all this with interest. Kirstie leaned over and stuffed another cola bottle into Heidi's mouth. Heidi made herself comfortable and leaned her head against the window, so she could watch the world go by. She was certain that one way or another, it was going to be a memorable day.

CHAPTER FIVE

The Distalgesic tablets lay scattered across the coffee table. An empty bottle of Bells Scotch whisky lay on the floor. Alex lay slumped on the settee. A knocking on the front door continued hammering out the intermittent, percussive rhythm it had been making for several minutes.

Outside, Norman waited between knocks; *Alex must be in bed asleep*, he thought. He began knocking again, looking round furtively, self-conscious that he was attracting the attention of neighbours. It was just turned seven and most people would still be in bed on a Saturday morning at this hour. He had left a message at work that he was feeling ill and gone straight home. Sitting in the car, he had considered whether he had done the right thing by going straight round to see if his friend was alright. He would probably be upset and needed some time alone, Norman concluded; probably needed time to calm down.

Norman had gone inside to explain the situation to Ann. She had begun to whittle about him getting the sack and how they would have to stay at home next year without a holiday, if he was going to keep turning down overtime. After half an hour of this, Norman decided the best plan was to go and check that Alex hadn't done anything silly. Norman felt he might do something silly if he continued this discussion with Ann.

After receiving no answer to his knocks at the door, Norman walked over to the living room window. The curtains were untidily closed, with a gap in the middle. The net curtains, which hadn't been washed for several years, impeded any further investigation. He knocked on the window, looking for signs of movement behind the nets.

The banging on the window made Alex jump up in alarm. 'Eh! What!' he called out, still not entirely awake. He must have fallen fast asleep while laid out on the settee. Norman noticed the sudden movement and heard Alex's voice.

'Al, it's Norm, you alraight or what?' he called out.

'What, no I'm – oh for fuck's sake, hold on!' Alex tried to compose himself quickly as he headed towards the front door.

The sudden realisation of what he had done before falling asleep led to a sudden sense of panic in Alex. Were the police outside waiting with Norman? He must surely have burned his bridges at work now. He took a deep breath and opened the door. Norman stood there alone, looking at him as if he might produce an axe at any moment. He nodded to Alex, then quickly decided he needed to play things down a bit.

'Are you going to let me in or what? You're looking at me like I'm a fucking Jehovah's Witness.'

Alex responded by turning back into the house, leaving the door open for Norman to follow. He followed Alex into the front room and immediately noticed the metallic strips of tablets and the empty bottle on the floor.

'You been having a party? You didn't invite me, you cunt,' Norman said, attempting to lighten the mood.

Alex stood in front of the fireplace and took a JPS Black cigarette from the packet on the mantelpiece. He lit the cigarette with a Zippo lighter, momentarily taking in the smell of lighter fluid before the smoke filled his nose and lungs. Looking at Kevin's army boxing trophies on the mantelpiece, Alex finally took a deep breath and spoke.

'I've really fucked up this time, haven't I?'

'No mate,' Norman said, trying to sound convincing, 'everyone knows things haven't been right for a long time. People are just worried about you.' Norman thought about Mitchell revelling in someone else's misfortune.

'I just had to get out! And then I saw that bastard's car and I just lost it,' Alex said, stubbing out his cigarette in an ashtray already full of dog ends.

'No mate, he had it coming, flash bastard, especially after what— well, he's lucky you didn't put him in hospital.' Norman had heard the gossip about Alex's woman running off with Mick Cooper. Some of the miners were like old washerwomen when a bit of juicy gossip became available.

Alex sat down on the settee and gestured toward the tablets. 'I was going to kill mesen, I couldn't even do that properly.' Alex broke down sobbing, cupping his head in his hands. Norman felt uncomfortable for a moment, and then becoming overcome with his friend's despair, he suddenly felt close to tears himself.

'Listen mate, we need to get you out of yoursen a bit,' Norman said, as he attempted to pat Alex on the back in a pitiful attempt to comfort him. Alex's sobbing continued, he began to rock backwards and forwards and Norman couldn't tell if he was laughing or crying. Struggling to know what to say or do, Norman offered to make a pot of tea, and without any response from Alex, continued regardless into the kitchen.

The first thing Norman noticed was the hole in the door leading to the kitchen. The cheaply manufactured interior doors of working-class housing were always an easy target for the frustrations of angry men. The sink was filled with pots that had lain idle for several weeks. On the kitchen table lay several rolled-up chip papers, and a more recent unfinished meal still on display amongst open newspaper.

After filling the kettle, Norman rinsed out a couple of mugs. In the absence of milk, he found a tin of Marvel in the pantry. There was little sign of any recent food shopping in the pantry. Old packets of Paxo stuffing, Bird's custard powder and a jar of mincemeat sat on the otherwise empty shelves. A chip pan sat in a corner, filled with hardened chip fat.

He considered washing up, but after testing the water found it too cold to clean the pile of pots. After making the tea he filled the kettle again, so he could do the washing up that now bugged him. He tidied up the chip papers and went out the back door to throw them in the dustbin. He found the garden lawn grown long after several years' neglect. A rabbit hutch, that Alex had once built himself, still sat unoccupied. The now rusting frame of a swing still occupied a corner of the garden, with the seat hanging from a single chain. The ground beneath the swing was still worn bare from the once constant scuffing of children's shoes.

Alex suddenly appeared at the door. 'I don't think there will be any test matches played here this year,' he said. Norman found this sudden attempt at humour encouraging.

'Well, you never were really Percy Thrower at the best of times,' said Norman, trying to continue the light-hearted banter.

'Drop a bomb on it and I could have another *Blue Peter* sunken garden,' said Alex, now smiling.

'That reminds me, while we're on the subject of cricket, how do you fancy going to the test match today?' Norman asked hopefully.

'Who are they playing?' asked Alex.

'You really are seriously off your feed, aren't you? It's the Ashes,' Norman answered incredulously.

Alex thought about this for a moment, then added, 'So have you got tickets then?'

'No, we'll get a ticket, you can always get a ticket on the day, it's not like the Cup Final,' Norman answered confidently. 'Remember when we went to see the West Indies play, we were bladdered that day.'

'I remember that bloke with the tea cosy on his head blowing that conch all day; gave me a headache,' Alex said, rubbing his head.

'There might be a streaker!' Norman offered, trying to gain Alex's enthusiasm.

'Like Erica Roe!' Alex's eyes lit up at this thought.

'More like Eric Roe,' Norman said, rolling his eyes.

'I bet she doesn't take much warming up,' Alex said, his mind now fixated on the memory of Erica's breasts bulging out of the Sunday newspapers. It suddenly occurred to him that this was the first time in over a year that he had felt aroused by the thought of a woman.

Alex walked back into the house and Norman followed him, hopeful that he was succeeding in raising his friend's spirits. It already felt like old times, pulling each other's leg all the time. He followed Alex through to the front room. Alex began searching through the old bureau that had once belonged to his grandfather. Norman sat on an easy chair, wondering if Alex might be sorting some money out for the cricket.

'There it is, the bastard, I thought it was in here!' Alex said triumphantly, pulling out some kind of booklet and waving it at Norman. On closer inspection, it turned out to be the programme for the match they had watched back in 1976. With the eagerness of a schoolboy, he took the programme and began thumbing through the pages. Looking through the player profiles he noticed a signature scribbled over Michael Holding's photograph. 'Hey, when did you get this!' He held the programme up for Alex to see.

'I don't know,' Alex said, shrugging. 'I think you might have gone for a piss; I was down by the fence when he was warming up, and I queued up with a bunch of kids for his autograph.'

Alex looked through the window at the clear blue sky and sunshine. It seemed like ages since he had actually taken any interest in the weather. He looked at Norman, who was still pawing through the pages of the programme enthusiastically. He decided that this was just the thing to take him out of his paralysing depression. So what if he'd burned some bridges today, he thought, trying to be optimistic. Maybe a change of scene was what he needed. His wife seemed to have moved on with Mick Cooper, so perhaps it was time for him to spread his wings.

'So what are we going to do if we can't get hold of any tickets?' he asked Norman, indicating that he was interested.

'Don't worry, if they don't have any at the ticket office, someone is bound to be trying to get rid of a couple; and besides that, we can just go on a pub crawl round Nottingham,' Norman said excitedly, sensing victory in his quest to conscript his friend into this expedition.

Alex clapped his hands as if to seal the deal. 'Right then, I'm going to nip upstairs and get changed and have a wash. Just give me ten minutes, shit, shave and shower and all that.'

Norman decided to tidy up while Alex was upstairs. He was just bending down to pick up the whisky bottle when he heard a car pulling up outside. Something made him nervous that it might be the police coming round to question Alex about the car. He rushed to the window and saw Mick Cooper climb out of his Jaguar, which didn't look as bad as he had envisioned. He quickly rushed to the front door to confront Cooper and try to sort things out without upsetting Alex. The whole day might depend on it.

★ ★ ★ ★ ★

The last thing Colin Townroe had expected when he walked out of Jackie Compton's house was to see a man with his face poking through the rear windscreen of his Ford Escort. He had just sneaked out of Jackie's house, trying not to wake her. He knew she would want him to stay longer if she collared him before he managed to escape. He didn't want Dawn to suspect him of messing around again so he had made sure he got out early.

It was almost like some divine retribution for his sins, some stupid twat on a pushbike flying head first into his car. There had to be easier ways of scrounging a lift, he thought. He had only just opened the front door when the man had crashed into his car. Then, of course, after shutting himself out, he had to knock Jackie up so he could phone the ambulance.

After the ambulance had taken the man away, Colin had felt quite shaken by the whole incident. He had ended up back inside Jackie's with a fag and a coffee. Then, of course, Jackie was so worried that she had to get him back to bed for another hour.

After finally getting away, he drove home in his car with the broken rear windscreen; he would worry about that later. First, he needed to figure out what he was going to tell Dawn. He was supposed to be doing a night shift at the pop factory, so for starters he was going to have to make up a story about where the car window had been smashed. He should have been home two hours ago, so that would need some explaining as well; hopefully the lazy cow would still be in bed asleep when he got in.

Colin's philandering had been found out before by his suspicious wife. Since she had had the kids, he felt that she had let herself go. He liked plenty of leg over and she rarely fancied sex. After her second pregnancy she had developed a serious case of the baby blues. The tablets the doctor gave her had completely killed her sex drive. Who could blame him, he kept telling himself, he had a right to his share.

He parked up outside the house. He looked to see if the curtains were open yet, and was pleased to see them still closed. He then remembered that she had gone out on some hen do and left the twins with her mum. She would be fast asleep now, making the most of being left in peace. The blond-haired woman who lived a few doors away came out into the street and got into her car. She didn't look bad in those ski pants, Colin thought, he could do worse; those black roots on her hair could do with touching up, though.

He quietly entered the house, expecting Dawn to pounce on him at any moment. All was quiet, so he decided to settle down on the settee; he could then tell her he hadn't wanted to disturb her when he had arrived at his usual time.

Dawn woke from a deep sleep, in which she had been having a pleasant dream in which her father had spoken to her. She missed him so much; it was such a comfort to see him in dreams, where he would reassure her that he was in a good place. She thought she had heard the door shutting, but couldn't be sure if it had been part of her dream as she passed between the worlds of sleep and consciousness. Looking at the clock, she noticed it wasn't yet eight o'clock. It suddenly occurred to her that Colin should be in bed with her, snoring his head off by now. What was the devious twat up to now? she wondered.

She decided to get up and see what he was up to. She still felt wet from earlier and decided to put on her big dressing gown. She put on a pair of knickers and fastened the dressing gown up tight. Last thing she wanted right now was him grabbing at her. Not that he seemed much interested any more, and when he did he was always trying to cram it up her arse. *Fuck that for a game of soldiers*, she thought. Tony was much more sensitive to her needs. She couldn't remember the last time Colin had gone down on her. He was getting a taste of his own medicine now, she concluded, attempting to justify her own unfaithfulness, which still troubled her.

Quietly, she came down the stairs and saw him there asleep on the settee. He had momentarily dropped asleep and woke up to find his wife staring at him.

'What time is it?' Colin said, rubbing his eyes and trying to look like he'd been asleep for some time. He brushed his fringe out of his eyes and looked around as if he'd been in a coma for months.

'It's nearly eight, why didn't you come to bed?' Dawn answered, wondering if maybe he suspected something and was sleeping on the settee because he knew something.

'Oh, I didn't want to wake you up; I knew you would want a lie in after going out last night.' Lying through his teeth was all just part of the game to him now. 'I think I will go and get my head down upstairs now you're awake, then,' Colin said, getting up and stretching. He kissed her chastely on the cheek as he passed her. As he scurried up the stairs, she heard him let out a huge fart. *Dirty fucking pig*, she thought.

He really thought he was God's gift, even after all these years. She remembered when they had got married, the same week that Charles and Diana had their wedding. He'd seemed like quite a catch back then. He still had that stupid moustache that he thought made him look like Midge Ure. She thought it made him look more like Blakey from *On the Buses*. They had all warned her that he had a bit of a reputation as a ram. Well, he definitely had the horns now. She remembered the Shakespeare play they had performed at school and how cuckolded husbands were always portrayed as wearing horns. Well, he was definitely a horny devil now, she thought triumphantly. Thinking about the play reminded her how dishy the black boy who had played Othello had been and the crush she had on him. His name was Michael, and he had ended up working down the pit like his dad and his brothers. She had given up the drama and dancing classes when she had met Colin. She had been so eager to grow up and be in a relationship. Now she came home smelling of chip fat to a husband she despised. She began to understand how Iago had ended up such a twisted character in that play.

Dawn went into the kitchen and made herself a mug of coffee. She still had a couple of hours to herself before her mum brought the twins home. Tony had given her a bar of Cadbury's Turkish Delight, which she had stashed away where Colin wouldn't see. She wasn't so worried about him asking when she had bought it, but knew he would criticise her about her weight if he caught her eating chocolate.

She settled down in front of the television and began devouring her chocolate. On the breakfast news they were talking about the Live Aid concert that was taking place later on. She reached over and picked up the *Radio Times* to see what time the concert was on. She was pleased to see that Status Quo and Queen would be playing, so things were bound to be rocking. She had always preferred rock to the electro-pop that Colin always played in the car. He used to fancy himself a bit of a New Romantic before they had got married. He still loved telling anyone who would listen how he had been mates with Steve Hovington from B-Movie. She didn't recall him ever meeting Hovington, though everyone seemed to claim they knew individual members from the region's answer to Visage. Colin had constantly played the 12-inch version of 'Nowhere Girl', which had managed to get into the lower reaches of the charts for a week or two. No doubt he would be out this afternoon, she thought, anticipating a peaceful afternoon watching the concert. She hated it whenever *Top of the Pops* was on and he criticised everything she liked, drowning out each song with his whinging.

Dawn expected Colin to be out with the football crowd he hung about with every Saturday afternoon. It had only been a couple of months since English football hooligans had made the news, when thirty-nine people had died as the result of a confrontation between Liverpool and Juventus supporters. A local man had been arrested and jailed in connection with the incident. Dawn remembered that Colin had nearly wet himself when he saw the man's photo on the front page of the local newspaper. Jabbing his finger at the picture he proudly claimed he knew the man. What had confused Dawn was why a Mansfield football hooligan had been in Brussels with an army of Liverpool fans. Colin excitedly told her how people representing different English football clubs would travel to big European games just for the thrill of going berserk across the continent. Each team had its own hardcore group of hooligans, and even Mansfield Town had its own contingent. Colin had been on the fringes of that circle of hooligans for several years, drawn into it by his friend Pluto Lockwood. Dawn never found out why people called him Pluto; she guessed it was because he was a bit like the stupid Disney dog. She thought he should be called Uranus instead because he was an arsehole. Colin wouldn't have anything said against Pluto, who was one of the central figures in the crew that indulgently named itself the Coocachoo Crew. If she knew anything about Colin, he would be the first to run and hide if any true violence ensued.

Colin's trainers were slung across the floor for someone to trip on. Dawn got up and threw them into a corner, out of the way. He had obviously been wearing them without socks, if the smell was anything to go by. She went to the window to let some fresh air in. As she opened the window, she noticed the missing rear windscreen on Colin's car. She began to wonder what the sneaky little bastard been up too.

CHAPTER SIX

I was woken from a deep sleep by Dad raving on about some cricket match. I'd had a troubled dream in which I walked down Leeming Street into the market square, passing dead birds. The birds I passed were at first small fowl, chickens and pheasants. As I walked on into the market square, the birds gradually became larger, dead swans and peacocks lay decomposing everywhere. Such dreams seemed to me to represent the despair that seemed to paralyse me in my waking hours. I would often wake up screaming from these dreams. On other occasions, I would find myself waking up laughing from joyful dreams that liberated me from the darker side of my consciousness.

I got up and went downstairs, still composing myself after this rude awakening. Dad and myself had hardly spoken a word to each other for months. He suddenly seemed to be jumping about like Scrooge on Christmas morning. Maybe he was experiencing some kind of middle-aged breakdown like Reginald Perrin. I had the sudden uncomfortable image of him stripping off and walking naked into the sea.

In the kitchen, Dad's old friend Alex sat at the dining table and greeted me. I had always liked Alex from when he used to come round and give me comics. He had come with us on a trip to Wembley to see England play Brazil in a friendly. I hadn't seen him since that evening. Somehow, he seemed to have lost his old sparkle. I recognised that scared shitless by life expression that I often felt and others attempted to conceal. Mum always looked that way; Dad was too thick to understand what it felt like. Seeing Alex here made me think that this trip to the cricket might actually be a good day out. Besides, I couldn't turn down the opportunity of Dad buying me free beer.

Dad had gone into the front room, and from what I could gather, Mum wasn't happy about him taking the morning off work to go to the cricket. To be fair, I couldn't remember him ever taking a day off work sick, let alone turn down a day's overtime. I could clearly hear Mum saying that she couldn't give a fuck about Alex.

51

As I sat drinking my tea, Alex looked sheepishly across at me. I raised my eyebrows and crinkled my mouth to communicate a kind of 'oh dear, what a shame, never mind' response to the argument. Alex's knee was shaking under the table, which was starting to irritate me.

I decided to switch the radio on to drown out some of the noise. I didn't recognise the voice on the radio that began speaking as a song I didn't recognise finished. What had happened to Ed Stewart?

'What's happened to *Junior Choice*?' I asked Alex, who looked at me as if I was cross-examining him in relation to a murder investigation.

'What… oh I don't know, I thought that had finished years ago. I haven't really listened to the wireless for ages,' Alex answered, after giving the subject a lot of consideration.

'I used to love that one by Terry Scott, what was it called?' I tried to remember.

'"Don't Jump off the Roof Dad",' Alex offered thoughtfully.

'No, that was Tommy Cooper!' It was frustrating me now.

'Your dad tells me you've got yourself a job now at the hosiery mills?' Alex asked, trying to change the subject from suicidal parents.

'"My Bruvva"'!' I clapped my hands in triumph as the song title suddenly came to me. Alex looked at me with some confusion.

'Oh, I thought he was talking about you,' Alex said. We sat silently, staring uncomfortably at the table before it dawned on me what he was talking about.

'No, I meant the name of the song by Terry Scott,' I said, smiling. Alex thought about this for a moment and then slapped his forehead and shook his head. We both began to laugh; I thought I saw tears in Alex's eyes as he shook with laughter.

Dad came in the room with the same sense of enthusiasm he had shown before his confrontation with Mum. He was obviously trying his hardest not to let the incident ruin his whole day. I said I needed to set the video recorder for a film that was on BBC 2 that afternoon. Dad asked me what the film was, and I told him it was *Giant* starring James Dean. Dad and Alex started talking about Rock Hudson and Elizabeth Taylor, who were both in *Giant*. I had no interest in either Taylor or Hudson, but Dad didn't seem to rate James Dean and began lecturing me on how Rock Hudson was what he called a 'proper' actor. He said he'd read in the newspaper that Hudson was now ill with some kind of cancer. I left them to carry on spiralling off onto something completely unrelated.

Mum was sat in an armchair next to the old radiogram, which sat in a corner like a coffin in permanent state. She had turned to her faithful friend QC for a shoulder to cry on. Things must be bad when it's sherry for breakfast. I hadn't seen the two of them have a catch-up like this since Christmas. Mum was staring right through the television as Timmy Mallet presented his *Wide Awake Club*. I messed about with the timer on the video recorder, trying to get out as quickly as possible. It was like defusing a bomb, nervously resetting the timer before the explosion took place.

I made the mistake of attempting to engage Mum in conversation, in an attempt to break the uncomfortable silence.

'You won't believe where I'm going today?' I said.

'I couldn't give a fuck where you're going!' Mother replied.

That was the end of that conversation; she had to be properly soused to resort to expletives of even the mildest variety. Any other day she would have been sat contentedly with a Catherine Cookson book. No doubt she would want to play her Edith Piaf LP at some stage. I was pleased that my records weren't to her taste, because the ones she played were all scratched to bits after years of abuse.

★ ★ ★ ★ ★

In the kitchen, Norman and Alex had moved on from Rock Hudson, through all the legends of Western films, gangster movies and Biblical epics. Alex suddenly became quiet again and began ruminating on the events of the morning. Norman picked up on this change of mood in an uncharacteristic moment of empathy.

'You're still worried about banging into that knobhead's car, aren't you?'

Alex looked up at Norman, raising his eyebrows and sighing. 'I've got myself in a right mess, haven't I? Up to my neck in shit,' he said, making a gesture that indicated the approximate height of the said excrement.

Norman looked out of the window, wondering whether to tell Alex about Mick Cooper's visit earlier that morning. He looked at Alex's pitiful countenance and decided that he couldn't cope with him being a mard arse all day.

'Tha'll be alrait, Mick won't be bothering you, I've sorted it,' Norman said, scratching his head with a sheepish expression.

'What? Why? What do you know about it?' Alex answered, with an expression of puzzlement.

Norman slapped his hands down onto his knees, took a deep breath and exhaled, blowing out his cheeks. 'While you were upstairs getting changed, Mick came round.'

'What! Why didn't you give me a shout?' Alex stood up and began pacing around the kitchen.

'I didn't want you getting upset again, so I went out and had a word with him, that's all,' Norman replied, hoping to put a quick end to the discussion.

'What did you say to him? What did he have to say?'

'Let's just say Mick owes me one,' Norman nodded his head and tapped his nose conspiratorially.

'What about the damage to his car, you're not telling me he's going to just let that go?' Alex said, shaking his head incredulously.

'Like I said, Mick owes me and he won't be bothering you about it, so let's drop it!' Norman concluded with a stentorian authority in his tone that succeeded in silencing his friend's cross-examination.

★ ★ ★ ★ ★

I returned to the kitchen to find the atmosphere had changed somewhat. Alex was pacing around the room and Dad was sat looking out of the window and tunelessly whistling. I recognised that stupid whistling expression from when he was usually trying to avoid some kind of confrontation with Mum. I sat down, and this dumb show seemed to go on for an eternity before Dad got up and suggested we got going.

★ ★ ★ ★ ★

Ged 'Myfanwy' Thomas headed for the smoking section of the train and made himself comfortable in a seat next to the window. He looked out of the window at Lincoln's modest train station, pleased to be free from the town's prison after a six-month stay. He greeted the clothes he had last seen when entering the prison like old friends. He wore his boating blazer with its stripes of varied hues of purple. He wore his white Fred Perry shirt, black jeans and black bowling shoes. These were the smartest clothes he owned, to wear when he appeared at court. He was glad that he hadn't worn his parka as well, he reflected, feeling the warmth of a fine July morning.

Ged had earned the soubriquet of Myfanwy due to his spurious Welsh ancestry. According to him at various times, he was a distant relative of Dylan Thomas, a veteran of Rourke's Drift and could trace his lineage back to the royal line of

Llywelyn the Great. He lived with his grandparents who, like him, were born and bred in Mansfield. He claimed that his mother lived in Wrexham and had abandoned him due to mental illness. It was never really clear who his father was, and the story often changed. Myfanwy always shouted for Wales when the rugby was on television and Richard Burton was his favourite actor. It never occurred to him, or anyone who knew him, that Myfanwy was a girl's name.

Myfanwy's favourite hobbies were stealing and sniffing glue. In truth, his passion for glue had been superseded by an infatuation for more potent drugs during his residency in Lincoln prison. His talent for stealing had been curbed somewhat in the time he had been locked up. He had been introduced to heroin whilst incarcerated and discovered that sucking cock was a good source of income for little luxuries like drugs and cigarettes.

Since the revival had begun at the tail end of the Seventies, Myfanwy had been a convert to the second coming of the mods. He was the king of the ragamuffin mods; a cross between Chalkie from *Quadrophenia* and the Artful Dodger. He was an avuncular character who attracted a following of pubescent urchins, all dressed in scruffy parkas. His magical mod coat could make anything disappear from a shop; without it, his powers faded and his luck finally ran out.

Myfanwy was a slimline John Falstaff, who led a vagabond company of mod foot soldiers. The aristocracy of the order rode their Vespas, wore their French macs and listened to rare grooves. The serfs played 'Pretty Green' and painted their parkas with Jam. Plastic mods, someone called them; yet wasn't all pop culture plastic and artificial? Something to be used up and thrown away when the next new thing came along. The grubby young imitators were what it was all about; just like the Sid Vicious lookalikes in their painted leather jackets who'd never heard of the Bromley contingent.

The train stopped at Bingham, and Myfanwy watched groups of people in floppy white cricket hats climb aboard. Several of them sat opposite him and began talking about the state of play. Clearly there was some kind of match on at Trent Bridge, and Myfanwy instantly saw an opportunity to make some much-needed money. Someone picked up a newspaper and it became apparent to Myfanwy that some kind of charity pop concert was taking place at Wembley. The passenger with the newspaper nudged his friend and tapped the article about the concert and began talking about charity beginning at home. Myfanwy remembered a charity record being released in December, before he got sent down. He remembered Paul Weller singing with his hair slicked back; something about starving children in Ethiopia. If it was good enough for Weller, it was good enough for him. He took note of the passenger who made the remark; he would get charity begins at home alright.

He felt in the inside pocket of his blazer and pulled out a piece of folded paper. He unfolded it and recognised the verse written in biro.

> In the time of Edward and Richard came
> Many great writers of literature;
> Boccaccio, Petrarch, Langland to name
> But a few; and the great Geoffrey Chaucer,
> He that wrote of Troilus and Criseyde,
> And he penned the grand Canterbury Tales;
> Not in French but English vernacular,
> Representing pilgrims varied travails.
> Cooks, clerks, squires, friars, painting vivid details.

Dean had given it him to read the last time they had met. He remembered that it had been the first occasion that Dean had ventured into the Blue Boar with him. Dean had drunk six pints of snakebite and then been violently sick. Myfanwy quickly scanned the verse but couldn't make head nor tail of it. Pete Townshend was the only poet he admired.

Settling back into his seat and looking out of the window, Myfanwy turned off the supercilious and pedantic chatter of his travelling companions. He thought about Sutts, the old school mod he had become so close to in prison. Nick Sutcliffe, or Sutts as he preferred to be addressed, had led an illustrious life. He had been a mod in the first wave of 1964 and had watched The Who at the Goldhawk Club, when they had still been the High Numbers. Mods had a voracious appetite for amphetamine tablets and Sutts seized the opportunity to supply them. Purple Hearts and Black Bombers kept the youngsters jumping about like monkeys all night long. During the bank holiday riots at Clacton, Sutts put the windows through of a jeweller's shop and was subsequently collared whilst trying to sell his stolen watches to day-trippers.

He spent his first spell in prison after pleading guilty to receiving and selling stolen goods, but denying that he had stolen them himself. In Pentonville Prison he made some useful contacts, before graduating and becoming an apprentice villain with the Richardson gang. After it was brought to Charlie Richardson's attention that Sutts was bisexual, he decided to surreptitiously introduce the pretty boy to Ronnie Kray. Richardson saw an opportunity to plant a KGB-style mole inside the

Kray camp, by appealing to Ronnie's peccadillos. Sutts was brought along to a party and was quickly spotted by Kray.

Sutts was like a Trojan hobby horse for Ronnie to ride. He learned very little in his time with the Krays, but was thrown about like a rag doll for six months. The police paid him for any information on both gangs. On the night that Jack McVitie was murdered, Sutts was part of the group that helped to lure him to the flat where Jack the Hat would be murdered.

In the aftermath of the murder, Sutts fled London. In 1970, he found work as a security guard at the Isle of Wight Festival, patrolling the fences that kept freeloading hippies from entering without a ticket. To supplement his wages, he sold acid to the festivalgoers, and by the end of the weekend Sutts was tripping in the back of a Volkswagen camper van destined for the hippy trail. He was a stranger to the shores of England for two years when he returned, and was immediately arrested in possession of a euphonium stuffed with cannabis and a bag of heroin up his arse.

After a long spell locked up, Sutts drifted from place to place, out of step with the changing world he was confronted with. He became a slave to the sadistic master that was heroin. He soon began to beg, borrow, steal and cottage, to support his addiction. He was arrested after he was caught driving away a stolen Sinclair C5. That was the point where Myfanwy made his acquaintance in Lincoln jail.

As Nottingham came into view, Myfanwy hoped that he might see his friend again, picturing himself meeting Sutts at the train station and then introducing him to his friends in Mansfield. He almost viewed the older man as the nearest thing he had ever known to a father figure.

When Myfanwy had found himself on the wrong side of some distinctly unpleasant characters, it was Sutts who had raced to his defence. Yet each time he thought about his friend, he had the feeling he was being confronted by a future version of himself. Maybe that was ultimately why they had been destined to meet. But he also sensed that it was a case of closing the gate after the horse had bolted, in terms of any moral lesson. Promiscuity and drug use in prison had left Myfanwy with a Faustian debt to pay. He resolved to make every moment count from then on.

He rose with the other passengers as they prepared to alight from the train. He had allowed himself to be distracted by his melancholy thoughts, and focused on the charitable chap who had been drawn to his attention earlier.

CHAPTER SEVEN

Feeling an elbow nudge her, Heidi jumped awake from a deep sleep. Sitting up straight and stretching, she looked out of the window. She groaned with the realisation that the car park they were pulling into was not Wembley but yet another service area. She felt the childish impatience that comes with interminable holiday journeys where the destination always seems to be tantalisingly out of reach.

She wondered who wanted to go to the toilet this time; why couldn't they tie a knot in it? They had already made an earlier stop at Leicester Forest services. Jeannette had spotted Heidi and Kirstie together and shoved herself between them, linking arms with Heidi. Jeannette's advances toward Gareth had clearly proven unrequited and she had decided to latch on to Heidi instead. She tried to hurry Heidi along and leave Kirstie behind.

'We're going to have so much fun today. Did you hear on the radio? Quo are coming on first, so we'll be down the front rockin',' she said, as she pushed herself against Heidi rhythmically. She had an irritating way of forcing a laugh at the end of every statement; a laugh which excluded any genuine sense of humour. She had got into the habit of punctuating her sardonic comments with this laugh to indicate that no matter how cruel or base her words, it was only a joke.

Heidi stopped dead in her tracks and turned around to wait for Kirstie to join them. Using this opportunity to pull away from Jeanette, Heidi rolled her eyes in despair, making Kirstie smile.

'Come on Crystal Tips, hurry up slow coach!' Jeannette called out to Kirstie.

'Oh, piss off,' Kirstie muttered under her breath. Heidi always thought that Kirstie's frizzy red hair was more reminiscent of the little red-haired girl who Charlie Brown admired from afar in the *Peanuts* cartoon strips.

'Have you started having your periods yet, Kirstie?' Jeanette asked with exaggerated concern.

'Why do you ask me that every time you see me, just drop it!' Kirstie replied, exasperated by Jeanette's need to keep asking this question like a menstrual inquisitor.

'Ooh, Kirstie, I'm sowwy!' Jeanette grabbed Kirstie, hugging her tightly.

Kirstie's mother had recently taken her to the doctor with regards to her absence of menses. The doctor had diagnosed Kirstie as having a benign tumour called a prolactinoma. Kirstie's late pubescent development had been a symptom of this, and she had been prescribed medication to eliminate this problem.

Once in the toilets, Jeannette began to preen her big blond hair and apply make-up in front of a mirror. She was by far the prettiest of the three of them, Heidi conceded, but something far uglier lurked beneath the surface of Jeannette's fair skin.

When Heidi came out of the toilet cubicle, she saw that Jeannette was still gazing at herself in the mirror with all the intelligence of a budgie. She hastily left the ladies' before Jeanette spotted her. As she hurried past the cafeteria she noticed Kirstie leaning against a wall, giggling coquettishly at something Gareth was telling her. He leaned across her with his hand resting on the wall against Kirstie's face; all a little too intimately, Heidi thought. She felt the sudden sensation of jealousy, even betrayal. She made to hurry past them both, pretending that she hadn't seen them. She turned round, quickly composing herself as Kirstie called out to her. Kirstie gently pressed her hands against Gareth's chest and pushed past him. Heidi would analyse this action in a hundred ways; was it a flirtatious push? Was it a subtle way of telling him that they would continue their tête-à-tête at some later stage? Kirstie led her by the arm back to the minibus, telling her how Gareth had been explaining to her how he had been fending Jeannette off all morning.

During the latest comfort stop, Heidi opted to stay put. Kirstie climbed out to stretch her legs for a few minutes. Gareth was stood on the opposite side of the minibus, talking to Tom. Heidi began to perk up again, concluding that she had been thinking irrationally about Kirstie and Gareth. The silence of the stationary vehicle amplified the rustling of a crisp packet behind her. It was starting to feel warm and she could smell the odour of cheese and onion crisps. She looked around to see Callum Yates devouring the crisps, almost biting his fingers off. He proffered the packet to her, but she politely declined the offer and quickly turned round again. Callum clearly ate too many crisps, judging by the condition of his face. It was red and blotchy, with skin peeling from his nose and cheeks. His greasy straw-coloured hair looked like it could do with a good wash. The lenses of his National Health spectacles were so dirty that it was a wonder he could see through them. Kirstie, with uncharacteristic cruelty, called him Calaban. Heidi secretly felt sorry for him and thought he was a nice and kind person. Peer pressure would always make it impossible to be seen to associate with a boy like Callum. He used to cycle to the church and would smell strongly of body odour when he arrived. Once he stood next to Jeannette and she told him he smelled like a yak. Heidi despaired at so-called Christians sometimes. Heidi imagined Jesus telling Callum to come and stand next to him in church, joking about how bad he had smelled after forty days in the wilderness. She turned around again, and with a friendly smile, said to Callum, 'I think I will have a crisp, if you don't mind.'

Everyone got back into the minibus after the allotted ten minutes, with the exception of Jeannette. Five minutes went by and everyone was growing impatient. Tom stood outside with Gareth, preparing to go and search for Jeannette. Then she came strolling out of the services, chatting with what looked like a couple of lorry drivers. She sauntered through the car park, waving to the two burly looking men as they headed toward the lorry parking area. Heidi saw Tom pointing at his watch and berating Jeannette, who shrugged her shoulders and seemed to be making some kind of feeble excuse. Gareth climbed into the passenger seat next to Tom. As Jeannette sat down next to him, he turned round, mouthing 'Help!' towards Kirstie.

★　★　★　★　★

Outside the old concrete bus shelter on Netherfield Lane, Saturday morning shoppers began to congregate. Luckily, with the warm weather, nobody needed to seek shelter in its interior, which reeked of urine. The sound of gossiping housewives woke Spike from a peaceful slumber. The verdant hawthorn hedge had kept him in the shade from the rays of morning sunshine. He could hear a woman complaining about someone who hardly ever showed her face at the club, having the audacity to win the snowball bingo game. Spike's head began to hurt listening to this tirade. He focused on the hedge sparrows, that were oblivious to the petty concerns of humanity.

The sound of people waiting for the bus reminded Spike of his plan to go and visit John. Without a moment's hesitation, he dragged himself up out of the field and staggered from behind the bus shelter. The gossiping housewives looked round in shock at the bedraggled figure, but immediately returned to their conversation when they recognised Spike. He asked someone the time and was told that it was nearly half past nine.

Stood leaning against a lamp post at the opposite end of the bus stop was Sammy's dad. He drew deeply on his Park Drive cigarette and looked at Spike through the haze of smoke. Spike figured that he must have an important appointment with his turf accountant, in order to be out and about at this early hour. Either that or he had shit the bed. He wore the black suede beetle crushers that seemed to be the only pair of shoes he owned. He had on a pair of grey trousers and an open-necked black shirt and brown braces. His once proud Teddy boy quiff had now receded into a greased-back combover; with his stubbly tanned face, he looked like a shambolic remnant of Mussolini's squadristi.

Spike made his way over to greet the man, and maybe beg a breakfast smoke. He nodded, and merely said, 'Tommy, giz a fag.' Tommy obliged by pulling out his packet of ten Park Drive and handed one over to Spike. When Spike asked for a light, Tommy offered his own cigarette as a light, with the ubiquitous, 'Do you want me to smoke it for you as well?' Spike took a deep and satisfying drag on the cigarette and then spat out a piece of loose tobacco. At that moment, the double decker bus came into view and people began to step forward toward the kerb. They watched the bus approach with eager anticipation of the brief interlude from the sense of paralysis of life in the village.

They both went upstairs so they could continue their smoke. Tommy found a seat and Spike stretched out on the seat behind him. Spike took the opportunity to extract twenty pounds owed to him by Tommy. They had recently stolen some items from a garden shed, and Tommy had promised him twenty pounds when they had been sold on. Tommy reluctantly began feeling around in one of his trouser pockets.

'Come on you tight cunt, I bet you could peel an orange in that pocket,' Spike said, grinning at the old rogue.

Tommy pulled out a couple of twenties and handed one to Spike, who held it up to the light to verify its authenticity. The bus conductor came up the stairs; a huge Scottish woman who put the fear of God into busloads of diabolical school kids. With her blue rinse hairstyle, she looked like a grotesque Ralph Steadman cartoon version of Molly Sugden. Even Spike and Tommy shuffled nervously in their seats. When it was their turn to pay, she approached them with an expression normally reserved for encounters with dog excrement.

Seeing Spike's boots on the seat, she snapped, 'Get your feet doon! Would you sit like that at hame?'

'I would,' sniggered Tommy.

'I wasnae asking you!' she roared into Tommy's face.

Spike quickly sat up straight, cowed by this fierce Caledonian dragon. They sat quietly until she began descending the stairs, and then looked at each other and began to giggle like naughty schoolboys.

By the time this unfortunate confrontation had ended, the bus had already arrived in Warsop. Tommy prepared to get off, nodding his head to Tommy.

'Lend us another fag then, till I can get some in town,' Spike pleaded.

'Fuck off, I've only got two left!' Tommy answered curtly.

'Well, you can give me one then,' Spike reasoned.

'I'll see you later!' Tommy called out, scampering away to avoid crashing another cigarette. The bus stopped outside the Hare and Hounds pub, and Spike looked out of the window when he heard the unmistakable noise of an unbaffled motorbike. He watched as Rollo Fenwick came roaring past on his Norton Commando. His shiny chrome German helmet gleamed in the bright sunshine. Rollo was the president and founder member of an outlaw motorbike club named Robespierre's Barbers. On the back of his leather waistcoat was a patch bearing the image of a guillotine, with a skull grinning maniacally from the stocks at the base of its frame. The club name had been conceived by Rollo after he had read a book about the French Revolution. He had first intended to call the club 'Reign of Terror'. When he sketched his idea for the club emblem, he decided that Robespierre's Barbers was a more pithy evocation of mass executions, whilst suggesting a bunch of cutthroats.

Spike was fascinated by Rollo and his freewheeling biker lifestyle. He would often drink with him in the Hare and Hounds, but remained cautious, not entirely sure what Rollo was capable off. Rollo commanded thirty chosen men in his club, all of whom would lay down their lives in the name of Robespierre's Barbers; or so Rollo would often boast.

Beginning to feel warm, Spike took of his coat, revealing his heavily tattooed arms. His sleeveless T-shirt bore the slogan 'Fuck the Tories' above a photo of Riot Squad, a punk band who hailed from Mansfield. 'Fuck the Tories' had been a minor hit for the band. The record had been released on Rondelet Records, an independent label run by a local record shop owner. Spike knew Dunk, the band's vocalist, and he remembered John and himself following the band at some of their first gigs. He smiled as he recalled them both being thrown out of one of the band's gigs at Pleasley Miners Welfare Club. They had been thrown out for making too much noise during a mandatory bingo session which interrupted the band's performance.

Feeling in his jacket pocket, Spike pulled out a bag of pork scratchings he had begun eating the previous evening. He began loudly munching the salty snack as the bus conductor appeared again to collect fares. She gave him a disapproving glance as he crunched on the tough pork rind. Fearing another confrontation with the fiery Scot, he quietly sucked the scratching until she descended the stairs again.

The saltiness of the scratchings began to make Spike feel thirsty, and he decided he would purchase refreshment once he arrived at the bus station. He would then be free to begin walking up Sutton Road, where the A38 began, and start hitching a lift onto the motorway and beyond. He felt a surge of freedom he hadn't experienced since the previous summer. He loved the freedom of hitchhiking and fending for himself. He was glad that he had set off that morning without any procrastination. Dog and Sammy had been mithering him for ages to take them on one of his journeys.

He was joined by Gladstone Roberts, who boarded the bus near the Gate pub. He was wearing his *Ebony* T-shirt. *Ebony* was a television magazine programme that focused on issues within Britain's Afro-Caribbean community. Gladstone and his family had appeared on the show in a segment about black families living in traditionally white mining communities.

Gladstone had been in the same year at school as Spike. He had never shared the athleticism of his brother Andy, who had gone on to play professional football for Chesterfield. He had always been overweight, but now put his large frame to use as a doorman at Mansfield's Sherwood Rooms. The Sherwood Rooms had a reputation for weekly brawls and needed hired brawn to remove troublemakers.

'I hear Myfanwy's out on probation,' said Gladstone, with an ironic smile that suggested that this would only be a temporary sabbatical from prison life.

'I didn't even know he'd been sent down again,' said Spike. 'What's he done this time?'

'Pinched a Subbuteo set from WH Smiths, then sold it in the pub and went back in to nick the accessories.'

'What do you mean?'

'You know, floodlights, the grandstand and all that shit; just stuffed them up his mod jacket; but this time he got caught. Broke his probation and got sent straight to Lincoln nick.'

'Sounds about right for him,' said Spike. He got on really well with Myfanwy. They had been best glue buddies at one time. Myfanwy would sniff anything. Spike remembered one occasion when Myfanwy had even taken the cap off someone's scooter and begun sniffing the petrol.

Gladstone got off the bus when it reached Mansfield Woodhouse. As he descended the stairs, Spike noticed the large scar on the back of his head that left a bald patch. The scar had been a souvenir of the Battle of Orgreave. Spike, Gladstone and Tommy had been amongst a group that had travelled to the Orgreave coke plant to reinforce the pickets there. Thousands were heading there to try to stop lorries from leaving the plant with coal destined for a steelworks in Scunthorpe. A pitched battle ensued after the police began to employ aggressive tactics. As a black picket, Gladstone made an irresistible target for the police in their riot gear. Despite giving as good as they got, it was a sore day for Gladstone and many others.

That day had been like a scene from the Peasants' Revolt in Spike's memory. He could remember every smell, sound and sight with perfect recall. He remembered the line of mounted police, charging on their horses. The terror-stricken crowd of men, fleeing like a routed army from the field of battle. He could still hear the noise of the horses' hooves, galloping behind him. He could still hear the snorting of the horses and the shouted orders to stay in line. Then he had gone over and thought that he might die. Somehow, the horses had ridden straight by him without trampling him. He lay there in a ball and realised that he'd pissed himself. He managed to compose himself and get up and keep running to the edge of the field, where some of the pickets still stood amongst some trees. He had gone there that day for no other reason but to revel in anarchy, directed against the police and the Tories. When he got to the edge of the field he vomited, shaking with fear and adrenaline.

Such heavy-handed tactics by the police seemed to be becoming commonplace. It had only been recently that a similar situation had occurred in Wiltshire, at what became known as the Battle of the Beanfield. The Peace Convoy was travelling to Stonehenge for the annual free festival. A High Court injunction had been obtained to keep the New Age travellers away from the site. A huge police presence had been brought in to prevent the travellers from getting near Stonehenge. When the convoy allegedly attempted to breach a police roadblock, violent scenes followed. Many were injured and hundreds were subsequently arrested.

When Spike and John had travelled to the festival at Glastonbury the previous year, they had hung out with some of the Peace Convoy. The travellers had been camped on the outskirts of the festival in their motley assortment of converted buses and ambulances. They had enjoyed the hospitality of the travellers, and had been entertained by their music and juggling. Both Spike and John had been enchanted enough to consider living such a lifestyle themselves.

Looking out of the window of the bus at the old Metal Box factory, Spike began to yearn for escape. The Metal Box factory was situated in an old quarry site that had provided much needed protection from the Luftwaffe during World War Two. Now, industrial bastions such as Metal Box faced destruction from another enemy, which viewed such places as economically unviable. The Industrial Revolution had almost turned 360 degrees. The factory's clocktower showed that it was ten o'clock; time to move on.

CHAPTER EIGHT

I followed Dad and Alex across the bridge, which led towards the cricket ground that borrowed its name from this impressive construction of iron and stone. We had parked the car under the tree-lined Victoria Embankment. There was no argument about who would drive home at the end of the day. Dad seemed to think that half a dozen pints of bitter was a perfectly reasonable amount to drink before driving home. He was normally so full of moral indignation, yet blissfully ignorant of any wrongdoing on his own part when it came to drinking and driving.

The gently flowing waters of the Trent gleamed in the sunlight. Outside the Nottingham Rowing Club, a team of rowers were preparing to take a scull out on the river. Behind the rowing club towered the City Ground, where Brian Clough had reigned for a decade. We walked across the bridge with a crowd of people, all heading to the cricket. Several ticket touts were asking if anyone had tickets to sell. None seemed to be selling tickets, which seemed to suggest to me that there probably weren't any available. The thought that we might not get in suddenly became very attractive to me. I could escape into Nottingham and search for some records, which seemed more agreeable than spending the day watching a game I had no interest in.

We turned onto the Radcliffe Road and, feeling peckish, I decided to go into a little shop across the road from the Trent Bridge Inn. It was busy inside and I had to join a growing queue of people buying snacks and newspapers to take into the cricket ground. I chose a beef and onion pasty and a bottle of chocolate milk. I joined the queue and waited patiently, surreptitiously studying the dirty magazines on the top shelf. Two elderly men joined the queue behind me. They began complaining about the lack of parking, and then began criticising the Trent Bridge ground staff for preparing a lifeless pitch. I considered whether there might be some kind of druidical ritual that might be performed to bring the pitch to life. A human sacrifice or two might do the trick;

the two gentlemen behind me would surely volunteer themselves. I was beginning to feel the wave of irritability that comes with lack of sleep, after a week of night shifts. The eyes would begin to sting and become sensitive to light. Random sounds would become unbearably irritating. Euphoria and depression would follow each other from moment to moment. Only a surfeit of beer could tame this demon.

When I finally emerged into the daylight once again, Dad and Alex were both looking pleased with themselves. They had succeeded in obtaining tickets for all three of us. My heart sank a little when I was given this news. I had begun thinking about buying some Frank Zappa records at Selectadisc, if we didn't get the tickets. My spirits were raised again when Dad suggested we adjourn to the Trent Bridge Inn.

As I walked through the doors of the Trent Bridge Inn for the very first time, I was ignorant of the worldwide renown of this pub. I discovered that a publican and cricketer named William Clarke had married the landlady of the Trent Bridge Inn. They had subsequently had the land behind the pub cleared so that cricket could be played there, and so began the illustrious history of Trent Bridge Cricket Ground. William Clarke would continue planting the seeds of cricket history by creating and captaining the first All-England Eleven. Clarke played in the 1830s and '40s, with notable players who had wonderfully Dickensian names like Alfred Mynn and Fuller Pilch.

The bar was snided with waiting customers, and Dad and Alex went to queue for drinks whilst I waited out of sight of any overzealous bar staff. I looked at pictures and memorabilia on the wall that commemorated notable moments in the ground's history. At the corner of the bar, an Australian was loudly holding court. He had long brown sideburns and a matching walrus moustache. He wore a yellow rugby shirt over a large paunch, knee-length shorts and flip-flops. He was draped in an Australian flag.

'This bladdy Pommy laaager tastes like piss!' he called out to anyone in hearing distance.

A young man who wore a pair of Union Jack shorts that barely concealed his testicles answered, 'They say that when the convicts sailed to Australia, they were forced to drink their own piss when they ran out of water, and that's how the Aussie brewing tradition was born.'

This remark was greeted with a loud cheer from many of the English supporters within earshot. The Australian and his companions laughed good-naturedly. He held up his pint glass to make a toast, 'Here's to the Old Dart, it's great to be back!'

Everyone cheered again, although many didn't understand that 'the Old Dart' was an Australian slang term for England.

After an interminable wait, the drinks arrived. Alex handed me a pint of bitter. 'Here, get that down you,' Alex nodded toward my drink. 'I wasn't sure whether to get you pop and crisps.' He winked at my Dad.

I laughed along with them, feeling the thin-skinned sensitivity that is common to most teenagers. I was getting used to worse at work. Taking the piss seemed to be what passed for wit amongst men like these. It was part of the rite of passage for a young man in the pits and factories to endure puerile 'leg-pulling' and initiation ceremonies.

After quickly quaffing our drinks, Dad hurried to the bar to get another round before we went into the ground. He went with the enthusiasm of someone who has just heard the four-minute warning siren. I said to Alex what a spot of luck it was, getting hold of the tickets. He explained that a dodgy-looking young man in a stripy boating blazer had sidled up to them and given them some bullshit about his grandmother dying and being unable to attend the match as a consequence. I wondered if perhaps he might have come from the rowing club.

Nobody seemed to be in any hurry to get to their seats in the ground. The Australian looked as though he was taking root at his spot at the bar. Dad weaved his way back through the throng of drinkers, holding three pints in his hands with the confidence of a seasoned drinker.

I'd only just got the glass in my hand before Alex suggested, 'We'd best sup up and get to our seats. I don't want to miss a ball.'

The Australian began to sing a spirited rendition of 'Advance Australia Fair'. A couple of his fellow countrymen linked arms with him and joined in. Most of the English drinkers didn't recognise the song, thinking that 'Waltzing Matilda' was the national song of the Aussies. They had hardly started the second verse before Alex had slammed his glass on the bar with a triumphant 'I won' expression on his face. I had hardly touched mine, which meant I would have to practically down it in one, while they stood and watched. There was nothing worse than a competitive drinker. Alex gave a loud belch and announced that he needed a piss. He gave me a parting look which suggested that he expected me to be ready when he returned.

★ ★ ★ ★ ★

It had been a most gratifyingly productive morning for Myfanwy so far. After exiting the train, he had followed the three men who had sat near him. He had been highly affected by their views and wished to learn more. Hunger in Africa, it seemed, was a product of post-colonial indolence. Unemployment was a product of post-imperial indolence. He had also learned that the Isle of Man had ceased to administer the birch to criminals in 1976.

He followed his three new friends past the shiny red-brick buildings of the station, to the buffet. Myfanwy had observed one of the group check his tartan holdall and exclaim proudly that he hadn't lost the tickets. He wore red shorts, green socks and sandals. All of his friends wore equally abominable raiment. An assortment of garish polo shirts was tucked neatly into each pair of shorts. An array of floppy hats was worn purely to keep off the sun, and not one was set at a rakish angle.

The man with the tartan holdall found a table whilst his companions went to the counter to queue for refreshments. Myfanwy observed all this from the doorway, leaning against the wall as if casually waiting for someone. Some kind of palaver was taking place between the two men and the waitress about tinned tomatoes. Myfanwy could hear cries of 'Really!' and 'Typical British Rail!' The young girl behind the counter, who was taking the order, looked on with indifference; water off a duck's back. The two men turned to their seated friend, shaking their heads. Momentarily distracted by the monumental decisions pending, concerning beans and tomatoes, he rose from his seat to personally investigate the situation. At the moment he walked toward the counter, a group of people entered the buffet. Myfanwy seized the opportunity to follow them inside. While the three men were preoccupied with ordering breakfast and were joined by the new arrivals, Myfanwy casually picked up the holdall and walked out.

He walked straight into the nearest gents lavatory and locked himself in a cubicle. He inspected the contents of the bag. He took the tickets and forty pounds from a wallet. He also took a membership card for Nottinghamshire County Cricket Club, which he decided might come in useful. Leaving the bag and the remainder of its contents, he made his way out of the station to the taxi rank.

Myfanwy climbed into the back of the first available taxi and instructed the driver to take him to Trent Bridge. The Sikh driver was obviously a keen cricket fan and began talking excitedly about the state of play in the current test match. Myfanwy sat forward in his seat, eagerly nodding his head. He had no idea who was playing in the test series and hadn't even looked at the tickets to see who it was between. He saw a group of people walking along the London Road in the direction of Trent Bridge. One of them wore a blue flag with stars and a Union

Jack on it. He couldn't remember the difference between the Australian and New Zealand flag. He checked the tickets to establish who was playing.

The driver asked him what he thought of the current Australian bowlers. Myfanwy remembered snatches of conversations he had heard on the train. He parroted something he had heard about there being a lack of quality leg spinners since the days of Benaud. The Sikh nodded his head enthusiastically in response to this comment. He began talking about India's heritage of spin bowling. Myfanwy's eyes were beginning to glaze over as the driver began to wax lyrical about someone called Bishan Bedi. Fortunately, the cricket ground was coming into view. As Myfanwy paid his fare and tried to drag himself away, the driver was still making conversation.

'It's all spinning, spinning, spinning in India!' called out the driver, making a rotating gesture with his fingers. Myfanwy felt as though his head was spinning.

Wandering round outside Trent Bridge for twenty minutes, Myfanwy couldn't give his tickets away. He decided to walk up to the bridge, in the hope of finding better luck. He quickly changed his mind and turned back when he saw a familiar face touting on the bridge. He recognised the club-footed walk and rat-like features of Rich 'Boz' Bosworth. Like Myfanwy, he was a sly little petty thief. They had both served in North Sea Camp at the same time.

The strict regime of farm work at this borstal on the exposed Lincolnshire coast hadn't been the holiday of a lifetime for Myfanwy. He had struggled to survive amongst the hard cases in the camp. Boz had given him a hard time in more ways than one. On one particular occasion, Boz had told Myfanwy what he intended to do to him later on that day. In his desperation, Myfanwy managed to steal a biro which had been left lying on a table by a warder. Boz's reputation as a sexual predator was well known and Myfanwy had no intention of being the prey. When Boz and his cronies grabbed Myfanwy and dragged him behind a silo, he had struggled and managed to free his left arm. With Boz behind him with his chin resting on his neck, Myfanwy pulled the pen from under his shirt sleeve. He jabbed the pen into Boz's eye. With the pen sticking in his eye, Boz screamed in pain. His two accomplices quickly fled the scene, not wishing to be implicated in any crime. When Boz was cross-examined by the governor, he had been forced to say that the injury had been a self-inflicted accident rather than be branded a grass. As a consequence, as well as losing the eyesight in his left eye, he was punished for the theft of the pen. He stayed away from Myfanwy after that.

As Myfanwy made a hasty U-turn, he was forced to smile at the eyepatch that Boz still wore. Lady Fortune once again gave Myfanwy a break as he turned the corner onto Radcliffe Road. A couple of flabby, gullible-looking middle-aged men stood on the corner and Myfanwy heard one say that they should try the ticket office next. They snatched up all three of his tickets at face value without any haggling. Myfanwy strode off toward Bridgford Road, feeling somewhat peckish.

He found a nice, pretentious little bistro called Foucault's and sat down at one of the little tables outside. A pretty honeypot of a waitress came out wearing a long white apron like the ones worn by French waiters. He ordered poached egg with cheese on toast and fresh coffee. Someone had left behind a copy of *The Times*, which he picked up, taking the opportunity to catch up on the latest news. Thatcher had been refused an honorary degree by Oxford University, and the *Rainbow Warrior* had been blown up. A seventeen-year-old German tennis player called Boris Becker had won Wimbledon. Myfanwy already knew about this; the previous weekend he had been allowed to watch the men's final with his fellow inmates. Nobody had really been interested in the tennis and many had complained that they hadn't been allowed to watch the FA Cup Final.

As Myfanwy enjoyed his coffee and relished the fresh air and sunshine, he was joined by another customer. An elderly man who wore a red and yellow striped blazer, white flannel trousers and a panama hat sat at the next table. His hat had a band of identical red and yellow stripes around it. These were the eggs and bacon colours, worn by members of the prestigious Marylebone Cricket Club. Some waited decades for the privilege of becoming a member of the MCC.

The gentleman leaned over, and asked Myfanwy, 'Could I trouble you to borrow your newspaper, I haven't had time to buy one yet?'

Myfanwy graciously nodded his head and passed over the newspaper. 'By all means.'

'You're a gentleman, sir,' the old man replied, raising a pair of pince-nez spectacles to his bushy-browed eyes.

The gentleman turned to the sports reports and began reading the cricket scores. He chuckled and shook his head at something he had found amusing. He looked up at Myfanwy, taking his spectacles off to study him more closely. 'Are you here for the test match?' he asked.

Myfanwy looked up from the cigarette he was rolling. 'Yes, this pitch is a bit of a dead duck though.'

The old gentleman considered this, and then replied, 'Quite right, but it's still terribly good, top drawer batting.'

He continued to study Myfanwy, taking interest in his boating blazer, which he mistook for a cricket club blazer. 'Can't quite place those colours, are you I Zingari by any chance?'

Puzzled by this strange comment, Myfanwy shook his head.

'No, you don't look like a Harrovian,' said the old man, shaking his head thoughtfully. 'Bunch of Harrovians, your I Zingari Cricket Club.'

'No, err, this is an Athenians blazer,' Myfanwy replied, remembering the name of a local scooter club that went by that name.

'Really, I haven't heard of that one.'

'Oh yes, they have a long tradition in this area. They originally started out playing at Newstead Abbey when Lord Byron lived there.'

'How utterly fascinating!' The gent was taking a fancy to Myfanwy now. 'And do you bat or bowl?'

'Leg spin; Benaud has always been a big influence on me,' Myfanwy was beginning to feel like he was getting into form at the crease now.

'Oh first rate, deceive them with the wrong 'un, eh?' The old gentleman was making gestures with his hand, reminiscent of the Sikh taxi driver.

'Oh yes, I can tell you a thing or two about wrong 'uns.' *Change the subject, quick,* thought Myfanwy. The gentleman got up and sat next to Myfanwy, offering his hand. 'The name's Edward Towton, honoured to meet you sir.' He held Myfanwy's hand tightly in both his own hot and sweaty hands and shook them enthusiastically.

Edward finished his tea, and then looking at Myfanwy thoughtfully, he said, 'I say, I don't know what your plans are for today but I was wondering if you might care to join me in the executive suite?' He licked his lips, coyly placing his fingers on his alcohol ravaged face, and then continued, 'I'm afraid I've had to leave my friend Freddy behind at the hotel. He's lying in bed with one of his migraines. He really is a frightful bore.'

'Well I appreciate the offer, but I'm not sure I have the wherewithal to pay you for the ticket,' Myfanwy replied, preparing to mount a thoroughbred free ride.

'My dear boy, I wouldn't dream of taking a penny from you!' He placed his hand on Myfanwy's knee. 'You will be my guest for lunch and you will drink only the finest wines that Jove himself is served by Ganymede.'

Myfanwy held his hands up in a gesture of surrender. 'Well, when you put it that way, how can I refuse?'

Rising to his feet with a theatrical flourish, Edward grabbed his walking cane and, pointing like a figure in a neoclassical painting, exclaimed, 'Let us make haste then to Trent Bridge!'

CHAPTER NINE

We entered Trent Bridge through gates which led into a large yard at the rear of the Trent Bridge Inn. The whole area was teeming with people, who were milling around the concourse of the ground. A beer tent was providing plastic pint pots of various brews to a large queue of people, many of whom would be slobbering drunks before the day was out. The tantalising smell of frying onions on a burger stand wafted a fairground smell. Our first priority was to empty our bladders. The urinals were already full of men, shoulder to shoulder, who had tried to consume as many pints as possible in half an hour. Our Australian friend was there, leaning against the wall as he set free a gallon of breakfast beer.

We found our seats on the upper tier of the Parr Stand. We were in the middle of a row of seats that were already occupied. People half-heartedly moved their knees to one side to let us squeeze past. As we sat down, I surveyed the scene of that historic ground for the very first time. On my right was the pavilion, with its members' enclosure full of spectators. The flags of England and Australia hung limply on a pole either side of the pavilion roof. A steward in a long white coat ceremoniously rang a bell which hung near the pavilion's entrance. The players and umpires would appear shortly. The stand we were sitting in was named after a contemporary of William Clarke, named George Parr. An elm tree had once stood on the Bridgford Road, which because the renowned batsman hit so many times, was christened Parr's Tree.

The two umpires appeared from the pavilion and walked down the steps with sacerdotal dignity. In their long white coats they might have been selling seafood, like the men who came round the pubs on a Friday night. The umpires were greeted by muted applause, which grew in intensity as the two England batsmen came onto the field. Finally, the Australian team took to the field to a mixture of cheers and booing.

The crowd became quiet in anticipation of the first delivery of the day. I studied the huge scoreboard at the opposite side of the ground, dwarfed by an even bigger office block behind it. I recognised the names of the two English batsmen. I had seen them when Dad had been watching the cricket on television. I recognised one who had blond curly hair which reminded me of Harpo Marx. The other stocky batsman with the neatly trimmed beard reminded me of a grumpy pub landlord. I didn't recognise the tall Australian bowler with long fair hair who thoughtfully made his way back to his mark after every ball. He would then charge into the wicket to launch the ball like a trebuchet trying to breach a fortified city.

We couldn't seem to shake off our Australian friend, who sat at the front of our stand with his flag draped over the advertising hoardings. He shouted some remarks about the dietary habits of the bearded batsman. He seemed to be even more critical of the Australian bowling and fielding. 'You've got hands like feet!' he called out to a clumsy fielder. After half an hour, my mind was beginning to wander. I drifted into my own personal fantasy world, where I knew I would be happy for a while.

The provincial arena, situated in the arsehole of the empire, was tiny in comparison to the Flavian Amphitheatre in Rome. What I would have given for some good Falernian wine instead of the horse piss on offer here. At least the weather was uncharacteristically pleasant for Britannia. The entertainment offered few surprises after seeing an arena flooded in Rome for the staging of a mock sea battle. At least Diocletian had revived Christian persecution, so it wouldn't be all that bad.

I was suddenly woken from my reverie when there was a big appeal for leg before wicket. All the fielding side leapt up in the air like a Cotswold Morris side, minus hankies and bells. The umpire, who also seemed to have been lost in his own private daydreams, looked up after several moments of reflection and shook his head. The Australian fan cursed the umpire for his ocular inadequacy.

Alex had perked up since his initial melancholia and seemed more like his old self. He suggested fetching another round of drinks and I offered to help carry them in a desperate bid to find a distraction from the cricket. The concourse behind the stands was busy with groups of drinkers and toilet seekers. The serene pace of the match gave people the opportunity to drift in and out of the action, to wander round the ground like lost dogs. Some people were already collecting passes at the gates, to wander off into West Bridgford for lunch. The event had the atmosphere of a festival of cricket, spanning four or five days. Alex asked me cheerfully how I thought the cricket compared to our Wembley trip.

'No, there's no comparison,' I said. 'Seeing the Brazilians play at Wembley beats everything.'

'I wouldn't know, all I can remember seeing was that flag you kept waving.' This memory always seemed to amuse Alex.

'I seem to remember John was waving his flag as well,' I said. I noticed Alex's expression change as he processed this memory. I'd heard that John had run off to London after they'd had some kind of row.

In hindsight, the match against Brazil had been a disappointingly tame friendly. Brazil's great star at that time, Zico, scored the only goal from the penalty spot. There had been none of the superb artistry of the side that would go on to play in the World Cup of 1982. Players like Zico and Socrates created football magic in Spain; a team that was ultimately too good to win that year's trophy, stifled by physical, European defensive play.

I stood with Alex while he queued for the beer. I was constantly amazed by how many pints some people could carry in their hands. A couple of public school types stood in front of us, dressed in short-sleeved rugby shirts with the collars up, knee-length denim shorts and deck shoes. One of them had a fancy pair of sunglasses perched in his hair. They were part of a larger group who were all sat at the back of our own stand. Everyone could hear their interminable moronic laughter and boisterous joshing. I felt pity for the poor souls who had to sit in front of them all day.

'Come on, you arses, we want some beer!' Sunglasses called out. The other young man then playfully pushed Sunglasses, who proceeded to push his friend in return. This puerile game began to cause a commotion when the two youths stumbled into Alex. I noticed that Alex was obviously becoming increasingly irritated by this horseplay. As soon as the tomfoolery impinged on his own personal space, Alex snapped.

He grabbed Sunglasses by the throat. 'Calm yourself down, youth, or I'll take your nappy off and smack your arse!' he growled into the terrified youth's face.

The incident seemed to have taken place relatively unnoticed by anyone else in the area.

'Come on,' Sunglasses suggested to his friend, 'let's go to the other bar.' They scurried away; the tanned face of Sunglasses was now white as a sheet.

Alex blew his cheeks out, taking a deep breath, and then smiled at me apologetically. 'Why don't we nip round to the TBI for a quick one?' he asked, and then added nudging me, 'Ha! A quick one with Swift, eh?' I wasn't going to argue with him.

We were given a couple of passes by a steward at the gate. It was still busy inside the Trent Bridge Inn. One reason for this was the superior quality of the beer, compared with the overpriced brews that were served up in plastic containers inside the ground. I opted for a potent-looking ale called Nobbe's Leviathan. Alex said he didn't normally do the top shelf but that he fancied a chaser with his pint of mixed. Mixed was one of those concoctions like Black and Tan or Snakebite, that by blending two drinks, makes neither palatable. It seemed to me that the potency of the cider in Snakebite was diluted, rather than being strengthened by the addition of beer.

After ordering the drinks, Alex quickly drained his whisky in one gulp. He lit a cigarette and began inhaling like an expectant father outside a maternity ward. Ash dropped from his cigarette and he brushed it from his jeans with his right hand with its missing ring finger. This instantly reminded me of the comedian Dave Allen, who also had a missing digit. Such accidental amputations were an occupational hazard for miners. My father had lost a big toe; such mutilations had fascinated me as a small child.

Looking at me with amusement, Alex said, 'Last time I saw you, you were canoodling with some bird in that bus stop near the church.'

'That's all water under the bridge now,' I said, unconvincingly trying to sound like a man of the world.

'Just get yourself another girlfriend, mate, enjoy yourself while you can,' Alex sagely advised me. He seemed to have deduced from my tone that the experience had not ended well.

My first teenage romance had been too rich for my sensitive soul. I had fallen head over heels for the first girl who had taken an interest in me. She had grown bored with me and finished with me after a month. I went to pieces and broke an acoustic guitar to pieces outside her home. When a friend and I had kept a drunken vigil outside her house, her father chased us away.

'I could do with another one of these,' Alex said, looking at his empty whisky glass. 'Are you going to have one with me? Mister's drink, this is.'

'Maybe we should go back and get Dad a drink, he'll be getting the cob on.' I could sense that Alex was going into the same insular world of alcohol that Mum inhabited when she started bingeing.

Alex suddenly looked very melancholy. 'Yeah, you're probably right, let's get back to the mardy twat.'

★ ★ ★ ★ ★

Edward and Myfanwy entered Trent Bridge through the Dixon Gates, which led to the members' pavilion. The short walk from the high street had seemed to take an eternity. Edward had taken his time, regaling Myfanwy with his life story. He had taken his new friend's arm for support, though he seemed quite spritely for a gentleman of advanced age. Myfanwy learned that Edward had led an illustrious life in the pursuit of both a career in law and also in politics. He had made his name as a barrister, taking part in several highly publicised court cases. He had then proceeded to take the silk of a Queen's Counsel, before successfully taking the Conservative seat of North Berkminster. Myfanwy sensed that there was something darker lurking beneath the surface of this upstanding member of the community.

Edward led him through the Long Room, which he pointed out wasn't as long as the Long Room at Lord's. Above and along the length of the pavilion bar were mounted an array of ancient looking cricket bats. Each of these treasures of antiquity had been wielded by such notable players as W.G. Grace and C.B. Fry.

The only time Myfanwy had been in a cricket pavilion was when he and Spike had broken into one that belonged to the colliery club near where he lived. They found nothing there of any value except a priceless tin of Evo-Stik. They had built a fire to keep warm, smashing a few chairs to serve as firewood. The resulting fire left the entire pavilion in ashes.

They walked through the room, observed by the faces that peered from team photographs. Solemn, hirsute-faced Victorians were succeeded by Brylcreem boys with clean-shaven faces. Faces wearing sideburns and collar-length hair signalled the arrival of the 1970s. Standing behind people who sat viewing the game from the windows, they took in the splendour of Trent Bridge on a sunny day, during a test match.

'I was here when Bredman played, you know,' said Edward proudly. He gazed through the window as if he could see that very same game again clearly.

'Oh yes, the Bread Man, he was the best,' said Myfanwy, completely lost again.

'Of course, Larwood and the boys had softened The Don up a bit when I saw him,' Edward continued, still in his own world of 1934.

Edward took Myfanwy by the hand and led him to a door with a brass knob fashioned to look like a cricket ball. On the wall above the door was a painting of a cricket scene. The painting showed a late afternoon scene of a cricket match drifting along into an inevitable draw. The painting was titled *Playing out Time in*

Fading Light. Myfanwy studied the picture and saw a metaphor for his own life. The sun was setting on his game already and there seemed to be no chance of a result. His only chance was to play a few lusty strokes and enjoy the last hour of play.

'Come on, let's find some refreshment,' suggested Edward, 'I've got a thirst that could put Charybdis to shame after this morning's perambulations.'

Myfanwy followed him to a door which led to the Executive Suite.

There was no trace of a sausage roll or a potted meat sandwich amongst the *amuse-bouche* on display in the Executive Suite. When he had walked out of jail that morning, the most Myfanwy had wanted was proper toothpaste instead of the prison issue tooth powder. The Chateau Lafleur tasted better than the poteen that he had imbibed while inside Glen Parva.

Edward greeted a man who he addressed as 'Kenny'. 'And how is the Right Honourable Member of Parliament for Rushcliffe today?'

The portly man with the pint in his hand politely stopped to speak briefly to Edward, before moving on quickly to speak to someone else.

'They're saying he's tipped to be Maggie's choice for the next Minister of State for Employment,' Edward said, conspiratorially.

'Excellent!' Myfanwy said, with a hint of cynicism. 'That's one off the employment figures straight away then.'

'Let's hope he gets some of these vagabonds off their arses!' Edward said, wagging his finger.

Let's get them off their faces, thought Myfanwy, draining his glass of wine.

'My dear boy, let's get you another!' Edward cried out in a tone of concern, as though addressing one of the starving Ethiopians.

'Oh, you're spoiling me sir, truly you are!' Myfanwy bowed his head graciously.

With a fresh drink in his hand, Myfanwy settled down to watch the cricket from an exclusive balcony. He and Edward were accompanied by Trent Bridge's very own dog-collared chaplain. The chaplain shared the same bibulous, alcohol ravaged features as Edward. As his companions discussed the impending demise of the Anglican Church, Myfanwy retreated into his own thoughts. He was startled from his soliloquising by the sight of Boz Bosworth and Nappy Daniels, trying to enter the members' enclosure. They were trying to gain access to the enclosure through a side gate, but were barred entry by a fierce-looking steward. Myfanwy feared that Boz must have somehow been alerted to his presence in the pavilion. He ruminated on this for a while and then his mood brightened as a plan began to form in his mind. Edward noticed Myfanwy's pensive expression and concluded that he was simply engrossed in the elegant stroke play of the England batsmen.

Making the excuse that he needed to visit the lavatory, Myfanwy set off to investigate the whereabouts of his nemesis. He was disappointed to have found Nappy Daniels in the thrall of Bosworth. The baby-faced rascal had been one of Myfanwy's band of diddy mods. He had worn the scruffy parka with pride and now he was in league with the cyclops.

Venturing furtively out of the safety of the pavilion, Myfanwy feared he might walk straight into the path of Boz. He didn't have to look far before he spotted him queuing behind a dozen or so people at one of the temporary bars. He looked round and saw Nappy leaning against a wall, round a corner where the bar staff wouldn't see his juvenile features. While Boz was distracted, he hurried over to where Nappy was loitering.

'Nappy, how's it going, youth? Listen, I can't stop; give this to Boz and tell him to meet me in the pavilion bar at one o'clock.' He handed Nappy the pilfered membership card.

Nappy looked surprised to see his old friend, and said, 'Hey Myfanwy, I heard you were due out! I didn't know you knew Boz?'

'You look well, mate; just tell him I've got an offer he won't be able to refuse!'

Myfanwy fled in fear that Boz would see him. He entered the pavilion via the same gate that Boz had tried to gain entry. He couldn't risk Nappy seeing him go back the way he had come out.

When he returned, he found Edward heartily applauding a cavalier square cut. The batsman had just rocked back with perfect timing and executed the shot with exquisite panache.

Seeing Myfanwy once again, he took his hand in his. 'Oh my boy, I thought you'd abandoned me!' Edward cried out, a little too loudly for Myfanwy's taste. All he could do now was wait until the lunch interval, to see if his plan would succeed. He drank some more wine and prepared himself.

CHAPTER TEN

The famous twin towers of Wembley Stadium hove into view as the minibus finally made its way into the busy car park. Heidi and Kirstie and the rest of the group had arrived with a full hour to spare. When they entered the stadium, they found the pitch area already thronged with spectators. The area in front of the stage was already packed with the keenest fans, who had been queuing since dawn for the gates to open at ten o'clock. Tom had given everyone instructions where to wait at the end of the concert if they couldn't find the coach.

Jeanette had wasted no time in finding a boy to spend the day with. She had hooked up with a young man with a dark spiky mullet, wearing a sleeveless U2 T-shirt and black jeans. As soon as Status Quo had taken the stage with 'Rockin' All Over the World', Jeanette was grinding herself against her new friend's crotch. He started to grope her buttocks and Jeanette grabbed his hand and began to gradually pull him into the multitude of people where she wouldn't be seen.

The Coldstream Guards had performed 'The Royal Salute' in honour of the arrival of the Prince and Princess of Wales. The royal couple entered the Royal Box accompanied by Bob Geldof. One or two people had booed at this point, but Heidi adored military bands. Heidi was a big fan of the royal family, especially Prince Andrew, who she would have loved to marry.

Status Quo were bashing out their unique brand of revved-up boogie rock. Francis Rossi wore a black waistcoat and collarless shirt that made him look like a member of Chas and Dave. The moustachioed bass player with the bubbly black hair reminded Heidi of Bobby Ball. She though that Rick Parfitt looked quite handsome with his long blond hair flowing. Heidi couldn't wait to see Spandau Ballet and some of the other current acts. She thought it quite ridiculous to see these aging rockers prancing around on stage. She tried to imagine Duran Duran or U2 still performing when they were all in their fifties. She thought that Tony Hadley might look quite dignified as a sexagenarian, crooning away like a New Romantic Tony Bennett.

It was hot in the centre of the pitch area of the stadium where Heidi and her companions were all stood, minus Jeanette. Heidi imagined that the stadium had never been filled to such a capacity before Live Aid. She wasn't aware that her own grandfather had attended the FA Cup Final of 1923, when the stadium had opened its gates to the public for the first time. He had come to cheer on West Ham United, who were playing Bolton Wanderers in the final. No one had anticipated the crowds to exceed the already huge capacity of the new stadium, but two or three times the estimated number arrived that day. The pitch itself became flooded with spectators as the terraces became dangerously packed. Mounted police were assigned the task of clearing the pitch of spectators. A policeman on a white horse called Billie cleared the spectators onto the track that surrounded the pitch, allowing the match to proceed. The day would always be remembered as 'The White Horse Final'.

None of this meant anything to Heidi, who was focusing her attention on what seemed to be Jeanette, mounted on someone's shoulders near the front of the stage. It was without a doubt Jeanette up there amongst waving flags of various nations. Heidi couldn't believe her eyes. *Please don't get your tits out*, she thought.

'Oh my God! Is that who I think it is?' Kirstie asked disbelievingly.

'Fraid so,' Heidi confirmed.

After Status Quo finished their three songs, it was time for The Style Council to perform their set. They were introduced by a middle-aged man with tinted glasses and dark shoulder-length hair. Heidi couldn't make out whether it was Mike Read or Simon Bates till he spoke. Then she recognised the voice of the 'Radio 1 Bits and Pieces' jingle. It was Tommy Vance, who presented the *Friday Rock Show*. It seemed a bit incongruous, him introducing The Style Council. Heidi thought Paul Weller looked really cool in his red top and white trousers. She though his sidekick on the keyboards needed a straw boater to match his boating blazer. Jeanette seemed to have disappeared into the crowd again.

Heidi looked round to see if any of their group was still stood in the same area. Gareth was chatting up a couple of Sloane Rangers who were dressed as though they were doing a photo shoot for *Harpers & Queen*. A group of girls were cavorting about, wearing nothing but skimpy bikinis. Even Callum was sharing some sweets with a plump blond girl in a West German football shirt. It seemed like everyone was copping off with someone.

It was great to see everyone having such a good time to save the lives of all those Ethiopians. Heidi reflected that at least the twenty-five pounds she had spent on her ticket might make some kind of difference. It would have made more sense for everyone to fast for twenty-four hours and raise money that way. At least then, people would be able to reflect on the pain and suffering that famine caused. Heidi had never really been a fan of Bob Geldof and The Boomtown Rats. She was even less of a fan of his wife, who always seemed to be sat with her legs open on *The Tube*, flirting with some pop singer. Geldof had taken on the Herculean task of organising Live Aid with a messianic fervour. Seeing him with his dishevelled clothes and wild hair reminded her of Jesus after his time in the wilderness. Geldof seemed to be the last person that she would have chosen for a task of such Biblical dimensions; but choosing someone so incongruous seemed to Heidi to be exactly the kind of thing Jesus would do. She remembered the Caravaggio painting, *The Calling of Saint Matthew*. She imagined Geldof in the role of Saint Matthew, pointing at himself as if to say, 'Not me, Guv, you've got the wrong bloke!'

* * * * *

Mansfield had woken from its dreamy slumber since Dean Swift had cycled home through its streets like a figure in a dream. The fruit and veg men had been the first to wake her at six o'clock. Weekend shop girls then crept in with their cheaply bought hangovers. The first shoppers of the day then appeared, with summer salads on their minds. The only food queues here were for the best butcher's shop.

The streets were full by midday. The busy market square was filled with stalls that spilled out as far as Westgate. A Morris side danced with sticks to the accompaniment of a melodeon player dressed in a coat of coloured strips of rag. As they danced to the tune of 'Constant Billy', a Fool in a coxcomb pranced around, hitting people over the head with an inflated pig's bladder on a stick.

Mister Splash the clown came riding down Westgate on his tricycle, waving at passers-by and squeezing his hooter. A hippy in a beret stood outside WH Smith with his guitar, singing 'Sunshine Superman'. On a corner of the market square, a carousel transported children in double decker buses and racing cars to their own personal fantasy worlds. The pubs were filling up with lunchtime drunks, eager to wipe the memory of the week's labours by imbibing the waters of Lethe.

Passing sullenly amongst the shoppers, Colin Townroe stopped at the little newspaper kiosk at the bottom of Regent Street. The sound of The Style Council performing 'Walls Come Tumbling Down' at Live Aid was coming from a radio. Colin perked up when he heard this; he preferred The Style Council to The Jam. He purchased twenty Berkeley Superkings and some chewing gum. He eyed up the lady behind the counter appreciatively. She must be in her late forties, he thought. He'd never been with anyone over thirty and the thought of trying out a mature woman began to arouse him.

He walked towards Church Street and began thinking about his confrontation with Dawn before he had stormed out of the house. Once she had seen the smashed window, she had obviously spent the whole morning stewing and waiting for him to wake up, so she could cross-examine him. She had drawn the conclusion that some cuckolded husband had smashed the window. When he told her the story about someone on a bike crashing through the window, he simply substituted the original location for one on his usual journey. He said he had popped into the newsagents at the bottom of Southall Road when the incident had taken place. Dawn accused him of telling her a pack of lies, so he had indignantly walked out of the house. He was now heading to the Bridge Tavern for his regular Saturday afternoon drinking session. As he approached the Church of Saint Peter and Saint Paul's, a wedding was taking place. The church's eight bells were ringing hymeneal peals of congratulation. The bride in her white trousseau and the kilted groom came out to a shower of confetti and cheering. Colin looked away disdainfully, wishing that he had never been foolish enough to fall into the trap of marriage.

He walked into the Bridge Tavern, breathing in the comforting aroma of stale beer and cigarette smoke. Pluto Lockwood was sat on a bar stool at the bar, holding court. Craig Strachan was by his side, wearing his Rangers shirt. Feggy Edwards was also there, wearing his old PE shorts and a purple vest; he was watching the Live Aid concert on a television on the wall. Paul Weller and Mick Talbot were being interviewed by Janice Long. Feggy was excited because he'd seen Janice Long at a Radio 1 roadshow at Llandudno the previous year.

Strachan was regaling everyone with a story about one of his escapades with the Rangers ICF. He was explaining in military detail how they had ambushed a group of Hibernian's Capital City Service firm outside the Easter Road stadium.

'So how come your Rangers crew uses the same name as The Hammers Inter City Firm? Why don't you get your own name?' Pluto interjected.

'It was they London poofs stole the name from Rangers actually, big man!' Strachan twitched his neck with irritation. An industrial accident had left his face badly scarred, giving him a sinister countenance.

Pluto winked at Colin, who shook his head with mock despair. Strachan looked at Pluto, then Colin, who he studied with scorn. He was sceptical of Colin's ability to stand in a fight and couldn't understand why Pluto seemed to rate him so highly.

Colin feared that Strachan knew that he was a coward. He felt that the Scot could smell the fear on him. Colin had earned Pluto's respect one day near the beginning of the preceding season when Stags had been playing Bristol Rovers. A gang of them had walked into a trendy new bar near the football ground called Bunter's. As they gathered at the bar to order drinks, Pluto noticed a couple of Rovers supporters, drinking near a window. Pluto strode across the room towards them, much to their dismay.

One of them held his hands up submissively. 'We're not looking for any trouble, mate.'

Picking up a chair, Pluto said calmly, 'Well, you've found it now.'

He swung the chair at the jaw of the nearest unlucky face. Suddenly, all hell was let loose as the landlord came from behind the bar to stop the trouble. As glasses and chairs were broken, Colin backed away into the toilet. He cowered behind the door of a cubicle while he listened to the noise outside. After several minutes, the noise died down and he furtively emerged from the gents. He quickly made his way past the casualties of the incident. 'I'm going to phone for an ambulance!' he called out.

No sooner had Colin left Bunter's, than a horde of Bristolian hooligans came running down the street towards him. He only managed to run a few yards before they were breathing down his neck. He turned round to plead with them that he was a Rovers supporter himself. As he began to attempt to parley in a vague West Country accent, Pluto and reinforcements came charging and scattering the Bristol crew. From Pluto's vantage point, Colin had seemed to be standing his ground, beckoning his foes with outstretched arms. He had become a legend that day amongst the Coocachoo Crew for his conspicuous valour against insuperable odds. As a consequence, he had become one of Pluto's inner circle of lieutenants and had been fortunate so far, in avoiding any major skirmishes. Colin didn't know that Strachan's scepticism was more due to jealousy than genuine disbelief in his capability in a fight.

Pluto's wife had dropped him off after a golf session, taking his clubs home with her. He was still dressed like a harlequin, in a motley assortment of designer golf wear. He considered himself an arbiter of football casual style, taking his cue from the first division football hooligans of London. The designer tracksuits he wore always reminded Colin of his old PE teacher.

The antithesis of the trendy football casual walked into the pub. Mungo Severns strolled up to the bar in a Marksman Lager T-shirt, brown cords and plimsolls. Mungo was a throwback to an earlier generation of football hooligans from the early seventies. All that was needed back then was a sturdy pair of boots and a scarf tied round the wrist to pass muster. Pillaging motorway cafes after away games had been his favourite sport.

Mungo ordered a bottle of Newcastle Brown and emptied some of its contents into a half pint glass to drink. Pluto suggested that they should adjourn to the benches at the front of the pub to enjoy the sunshine. Now joined by several more of their crew, the assembled group began to drink in earnest.

'Plenty of fanny about today, Mister Townroe,' observed Pluto.

'I bet she likes her gravy,' said Colin, studying a particularly attractive specimen of the female species.

'He's prick-happy, that lad,' said Mungo.

Pluto slapped Colin on the back. 'He's a stallion, that's what he is!'

'When Colin fucks 'em, they stay fucked!' Colin declared proudly, warming to his favourite subject.

'That wee girl in The King's Head wasnae so enamoured by your charm, eh but!' Strachan sneered.

Pluto remembered the girl slapping Colin round the face, and laughed. 'What did you say to her, Stallion?'

'I said, do you like it up the arse, duck? You will do when Colin's fucked you.' Colin often referred to himself in the third-person. This habit seemed to suggest some kind of Freudian dual personality.

All of a sudden, the roar of a motorbike engine interrupted the jovial banter. Rollo came to a halt outside a tattoo parlour across the road from where Pluto's party watched. Rollo soon emerged with his wife, Doll. With her long flowing red hair and breasts down to her waist, Doll was the embodiment of the virago queen of the Iceni. This formidable biker Boudicca stepped out to hoots of derision from Pluto and his legionaries.

'Oi, Captain Caveman, giz a ride on your bike!' Colin bravely called out.

'Careful, duck, them tits will be dragging on the road!' Mungo added.

Rollo didn't condescend to even offer a glance at the odious crew, simply offering his raised middle finger in salutation. Feeling a confrontational mood coming on,

Pluto picked up a Newcastle Brown bottle and slung it across the road, where it smashed inches from Rollo's bike. Rollo continued to pull away stoically from the scene. Doll screamed bloodcurdling threats of castration. A pint glass smashed close to the bike as it raced away from the scene. Pluto and the boys cheered and then began singing a medley of football terrace anthems.

Pluto got out some calling cards he'd had printed and started handing them out. 'All the top firms hand out calling cards when they give someone a good hiding.'

The cards had the phrase 'We Just Want You!' accompanied by a photo of Alvin Stardust pointing with his gloved hand. Everyone eagerly accepted half a dozen or so of the cards.

A young couple walked by, carrying bags of shopping. The young man glanced across the road in the direction of the pub; he quickly averted his eyes in front of him as he saw the gang of thugs leering at his wife.

'Giz a gobble, duck!' shouted Mungo.

'Piss off!' the young woman shouted back.

'Just keep walking!' her boyfriend hissed, keeping his head down.

'Well, I'm not taking that shit off anyone!'

'You're going to get my head kicked in if you don't shut up!'

Pluto got up on the bench and shouted, 'Oi, twat! Turn around and look at me.'

'Come on, hurry up,' the young man pleaded with his girlfriend.

'I'm going as fast as I can,' she grumbled, ignorant of the looming threat of violence..

'Come on, I dare you to turn round!' Pluto shouted again, and then sat down again, bored with the game.

Mungo was enjoying this game of heckling and terrorising passers-by. A middle-aged woman came down the street pushing her teenage son in a wheelchair. As they passed the Bridge Tavern, her son, who had cerebral palsy, noticed the gang of surly-looking youths glaring at them.

'Well if it isn't Lockwood the dunghill cock and his band of stinkards!' he called out, knowing full well that they wouldn't be able to understand a word he was saying.

'Ayup, Joey,' said Mungo, waving his hand up and down limply, as if to a child.

'Thy Worst. I fart at thee,' quoth the plucky youth; an aficionado of Ben Jonson.

'Yeah, see you Joey!' said Mungo, who was clearly not conversant with early modern drama, and carried on waving moronically.

'How do you know his name's Joey?' asked Strachan.

'Don't you remember Joey Deacon on *Blue Peter*?'

'Do I fucking look like I watch *Blue* fucking *Peter*?' said Strachan.

'I thought you were more of a *Jackanory* man, actually,' said Pluto, amused by the irony of his retort.

Mungo began doing playground spastic impressions.

Meanwhile, the young man with cerebral palsy continued his journey towards the library with his mother. His name was Steve Tompkins and he was going to the library to do some research for the historical novel he intended to write, with his mother acting as his amanuensis. He planned to set his book during the Battle of Lepanto, with Miguel de Cervantes as his main character.

Steve had found inspiration to write after seeing the television appearances of Joey Deacon, who also had cerebral palsy. He had been fortunate enough to meet Deacon before his death in 1981. Steve kept Deacon's autobiography, *Tongue Tied*, as a reminder that anything was possible.

CHAPTER ELEVEN

When the lunch interval arrived, Myfanwy once again made his excuses to Edward, who told him to hurry back for lunch. He knew that Boz would only be able to gain entry to the bar from the rear of the pavilion, access to the enclosure being restricted to ticket holders only. He once again approached the door with the brass cricket ball handle. Aware that Boz could be stood right behind that door, he opened it with stealth. He was about to peer through the gap when a tap on the shoulder made him jump with fright. Turning round, he was relieved to see that it was a white-coated steward.

'Is everything all right, sir?' asked the steward.

'Err,' Myfanwy glanced again through the door and instantly spotted Boz waiting near the bar. 'Well no, actually, there's a gentleman in there who tried to sell me some tickets and a membership card earlier today. I have reason to believe he might be some kind of criminal.'

'Oh, I see,' said the steward. 'We've had some reports of stolen property this morning, could you describe this person?'

'Oh yes, I couldn't forget that face. He wears an eyepatch and walks with a pronounced limp.'

The steward offered his sincerest apologies and proceeded to find police assistance to apprehend the villain. Myfanwy raced back to take lunch with Edward. He was feeling ravenously hungry now, after eating only *amuse-bouche* for sustenance. A lavish buffet was laid out and once again, Myfanwy noted the absence of boiled ham and Battenberg cake.

As he tucked into the ostentatious repast, Edward approached him with a new arrival.

'May I introduce my new friend, Myfanwy; Myfanwy, meet the one and only Mister Tip Topley.'

Myfanwy's jaw dropped with the realisation that he was standing before one of his musical heroes. He was dressed in a pair of cricket flannels, held up with an MCC tie. He wore a distinctly Byronic-looking white shirt and a wide-brimmed straw hat; with his neatly trimmed beard he looked like a character from *Brideshead Revisited*. Myfanwy couldn't help noticing that he had a habit of sniffing and pinching his nose.

Myfanwy pointed at Tip's nose. 'Touch of the old hay fever, eh?' he asked with a knowing wink.

'I'm a martyr to it,' Tip replied. 'Pleased to meet you,' he said, offering a limp hand to shake.

'I once successfully defended Tip in a very highly publicised drug case,' Edward said proudly.

'Oh yes!' Tip recalled. 'The notorious "Acid Bath Orgy" drug bust.'

Tip had been arrested in a drug raid in 1967, labelled by a leading tabloid newspaper as the 'Acid Bath Orgy'. The police had found, amongst other things, a bath generously laced with LSD, containing Tip and a groupie.

Myfanwy was more of a fan of Tip's earlier recordings with his first band, The Prentice Boys. He found his later albums with the psychedelic rock band, Toy Mistress, too far out for his orthodox mod taste. Tip had once been a promising English literature undergraduate at Oxford, until he was sent down for smoking marijuana. He then formed his first band, The Prentice Boys, playing lead guitar. The band's interpretations of Chicago blues classics became a big hit with the nascent mod scene. In 1966 he founded Toy Mistress. Their 1967 album, *The Valediction*, became an all-time classic. Tip's obsession with the Metaphysical poets permeated much of Tip's work during that decade.

With his ego pulled down a few pegs by LSD, he took a back seat, playing lead guitar for several American bands. First, he played guitar with a laidback Southern rock band. He then played with an even more laidback Californian rock band. Drugs, religious cults and finally mediocracy characterised the 1970s for Tip.

After several years spent in obscurity and in and out of rehab centres, he finally emerged again. Still mediocre, he was now relying on a trendy young producer to sell his new album to a new audience. His performances at the South African Sun City resort left him blacklisted. Consequently, he was omitted from the list of artists asked to perform at the Live Aid concerts that were taking place in London and Philadelphia.

Tip looked around and yawned, then raising his eyebrows at Myfanwy as if he'd just materialised before his very eyes, and said, 'So are you Edward's latest nephew then?'

Myfanwy was still a little star struck by the presence of Tip, but composed himself enough to answer. 'Err, no, actually I just met him this morning. We just got talking about cricket and things kind of progressed from there.'

'Of course they did,' said Tip with a sardonic grin. 'So what's he done with Freddy then?'

'I think Edward said something about him not feeling very well.'

'Yes, there's a lot of it about at the moment.'

This time it was Myfanwy's turn to grin sardonically. 'Yes, I can see you're suffering right now.'

'I'd hazard a guess,' said Tip, waving his finger with a thoughtful expression, 'Freddy threw a tantrum because Edward wouldn't buy him any more coke and he will be climbing the walls of his hotel room right now. Meanwhile, Edward's found another little boy to play with.'

There was an uncomfortable pause as Myfanwy struggled to think of something to say while Tip adopted a disinterested pose.

'The Prentice Boys were the reason I got into the whole mod thing,' Myfanwy said, holding out the collar of his boating blazer, which had a Prentice Boys badge pinned onto it. 'Even The Who and The Yardbirds can't compete with The Prentice Boys,' he said, proudly pointing to the badge.

'We were never really mods,' Tip reflected. 'It was just a gimmick, really; we were just jumping on the first bandwagon that came along.'

Myfanwy felt the existential despair of a Christian who has just discovered that God doesn't exist. With one flippant statement, his hero had shattered his illusions.

Edward was chatting to a woman who spoke with an American accent. Myfanwy recognised her as Tip's new wife. He remembered seeing the couple in a newspaper, getting married. Tip was twenty years her senior. Her name was Lucy Bahramov, heiress to the multimillion-dollar Bahramov Department Store fortune. There had been talk in the newspapers about her father threatening to cut her out of her inheritance if she married Topley. Some said that she had married the rock star simply as an act of rebellion.

Tip began looking around furtively and rubbing his nose again.

'Seems like your hay fever is playing up again?' Myfanwy inquired.

'Yeah, I need my medicine,' said Tip with a cheeky grin. 'Do you suffer with hay fever at all?'

'Oh yes,' replied Myfanwy, shaking his head, 'I get afflicted with stomach cramps and fevers when I get it bad.'

'I've got it bad right now,' Tip said, looking round and licking his lips. 'I need to go to the toilet and have my medicine, perhaps you could show me the way? I don't seem to remember where the lavatories are in here.'

'Follow me, Your Modness,' said Myfanwy, obsequiously bowing and scraping and gesturing with an outstretched arm. As they passed through the Long Room, Tip glanced around at *Playing out Time in Fading Light*. Unlike Myfanwy, this was not the first time that Tip had seen this painting. Like Myfanwy, he attached a great deal of poignancy to the metaphor that the painting represented. With Myfanwy as his batting partner, maybe it was time for them both to cut and pull a few shots before the close of play.

They found a cubicle and Tip began to chop several very generous lines of cocaine. They emerged several minutes later, feeling refreshed and recovered by the efficacious powder. Tip had completely redeemed himself in Myfanwy's eyes and regained his heroic status. He decided that he wouldn't take off the Prentice Boys badge after all.

'Edward, you old queen!' Tip called out to the eminent barrister. He then grabbed Edward and gave him a big kiss on both cheeks.

Lucy gave Myfanwy a contemptuous look. 'He was okay a few minutes ago, have you been feeding him that shit?'

'Not guilty!' said Myfanwy, holding his hands up. 'I think he might have had a few too many of those margaritas,' he said, pointing at the glass of green liquid in her hand. The glass with salt and a slice of lime on its rim looked like some kind of cold remedy to Myfanwy.

She poked a finger at Myfanwy's chest. 'I've seen scum like you hanging round Tip before, you're like leeches!'

Myfanwy was beginning to feel decidedly uncomfortable now, with all the attention he was getting from this heated exchange. 'Honestly, you've got me all wrong, duck, I'm as straight as a die, me!'

'Well, I think we should see what the cops have to say!'

Myfanwy looked round for support from Tip and Edward, but the two of them were doing some kind of waltz together. Edward was singing 'Why am I Always the Bridesmaid'. The image of the Sikh taxi driver came into his head, 'Spinning, spinning, spinning!' The whole room began to spin and the eyes of everyone seemed to be on him as paranoia replaced the euphoria of the cocaine. He stumbled across the room to a table laden with food and drink. Trying to compose himself, he took a few deep breaths and picked up a glass of champagne. He turned around in the hope that Lucy had backed away from him. He was once again filled with panic as a gentleman in a grey suit accompanied by two police officers came into the room. Everyone turned to look at the new visitors apart from Lucy, who looked angrily across at Myfanwy. The man in the grey suit walked across the room towards Tip and Edward, accompanied by the two officers, producing police identification from his inside pocket. Myfanwy saw the look of terror on Tip's face, while Edward looked quite nonplussed. Myfanwy's disorientation was replaced by bemusement as the plain-clothed police officer seemed to caution and arrest not Tip, but Edward. It was Edward who was then led from the room by the two uniformed policemen.

Edward looked round at Myfanwy with an attitude of complete stoicism and called out to him, 'I won't be long, dear boy; just need to assist these officers of the law with some legal matters.'

★ ★ ★ ★ ★

The northern extremities of the monstrous organism that was London came into view. Spike had successfully hitched there in three hours, in easy stages. He had begun his journey at the side of the A38, where he had shared some cider with a tramp. Spike had only walked a few hundred yards from Mansfield's bus station before this liquid brunch took place. The tramp was sat against the wall of the Mansfield Shoe Company. He wore a long black overcoat and his face was blackened by dirt and bonfire smoke. By his side was a briefcase that contained all his worldly goods. He spoke complete gibberish but had the good manners to share his bottle of cider.

Spike had been fortunate to hitch a ride as far as Leicester Forest services with a lorry driver who talked about nothing but sex. He talked constantly about his conquests, which beggared belief from a man who looked like a gurning champion.

When he arrived at Leicester Forest services, he took the opportunity to do his ablutions. When he came out of the toilets, a little black girl let go of the string which held her balloon. Spike retrieved the balloon, as the breeze from the entrance door blew it towards him. Her beaming parents held her up and told her to thank the man. Spike discovered that they were from a Pentecostal church in Leeds and were travelling to a gospel choir competition in London. He was told he would be welcome to travel with them on their coach if he would play the tambourine.

He had a ball, bashing that tambourine while the choir sang their songs all the way to London. The little girl kept peering over her seat at the friendly giant who had rescued her new balloon. Tea and sandwiches were constantly administered to him at regular intervals. Whether God above or pagan spirits sent that breeze his way, he had to conclude that there was definitely something in the air that day. These people in their Sunday best suits and dresses seemed to be the kindest and happiest he had ever met. They had taken him in and hadn't judged him, with his impotent Mohican hair and confrontational boots. He had to respect their faith, which hinged on something that seemed so ludicrous, at least as far as the materialistic minds of modern society were concerned.

When it was time to say farewell, the whole coach seemed to want to either kiss him or shake his hand. The little balloon girl even wanted to give him a hug. He was dropped off near the Swiss Cottage tube station. The choir was travelling eastwards toward Camden Town and he needed to travel west along the Belsize Road, which would lead him to Kilburn High Road. He didn't feel confident enough to take the tube and preferred to conserve his meagre resources anyway. So he began walking westwards towards his destination.

This was the first time that Spike had ever been in London, and he was already feeling overwhelmed by its immensity. It seemed like a place that could swallow you up, and where you might never see open fields or the sea again. He was starting to feel sweaty in his Riot Squad T-shirt and hoped that John still had the Peter and the Test Tube Babies T-shirt he had borrowed him. He came to a crossroads and saw a sign for Abbey Road. The sudden image of the four Beatles walking across the zebra crossing raised his spirits.

Outside a Littlewoods store, a drunk was singing 'Jake the Peg'; he waved the third leg which he had taken from a mannequin. A procession of Hare Krishna devotees dressed in saffron robes came down the street, chanting their mantra and banging drums. With a single lock of hair at the back of their shaven heads, they didn't look that different to Spike.

A girl sitting on a blanket asked him if he could spare any change. She wore her auburn hair in the style of a skinhead girl, now slightly overgrown. She wore Doc Martens shoes, bleached jeans and a Blitz T-shirt. He found some change and sat with her and they shared a cigarette that they had begged from a passer-by. She was a gregarious girl and was pleased to have someone to talk to. She went by the incongruous name of Podge; she didn't appear to be the slightest bit podgy. Spike couldn't quite place her accent; to his ears it sounded a bit Geordified. He discovered that she had come down from Darlington. She began to summarise her story:

'I started seeing this bloke called Fritch who I was introduced to at a National Front meeting. I was never really into all that stuff, but a few of the skinheads who I was hanging around with wanted to impress the big boys; peer pressure and all that. Fritch wasn't a skin, he was really into the Nazi thing though. I was only fifteen at the time and there was something really charismatic about him. He had this neat moustache that he was always pruning away at. He used to have this slicked-back hairstyle, shaved round the sides, looked a bit old-fashioned. He always used to wear a black shirt and pegged trousers. Anyway, whatever it was, he reeled me in.

'I started seeing him and at first it was great, he was spending all this money on me and picking me up in his car. I never really got the Nazi thing though; he used to play these records of Hitler's speeches and kept weird things like SS daggers. Mum and Dad were really wary of him; not just because he was seven years older, but they didn't like the Nazi stuff. I couldn't see it at the time, but he was becoming really manipulative and caused a big fall out between me and Mum and Dad. Then he stopped letting me see me mates.'

Spike was wondering if Podge would ever stop to catch her breath, so he stuffed the cigarette in her mouth. She took a long pull on it and inhaled the smoke deeply into her chest, squinting from the smoke that got into her eyes. She then carried on with her story.

'Things started to take a really nasty turn when he started knocking me about for really stupid things like not folding the tea towels properly. Then after a year he brought this other girl called Suze home and I basically had to share him with her. After a bit he started wanting us to do stuff in front of him. That wasn't actually that bad and as Suze started getting the same treatment as me, we started getting really close.

'That was when we decided to make a run for it and get as far away from him as we could. We pinched a wad of his cash and got on a coach down to London. As soon as we got here, I realised things weren't going to be easy. As soon as we got off the coach at Victoria there were predators from either some religious cult or wherever, trying to offer us somewhere to stay. We got a room the first night we stayed but when I woke up the next morning, Suze had gone and taken what bit of money we had. I was hanging round where all the tourists go for the first few weeks trying to get a bit of money together for something to eat. I was that desperate I ended up going with this bloke; it was disgusting and I threw up afterwards.

'I started getting paranoid that Fritch was going to come looking for me, so I figured I should move away from the centre of London. I was sleeping on Primrose Hill one day when these hippy types took me in and I've been staying at their squat for the last fortnight.'

Spike felt quite choked up by Podge's tale and admonished himself for being such a soft twat. He went to a nearby off licence and bought ten cigarettes for Podge. The owner of the shop came out shortly afterwards, and warned Podge that he would call the police if she didn't stop loitering outside his shop. Spike became quite aggressive at this point and the shop owner backed away, threatening to call the police. Podge suggested that this might be a good time to move on. Spike told her he was heading to Kilburn to meet his friend and invited her to join him.

CHAPTER TWELVE

Sunlight was filtering in through the pink sheet that served as a curtain in John's bedroom. He had slept deeply, and his bladder had been busy doing its job for the last eight hours. He went across the landing in his T-shirt and pants to the toilet, scratching under his armpits like an ape. He could smell bacon frying and what sounded like Spandau Ballet performing 'True' on the radio. As he passed a satisfying stream of piss into the toilet bowl, he remembered the concert.

He dressed and crossed to the kitchen where Jean Louis, his Senegalese flatmate, was preparing the belated breakfast. John placed several pieces of bacon between two slices of bread, bid Jean Louis farewell and hurried out the front door. He returned two minutes later, minus the sandwich, and grabbed a book.

John had arranged to meet his friend, Ray Keaton, at the Bonaparte's Retreat pub on Kilburn High Road. He had borrowed a book from Ray which he wanted to return. He had just finished *Dubliners* by James Joyce and was eager to discuss the book with Ray. He was developing an insatiable appetite for literature and Ray, or 'Keats' as he was better known, dealt books to him like an erudite drug pusher.

Ten years earlier, Ray had been leading an academic life. He had studied English literature at Dublin's Carysfort College. While studying there, Ray had got to know the poet Seamus Heaney, who was head of English at the college. He had shown promise as a poet himself, gaining attention from Heaney. The literary critic Edna Longley had referred to what she called Heaney's 'skinny quatrains', and Ray liked to think of his own stanzas as Rubenesque. Ray's life changed when he fell in love with Mary Cochrane. Mary had been the girlfriend of a Dublin gangster called Tamburlaine Doyce. After an apprenticeship taking part in several major armed robberies in the late 1960s, Doyce turned his attention to protection rackets and money laundering. He emerged victorious after a bloody gangland feud, which left him the undisputed king of the Dublin underworld of the 1970s.

Whilst still studying, Ray took a job as a barman in a pub run by Doyce. Tamburlaine was living upstairs at the time and it was here that Ray became acquainted with Mary. They began a dangerous love affair, which resulted in a secret marriage and the birth of a son whom they named Caedmon. Doyce regarded Mary as his own property, and Ray and his new wife and baby were forced to flee to Belgium, after the gangster had made it clear that there would be retribution for the two lovers.

Ray and Mary got on a ferry to the Belgian seaside town of Ostend and stayed there for two years. Ray found work as a barman in a bar called Habsburg's, located in a house that dated back to the Spanish occupation in the seventeenth century. A regular visitor to Habsburg's during this time was the Motown legend Marvin Gaye. Out of shape and out of creative energy, Gaye had fled to Ostend to get his head together. The two of them would often go for walks along the blustery promenade. Marvin Gaye would rediscover his creative muse in Ostend and begin writing the songs for his swansong album, *Midnight Love*. During his stay in Belgium, Ray himself managed to gain modest success with a slim volume of poems entitled *Trappist Nectar*.

Ray and Mary came to stay with Mary's brother in London in April of 1984. It was during this time that Ray heard about the death of Marvin Gaye; shot dead by his father, after trying to intercede in an argument between his parents. Ray continued to write his poetry whilst taking various labouring jobs. John met Ray one day when they had both found a day's work clearing a warehouse.

Bonaparte's Retreat was an old Victorian pub; it was built in the ornate style of the gin palaces of that period. John was always impressed as he approached the pub, with its multi-coloured tiles and stained-glass windows. Entering the pub, he walked across the mosaic floor to the ornately carved wooden bar. He looked at himself for the first time that day, through the etched mirrors at the rear of the bar. Next to his image sat Ray Keaton, looking at John looking at himself.

'Excuse me, Lewis Carroll, I think it's your round!' Ray said, tapping his empty glass on the bar.

John ordered a pint of Harp lager and gestured to the barman to get Ray whatever he wanted.

Ray pushed his pint glass of creamy Guinness towards the barman. 'Squeeze us another one in there, will you.'

The barman gave Ray a sour look and began pouring a fresh glass of Guinness. The barman was an ill-natured and grossly overweight man from Cork. Ray enjoyed baiting the barman, who was easily provoked into a hostile reaction.

'Hey Eddie,' called out Ray, 'you could actually wear a T-shirt big enough to say "Belligerent bastard" across the chest.'

This remark raised a few laughs from the regulars that clung to the bar. Eddie glared at Ray, but remained silent; not wishing to give away that he didn't understand what 'belligerent' meant.

When the pint of stout was reluctantly served, Ray held his glass aloft to toast John. 'You're a lovely bloke and I forgive you your race.'

They both quaffed their pints, leaving them half empty after the first long gulp. Both were aware that there was only another hour until last orders and that any conversation must be tempered with serious drinking. Ray lit a cigarette and threw the open packet on the bar with another cigarette protruding from it for John.

Ray nodded at the copy of *Dubliners* on the bar. 'So what did you think of your first encounter with Mister Joyce, then?'

John took the cigarette from the packet and lit it with the proffered lighter in Ray's hand. He took a long thoughtful drag on it, narrowing his eyes as the smoke penetrated them. 'Does that old bloke go and have a wank in "The Encounter"?'

Ray laughed, 'Yeah, people are always fiddling with themselves in Joyce. Leopold Bloom does it in *Ulysses*.' He took a quick puff on his cigarette then continued, 'For all I know they might be doing it in *Finnegans Wake*, but I'm fucked if I can understand a word of it.'

'The people in the stories remind me of the people from where I come from,' John said. 'Nobody seems to be able to get out of the rut they're in.'

Ray nodded his head. 'You've got it!' he wagged his finger at John. 'You know when you have those dreams where you're trying to get somewhere and you just can't seem to get your legs moving; well, that's *Dubliners* for you.' Ray was warming to the theme now, 'It's like a metaphor for Dublin itself at the beginning of the twentieth century; still stuck in the nineteenth century, while every fucker else in Europe is moving on.'

John nodded his head. 'It always felt like that in Mansfield.'

Ray slapped him on the back. 'Ah, but you've had the courage to broaden your horizons!' He finished off the remainder of his drink before continuing, 'All Joyce's books are about people kicking around Dublin, but he fucked off around Europe to write them all.'

Ray gestured to the barman to refill their glasses, then got up, passing John another well-thumbed paperback. 'I need a piss. Here, see how you get on with this'.

John inspected the cover of the book which was called *Candide* by someone called Voltaire. The illustration on the cover showed a young man in a tricorn hat, a long red coat, britches and stockings. Under his right arm he held a potted plant and in his left hand was a watering can.

Paying for the fresh refills, Ray nodded towards the book. 'That'll start putting some intellectual hairs on your chest.'

'Hmm, looks interesting,' John said, reading the blurb on the rear cover.

'It's a satire of certain philosophical ideas of the eighteenth century,' said Ray. 'Your man Leibniz said that everything that happened in the world, good or bad, was all part of the greater good; all part of God's great plan, so to speak.' He took another big gulp of stout, checking the big clock on the wall. 'Anyway, Voltaire looked at all the horror that was happening at the time with the Lisbon earthquake and the Seven Years War and decided that Leibniz was full of shite.'

John choked on his drink as he began laughing; he loved Ray's unique way of describing things. An old man who was seated further along the bar began singing 'Give Me the Moonlight'. A blind man who sat at a nearby table began to join in.

Ray rolled his eyes. 'They're like a pair of fucking canaries, them two, when they get going!' Pointing at the jukebox, he said, 'Put something decent on John, for fuck's sake, let's liven this shebeen up a bit!'

Passing Ray a fiver to buy the next round, John walked over to the jukebox to choose some music. He selected 'Should I Stay or Should I Go' and 'Silver Machine'; after some thought he made his final selection, choosing 'She Sells Sanctuary' by The Cult. The doors opened and in walked Jean Louis, which was unusual, as he didn't normally go to pubs. John was infinitely more surprised to see his best friend Spike follow Jean Louis through the doors. For a third time John was surprised, when Podge, the street girl he had recently taken to bed, entered the pub.

★ ★ ★ ★ ★

When Pluto and his lieutenant Strachan decided to go back inside the Bridge Tavern to play a game of pool, their camp followers weren't far behind. Feggy Edwards was only too keen to resume watching the Live Aid concert on television.

He was disappointed to find the spiky-headed Nik Kershaw singing 'The Riddle'. Feggy was hoping that Madness or UB40 would be playing.

'Fuck this, I'm going outside for a fag!' he snapped irritably.

'Why don't you smoke it in here, you numpty?' Strachan asked.

'I don't like Nik Kershaw!' said Feggy as he stormed out.

Strachan shook his head, 'What a gobshite.'

Colin was standing at the bar with Mungo, who was telling one of his racist jokes. Colin always considered himself above the racist attitudes of people like Mungo. 'I'm partial to a bit of midnight,' he would always say, thinking that he had the moral high ground over his uncivilised friends. He put most male white racism down to insecurity about the size of black penises. Considering himself well endowed, he felt no anxieties in that department.

'So he says, you're not black, you're not white, you stink, you must be a skunk!' Mungo roared with laughter at his own joke while Colin forced a smile.

While this tranquil scene of conviviality was taking place, a Ford Transit van was driving into the car park of the Bridge Tavern. In the rear of the van, a dozen men in ski masks prepared for an assault on the pub. Three more men in the front of the van quickly pulled similar masks over their faces. The van's occupants carried an assortment of pickaxe handles, crowbars, baseball bats, coshes, cudgels and clubs.

Rollo nursed his blackthorn shillelagh, eager to break a few impudent heads. The provocative behaviour of the so-called Coocachoo Crew earlier in the day had signalled a prelude to war. Rollo did not intend to wage a prolonged vendetta with mere football hooligans; he intended to administer arbitrary justice that would end the dispute once and for all. Without a word, Rollo raised his hand as a signal to commence the attack. The van doors burst open and the breach of the enemy stronghold commenced.

Colin was just raising his glass to his lips as the first of the biker berserkers came through the door swinging their weapons at anyone who stood in their way. Colin dropped his glass and instantly tried to dive under a table. Mungo broke his bottle on the bar and brandished it, shouting, 'Come on then, you fuckers!' His request was answered with a pickaxe handle round his face. Smashed teeth and blood flew out of his mouth as the stout piece of wood made contact with the side of his face.

As the invaders began to spread out, Pluto and Strachan leapt onto the pool table, clutching their cues for protection. Standing on their citadel they began to pelt pool balls at the oncoming aggressors. Strachan managed to make one connect with a masked head. Pluto threw a second ball which caused another biker Aunt

Sally to stagger and fall. Around them was a scene of carnage but they both felt the familiar sexual thrill of violence. The football season was long gone but here they were, standing their ground.

Unfortunately for Pluto and Strachan, this wasn't to be another Rorke's Drift. This last bastion of baize was about to fall as Rollo prepared to outflank its defenders. The ammunition had run out with the last of the balls and Pluto and Strachan struck out with legs and cues. All around them lay their comrades; some unconscious, some moaning in pain, others still crying out as blows rained down on them. With Rollo on one side and another of his men on the other side of the table, Pluto was knocked down by blows to the legs. He was then dragged from the table, kicking and cursing. Rollo thrashed Pluto mercilessly with his shillelagh.

'I've had enough!' Pluto soon cried out in submission.

'I'll decide when you've had enough!' Rollo said, although he had to confess, he'd had enough himself; his stamina not being what it used to be.

The moment that his general was dragged from the table, Strachan went into Kamikaze mode and leapt from the table and clung to the nearest attacker like a psychotic monkey. Dragging his opponent's mask far enough to clear his face, Strachan bit his nose and would not let go until he had been clubbed unconscious.

Feggy Edwards had stood outside with his cigarette, sulking. He really didn't like Nik Kershaw and the whole episode had spoiled his afternoon. When he heard a commotion inside the pub, he concluded that the rest of the lads had also grown sick of Kershaw and decided to wreck the pub. Truly believing that they had come round to his way of thinking, he approached the door in the hope of joining in the mayhem. It only took a moment for him to realise that he had miscalculated the situation terribly. He turned round and leapt over the fence, running away up Southwell Road. He didn't stop until he reached the Reindeer Inn just in time for last orders. On the television, Sade was performing 'Your Love is King'. As he composed himself with his pint of Marksman lager, the serene sound calmed his nerves. As he began to relax, he concluded that he wouldn't be where he was if it hadn't been for Nik Kershaw.

He decided that this was the last straw with the football hooliganism. People like Strachan took the whole thing far too seriously and he didn't like the way the Scot always tried to bully him. Feggy had enjoyed the night when he had walked home with Dean Swift and his gang, doing the Madness walk. Swift had turned out to be a pretty sound youth since Feggy had had the chance to get to know him since leaving school. He felt bad about bullying Swift all those years ago in junior school.

Colin's attempt at evading a battering had been less successful. He had dived under a table and curled up into a foetal position, which made him wish his mother was there to help him. His hiding place was destroyed when someone was sent crashing onto its top. Two masked men dragged him from the wreckage and he prepared for the oncoming pain. He was momentarily surprised to find himself being lifted up by the arms and legs. It reminded him of being given the birthday bumps at school. He then felt the sensation of flying through the air and then the sound of breaking glass. He felt winded and disorientated as he landed in the car park. At this point, his instincts took hold of him and he leapt up and began running as fast as he could. He finally ran out of steam at the top of Toothill Lane and rested behind the wall of a car park. He finally succumbed to shock and began sobbing uncontrollably.

After sitting there a few minutes, he began to feel the pain of the cuts and bruises he had received as a consequence of his defenestration. It seemed to be a day for people to be flying through windows. He decided he needed to carry on walking to the casualty department at the nearby General Hospital. As he began walking again, it dawned on him that he had shat his pants.

CHAPTER THIRTEEN

The day had so far gone quickly from screaming orgasms to screaming arguments and screaming kids for Dawn Townroe. After Colin had stormed out of the house, Dawn had managed to switch on the Live Aid concert long enough to nod off for half an hour, before being woken by the arrival of her mother and the twins. Her mother informed her that her grandma, Rosemary, had been taken into hospital with a suspected bladder infection. Dawn listened to her mother complain about how long she'd had to wait for the ambulance and the trouble she'd had getting Rosemary to the toilet.

They had all then gone out to the hospital for the commencement of the visiting time, which began at two o'clock. When they found the ward where Dawn's grandma had been admitted, they were greeted by a sight more reminiscent of an eighteenth-century Bedlam than a modern hospital. The ward had been set up for elderly people who were at risk of falling and as a consequence needed to be monitored constantly. Shrieks and cries of 'Where am I?' and pitiful calls of 'When can I go home?' would regularly be heard. The smell of boiled vegetables blended with the overpowering odour of urine and faeces.

They found Rosemary in a state of delirium. She seemed to be confused about where she was, saying that she needed to get dressed because the undertaker was coming round to discuss her husband's funeral details. Dawn was also confused as to how her normally sharp-witted grandmother could have succumbed so quickly to what appeared to be senility. When the doctor finally came on his rounds, he explained that delirium was a common side effect of bladder infections in the elderly. He told them that a course of antibiotics would treat the infection, but Rosemary would need to stay in the ward under observation for at least a week.

'Well, I'm going to Ingoldmells next Saturday,' said Dawn's mother, as soon as the doctor had moved on to the next bed, 'and you've got the kids to sort out, so that lazy cow Marie will have to do her fair share for a change.'

Dawn's moment of relief when she had heard the doctor's prognosis had evaporated with her mother's querulous whittling. 'The doctor said it's going to be fine, Mam, me and Marie will keep an eye on things when you go to Jingle Bells.'

'When are we going away?' Rosemary asked.

'We're all going to have a nice holiday soon,' Dawn reassured her grandma, stroking her hair. 'Come and give your great-nana some love, Beverly.'

Dawn picked up Beverly and sat her on the bed with Rosemary. 'Hello blondie,' said Rosemary, smiling. 'Is this Dawn?' she addressed this question to Dawn, who she seemed to think was her own daughter.

'Oh, what a life!' Dawn's mum said, shaking her head.

Melanie, Dawn's other three-year-old twin, had found a box full of jigsaw puzzles. An elderly lady, who was sat up in a chair, watched her. Watching this little girl felt like spring had just arrived in the room to this lady who waited patiently for her winter to end. Dawn told her to leave the box alone, but Melanie picked out a puzzle and took it to the old lady. Seeing that Melanie had made the lady's day with this little act of kindness brought tears to Dawn's eyes.

'Melanie, come and sit with Grandma now while Mummy goes to the shop.' Melanie came running over to the bed and Dawn sat her next to her sister. Rosemary gazed at their T-shirts: Melanie had a picture of Noddy on hers, and Beverly's had Popeye on it. Dawn went out to fetch a bottle of Lucozade for Rosemary and some sweets for the kids for being good.

She made her way along the squeaky floor of one of the labyrinthine corridors so characteristic of hospitals. Down a side corridor, two women and two teenage girls were stood in a group hugging each other; all of them were weeping tears of sorrow. Dawn was reminded of the day when she and her sister Marie had arrived at the hospital to find their mother inconsolable with grief. They had visited their father every day for six weeks, watching the cancer that had claimed his lungs gradually invade and conquer his entire body.

Distracted by this memory for a brief moment, Dawn suddenly realised she had taken a wrong turning. Turning back to retrace her steps, she noticed a woman and boy of six and a girl of similar age to the twins. There seemed something familiar about the woman. As she followed at a distance, trying to remember why she recognised the face, it suddenly became clear where she knew the woman from.

Dawn remembered seeing her with the two children, waiting at the factory gates one day as Dawn was leaving. Then she remembered seeing Tony come and lift the little girl onto his shoulders.

Dawn suddenly stopped, with a sudden sick feeling in her stomach. She suddenly feared that something might have happened to Tony. She turned around and walked back to where the ward was. She looked through the door to see a ward full of men. Looking down a row of beds, she saw men in various states of injury or illness. She couldn't recognise Tony amongst them, so she began to look down the row of beds on the opposite side. Once again, she saw some with bandages and casts; others who were laid resting in various states of illness. For a moment, she felt relief that she couldn't recognise Tony amongst the invalids. Then, as her gaze crossed to the other side of the ward again, she recognised him. He was lying in a bed near a window, his face swollen with bruising. She rushed over to him, recognising him now clearly, despite his swollen eyes and the cuts on his face. He was awake but was woozy due to the morphine that he had been given. He tried to speak but didn't make any sense.

'Ssh!' Dawn held his hand, looking around, suddenly realising that his wife might return. He began to try to speak again and it suddenly occurred to Dawn that his teeth seemed to be wired together.

A nurse began doing her rounds, and when she finally arrived at Tony's bed Dawn asked her what had happened.

'He was brought in this morning after his bicycle hit the back of a parked car,' the nurse began explaining, 'we think he might have dropped asleep for a moment. He was riding down that big hill on Bath Lane and must have hit the vehicle with some force.'

Dawn began sobbing. 'Is he going to be alright? What's happened to his mouth?'

The nurse put her hand on Dawn's shoulder. 'Don't worry, he's got a proper Mansfield thick head, this one. He's got a fractured jaw and his teeth have been wired up till his mandibular bone heals up.'

Dawn thought about what Colin had said to her about the incident with the smashed windscreen. 'Did the accident take place at the bottom of Southall Road?' she asked.

'I don't think so,' said the nurse, trying to remember. 'I seem to remember it was Bath Lane where the ambulance was called out to.'

The nurse continued with her rounds and Dawn looked at Tony, who looked back at her through sleepy eyes. She thought about what the nurse had said, and concluded that it was too much of a coincidence that two identical accidents should take place in close proximity on the same morning.

'I'd better go in a minute,' she said, looking nervously at the door, 'Mandy might be back any minute. I only found out because I saw her and the kids leaving the ward. I came in to see my Nana Rosemary; she's got a bladder infection.'

Tony seemed to have dropped off to sleep, so she took the opportunity to leave. She retraced her steps to the hospital shop. As she walked along the corridor towards the reception area, she passed Mandy and her children. Dawn hardly dared to look at them as she passed by. Mandy didn't seem to notice her as they passed each other. She had her arms around the children and was telling them how their Daddy was going to get better soon. At that moment, Dawn made her mind up that she couldn't continue seeing Tony.

Returning to Rosemary's ward, Dawn realised that she had thrown herself at Tony in a desperate bid to find some happiness for herself. To have something special just for herself; not for the kids, her mother or Colin, but just for her. She had to confess that she had never felt so alive in all her life. Seeing Mandy brought it home to her how wicked all the lying and cheating had been. Colin had dragged her down to his level and she had been given a view of life from his perspective. The only way forward was to get away from Colin and make a fresh start; all that mattered now were her and the kids.

She arrived back at the ward to find that her younger sister, Marie, had arrived. Marie was her usual bouncy and jovial self. She had earned the nickname of Tigger whilst at school, due to her effervescent personality. She looked very summery in her denim shorts, flip-flops and fluorescent lime green gym vest. She had a pair of sunglasses perched on top of her short burgundy hair. Her skin was tanned from her recent Club 18–30 holiday to Corfu. One of the twins was stood on Rosemary's bed, climbing onto Marie's back, whilst another sat on her knee.

Dawn ripped off the yellow cellophane from the bottle of Lucozade and poured a glass for her gran. Rosemary accepted the drink as though she had just been offered a gin and tonic. In her delirium, she though that she was having a party with so many of her family around her.

'Where's Colin?' she asked.

Dawn thought it was typical that even in her confused state, her gran should observe that Colin wasn't present. Like her mother, her gran thought the sun shined out of Colin's arse. He could always flatter and flirt with them both, make them buy the lovable rogue routine.

Marie noticed Dawn's expression change as soon as her gran mentioned Colin's name. She alone saw through Colin's act, and it had been her who had first alerted Dawn to his womanising ways. She had omitted to tell her sister that he had tried it on with her at his own wedding reception. At the time she hadn't wanted to spoil her sister's wedding day, but she had later raised her suspicions about his affair with Jackie Compton.

Dawn and her sister didn't speak to each other for several months after Marie had first voiced her suspicions about Colin. Early on in their relationship, Dawn was blinded by her love for Colin and wouldn't have a word said against him. She accused Marie of jealousy and her mother had also been of the same opinion.

One day, Dawn had had to come home from work, after an accident at work left her needing stitches in one of her fingers. After cutting herself with a sharp knife, her supervisor had driven her to the casualty department. She had been concerned enough to wait for Dawn and then give her a lift home. Arriving home three hours earlier than normal, she walked through the front door and found Jackie, naked apart from fishnet stockings and a suspender belt, riding Colin on the settee.

After apologising to Marie, the two sisters had become closer. Marie had remained openly hostile towards Colin and thought Dawn was foolish for giving him a second chance. He had got down on his knees, weeping and begging Dawn's forgiveness; he had claimed that Jackie had thrown herself at him and he admitted that he had shown weakness on that one occasion. It had taken several such occasions before Dawn fully woke up to the reality that she had deceived herself into discounting. She had even been foolish enough to blame herself for her husband's adultery.

The twins were starting to get restless, so Dawn's mum decided to take them for a walk down to the shop for some sweets. Marie pulled her chair up to get closer to Dawn, and looked round with a conspiratorial air.

'Come on, you can't kid me, that's a Colin look,' said Marie, putting her hand on Dawn's knee. 'What's the sneaky little bastard been up to now, or should I say who?'

Dawn looked over at her gran, who seemed to be asleep, and leaned closer to Marie so as not to be overheard.

'Where did you say Jackie Compton lived again?'

'Oh, don't tell me he's shagging her again,' said Marie, a little too loudly.

'Shush!' hissed Dawn. 'I don't want everyone knowing my business.'

'Oops, sorry,' said Marie, putting her hand over her mouth, 'me and my big gob. Yeah, she lives at the bottom of Bath Lane; her ex told me after they split up.'

'Yeah, thought so,' said Dawn, pensively.

'You need to fuck him off this time,' said Marie, shaking her head.

'I know,' said Dawn, sheepishly. 'Thing is, I've been seeing someone myself; what's good for the goose and all that.'

'You dirty cow,' whispered Marie, nudging her sister with a dirty grin on her face. 'I can't fault you though.'

Dawn felt relieved that she finally had someone to share the secret which had been bottled up inside her for months.

'Who is it then?' said Marie excitedly. 'Anyone I know?'

Dawn looked at her sister with a wry smile, shaking her head. She didn't bother to explain about the accident, or her irrational theory that Colin had somehow planned for Tony to hit the back of his car. She would have given anything at that moment to be able to get away with Marie and just get totally drunk.

★ ★ ★ ★ ★

The casualty department seemed unusually quiet to Colin as he looked around the waiting area. He had taken off his soiled underpants in the toilet and shoved them in the cistern. While he was in the toilet, he had felt a wet patch on the back of his head. When he touched the wet spot it felt sore, and he realised he'd probably taken the injury when the table had collapsed on his head.

He looked around at the other people awaiting treatment. He half expected to see a boy with a saucepan stuck to his head like in the *Carry On* films. A boy of about thirteen was complaining of a pain in his ear. Apparently he had shoved some cotton wool too far into his ear. A young man in football kit came hobbling in, assisted by an older man in a tracksuit. A woman with Downs Syndrome had burned her arm whilst cooking.

As Colin sat looking round, he sensed someone sit down nearby. He looked round to see a large bearded man wearing a sleeveless denim jacket. As the man leaned forward, Colin noticed, on the back of the jacket, the insignia of the Robespierre's Barbers Motorbike Club. The biker had a large bruise on his forehead and was holding a tea towel over his nose. Colin was relieved that it wasn't the same biker who Pluto had thrown a beer glass at.

'You look like you've been in the wars,' Colin said, desperate for some kind of distraction from the interminable waiting.

'Yeah, been playing rugby,' said the biker unconvincingly.

Looking around, Colin noticed two police officers walk through the entrance. It suddenly occurred to him that they might be looking for people involved in the incident at the Bridge Tavern. Anxious not to get involved with the police, Colin headed down the corridor to the toilet he had used earlier. When Colin saw a cleaner walk into the toilet with a mop and bucket, he decided to carry on walking. He turned a corner and walked down another corridor. As he passed a ward, he saw a very attractive nurse attending to a patient. He stopped to take a better look at the nurse as she bent over the bed. It was at that moment that he also saw another woman leaning over a bed and kissing its occupant chastely on the forehead. Puzzlement was quickly replaced by shock at the realisation that he was looking at Dawn with another man. Seeing his wife begin to move away from the bed, Colin hurried away the way he had come. When he arrived back in the casualty waiting area, the police were nowhere to be seen.

He found a seat once again and noticed that the biker had been joined by another member of Robespierre's Barbers. He wore almost identical denim and leather to the other biker and had the same unkempt hirsute features. He also seemed to have some kind of injury to his nose, which he covered with a red bandana.

When Colin was finally called to be treated, he was given stitches for the cut on the back of his head. He was vexed to learn that the injury would leave a scar and consequently a permanent bald patch; this was a great blow to his vanity. He was given a course of antibiotics, further adding to his woes when he learned that he should avoid alcohol when taking the medication.

As he walked out of the casualty department, he decided that his only chance for succour was to go and see if Jackie was at home. In the hospital shop he bought himself a can of Lilt to wash down his antibiotics. As he was choosing his drink, he noticed his mother-in-law with the twins, on the opposite side of the shelves. He hid behind a carousel rack of greetings cards and surreptitiously watched Dawn's mother paying for some sweets. He had once thought that she might be worth giving one too, but he concluded that she had let herself go in the past couple of years. It seemed to him that Dawn and her mother had given up making an effort after he had tied the knot, as part of some kind of conspiracy. He looked at the dark shadow of facial hair above her top lip and thought that she looked like Burt Reynolds. He consoled himself that at least Dawn's sister still knew how to tease him. It was still an ambition of his to finally get Marie into bed. He perceived that her rejection of him at his wedding was merely an act of loyalty towards Dawn, on her wedding day; she was chief bridesmaid, after all.

Once the coast was clear, he paid for his drink and hurried out into the bright sunshine. He wondered if Jackie might be watching the Live Aid concert; he quite fancied seeing Simple Minds playing in Philadelphia. He crossed over Woodhouse Road and headed towards Bath Lane, where he would be guaranteed some sympathy. A long queue of people stood by the side of the ABC cinema. He wondered if they were queuing to see *Back to the Future* or *Rambo II*. He doubted whether they would be queuing to go and see *Silverado*.

He was beginning to feel refreshed after finishing his can of Lilt. He threw the empty can on the floor and began kicking it down the pavement. Through an open window he could hear Paul Young singing 'Come Back and Stay'. He looked up at the clear blue sky and imagined what a great day it would be at Wembley. Jane Cresswell had come round at the pop factory the day before, collecting money to pledge for the famine relief. He had been loath to part with any of his pay packet, but he thought it might impress Jane if he casually handed her a tenner; that wasn't all he wanted to hand her.

He crossed the road near Jackie's house, feeling the crunch of glass from his rear windscreen under his shoes. For the second time that day he passed the broken garden gate that led to Jackie's front door. The garden was overgrown with rampant July grass. Colin concluded that Jackie rarely had time to cut the grass, with him keeping her otherwise occupied.

He knocked on the door and turned round and leaned on the wall. He reflected that there was still time to salvage something from his day from hell. After a few moments, in which he had received no answer, he knocked again. A window was open in the living room and he could hear the sound of the television. He walked over and could clearly see and hear Paul Young singing 'Every Time You Go Away'.

He thought for a moment he heard someone call out from the depths of the house. He tried to open the front door but found that it was firmly latched shut. He decided to have a look round the back of the house, thinking that Jackie might be sunbathing in the garden. He found the garden deserted, unless Jackie was hidden in the jungle of overgrown grass and weeds. He looked in through the kitchen window and tapped on the glass; all he could see was a sink full of dirty pots.

He tried the back door, which to his delight, he found was unlocked. His heart was beating quickly now, it was like a game. He decided to call out again to avoid being mistaken for a burglar. He stepped into the passageway and thought he heard a voice upstairs. He strained to listen over the noise from the television.

He crept up the stairs, confident that Jackie would appreciate him surprising her for a repeat performance. At the top of the landing his heart suddenly sank as he recognised a male voice exclaim, 'That's what you want!' The door to Jackie's bedroom was slightly ajar, so he decided to look inside. Peering through the gap in the door, Colin was shocked to see not one, but two men on the bed with Jackie. She was facing away from Colin, on all fours. His view of Jackie was obstructed by the sight of the hairy arse of a naked man with a dark mullet. He pounded away at Jackie's rear while the other man enjoyed the pleasure of Jackie's mouth. He suddenly recognised both men as mechanics from Mandora.

The sight of his lover cheating with two men was too much for Colin to bear. He fled down the stairs and ran into the back garden, where he collapsed in the long-neglected lawn. At that moment, Colin wished the grass had been twice as long for him to crawl into and hide. He heard the unmistakable sound of one of Jackie's screaming orgasms from upstairs and he covered his ears and began to sob. He was forced to quickly compose himself when he realised that the two men might not appreciate his presence if they found him laid in the garden like some kind of pervert.

He got up and ran, and didn't stop until forced to by exhaustion halfway up Bath Lane. His day couldn't possibly get any worse after what he had witnessed in Jackie's bedroom. The image of her making a beast with three backs was imprinted on his mind. Two building bricks could not have made him feel any more painfully emasculated at that moment. She had always made him feel as though he was the only man in her life. He might have resigned himself to sharing her with another man, but two seemed to be abusing the privilege. He knew both of the mechanics to be married men like himself. On reflection, Colin remembered Jackie becoming infatuated with him shortly after his wedding. It seemed as though she had an obsession with married men. He walked down Woodhouse Road, and decided to go into the Black Bull and lick his wounds before facing another bout with his wife.

CHAPTER FOURTEEN

The reunion of John and Spike at the Bonaparte's Retreat had been as charged with emotion as was possible for two punk rockers from a Nottinghamshire mining village. John introduced Spike to Ray, who had heard the sagas of the spiky one and was intrigued by what he had heard. He was amazed when Spike told him that he had hitchhiked to London that same morning.

'Your man Spike is like a punk Kerouac!' said Ray.

'Why does your Irish mate say I'm a punk Caramac?' Spike later asked John as they were taking a piss. John had attempted to summarise who Jack Kerouac was and Spike seemed quite pleased with the comparison.

Ray had also warmed to John Louis when he discovered that he was studying English at Middlesex University. The two had become engrossed in a conversation about the Nigerian poet, Christopher Okigbo. While Spike told John about the latest gossip around Mansfield, Podge quietly made the most of the free drinks. When Spike had introduced her to John, he had merely nodded his head in acknowledgement. She had been as shocked to see him, as he obviously had been to see her walk in the pub with Spike.

She had met him a few weeks earlier when he had turned up at the flat with an aging hippy type, who seemed to know a few of the residents there. After a few drinks, he had invited her back to his room. It had been the first time she had been with a man since Fritch, and she had found the gentleness of John's lovemaking a pleasant contrast to her former lover. She hadn't been left with bruises on her thighs and neck, which had been the hallmark of Fritch's foreplay. Podge was waiting for John to raise the subject of the twenty pounds she had taken from his jeans before she had crept out of his flat.

Last orders had soon created a sense of urgency in the reunion. After finishing their drinks with the landlord breathing down their necks, John suggested they all go round to Al's place.

'You'll love Al,' he told Spike, 'he used to be a traveller like the ones we met at Glastonbury. He used to be a roadie for The Clash!'.

Spike put his arm round John as they walked up Kilburn High Road. 'Hey, this is where Ian Dury got the name for his band before he started The Blockheads.'

'Yeah, Kilburn and The High Roads,' said John, as the penny finally dropped in regard to Al's earlier ambiguous comments.

'I watched GBH play a gig down here a while back.' John slapped Spike on the arm. 'Remember when we went to see them at the Porterhouse with Discharge, and we got fighting with them skins who kept *Sieg Heiling*?'

'Was that the night you got hammered and fell asleep at the front of the stage, and the bouncers had to wake you up after the gig, covered in piss and beer?'

'Aye lad, them were't days, eh!'

Podge walked along behind them, wondering whether to just disappear while no one was looking. Then Spike looked round to check that she was okay, realising that he had been so engrossed in his own nostalgia that he had forgotten her.

'Have you ever seen GBH, Podge?' he asked in an attempt to draw her into their conversation.

'No, the last band I went to see was The Cockney Rejects.'

John didn't want to spoil the atmosphere by bringing up the subject of the money. After all, he couldn't be certain that Podge had taken it. Part of him was excited to see her again. If she had needed the cash, he would have given it to her. She was obviously pretty desperate. She had given him her entire life story in one mouthful, like she had with Spike.

They stopped at an off licence and bought beer to take with them to Al's. John and Spike each bought a three-litre bottle of Jager lager. They turned off onto a terraced street and walked to the house where Al's flat occupied the ground floor. Loud music emanated from within, so John knocked as loudly as possible. A face peered through the net curtain in the bay window. Al shortly appeared at the front door, recognising some faces and noticing new ones amongst them.

'I thought it was the fucking Jehovah's Witnesses, man,' Al said with a slightly stoned grin. 'Get your arses inside.'

Angel's Egg by Gong was blasting out from the speakers in the living room. A man and a woman were sat on an old settee, which was covered with a blanket with some kind of Persian carpet design on it. A tapestry with a psychedelic blue floral design hung on a wall; all in all, a typical hippy abode. The woman had long curly red hair and wore a flowing orange dress that went down to her sandaled feet.

The dress was adorned with giraffes, which were grazing amidst trees and a blue lake. The man's head was completely shaven and he wore a saffron-coloured shirt and purple and blue cotton trousers. Al introduced the man as Dominic and the woman as Alicia. Spike had expected them to be called Sunflower and Dolphinella. Al explained that the two had recently returned from the Peace Convoy after the recent trouble at Stonehenge. They were attempting to sue the Wiltshire police for criminal damage to the converted ambulance that served as their home.

Al produced a bong made from a coconut and it was handed round everyone. Ray politely declined the offer of a smoke; he was happy with the half bottle of Bells whisky he had bought and his cigarettes. His experiences with drugs hadn't been entirely enjoyable; cannabis just made him paranoid and nauseous.

'I first met Dom and Alicia at the Isle of Wight Festival in 1970,' said Al.

'Yeah, that was when the fat cats started trying to turn the festivals into capitalist picnics,' said Dominic.

'Pignics!' added Alicia. 'Yeah, we met Al when we were trying to pull down the fences and make it into a free festival.'

Ray knelt down and began looking through Al's impressive collection of albums. After two minutes with Dominic and Alicia, he sensed the pretension levels in the room getting more stifling than the cannabis smoke.

'Take That Phone Book Coda' was bringing *Angel's Egg* to an end.

'Get us some more tunes lined up, Keats!' Al called out.

Ray was admiring the Paul Whitehead artwork on Genesis's *Nursery Cryme*.

'That's a classic, alright,' said Al.

Ray held up the album. 'I remember seeing Genesis play at Carracalla in Italy. Peter Gabriel came out dressed in a red ball gown, wearing a fox mask on his head.'

He carefully took out the Gong album from the music centre and replaced it with the Genesis album. Al owned a Sharp music centre with a vertical turntable. The stylus landed on the vinyl with a bump and a crackle before the understated introduction to 'The Musical Box' began.

Everyone in the room listened entranced for several minutes, before Dominic began to give his opinion on Genesis.

'Genesis were okay until Gabriel left the band, and then they just turned really commercial when Phil Collins took over the vocals.'

'I disagree,' interjected Ray, '*Trick of the Tail* is the equal of any Gabriel-era Genesis.'

'Well, I think they just sound like they're playing for the money,' said Alicia, sticking in her two-penneth.

114

Alicia seemed to have killed the conversation before it had even grown teeth and walked. Dominic looked at the new arrivals and asked, 'So where are you lot from then?'

'Notts,' answered Spike.

'Oh right, proper northern lads, eh!'

'No, we're from the East Midlands,' said John, irritated by the way people in London always referred to anyone north of Watford as northerners. 'We're from a small town called Lilliput.'

'These lads come from mining country, same as me,' said Al.

'Well, I hope you supported the miners' strike!' snapped Alicia accusingly.

John was growing increasingly irritated by this pair of hippy posers. 'No, actually my dad worked during the strike. I came down here to get away from all that bollocks.'

Spike offered his contribution to the debate by cocking his leg up and farting loudly. Podge found this Rabelaisian interruption highly amusing and began to giggle uncontrollably.

'Why do people always say "More tea, vicar?" when someone farts?' said Al to no one in particular.

John attempted to change the subject. 'Al says you were on the road with the Peace Convoy?'

'Yeah,' said Dominic. 'Of course, the "Peace Convoy" is just a name that the press labelled what was basically several different groups of travellers.'

'We had a few beers with some of your lot at Glastonbury last year,' said Spike. 'Do you know Biffo? Always wears a bowler hat and plays the fiddle.'

'We don't do Glastonbury now,' said Alicia. 'It's getting too commercial now. We don't have anything to do with Biffo and his crowd. They just want to sit around getting pissed on Special Brew and have a good time. We're committed to smashing the system.'

'I remember the first Glastonbury Free Festival in 1971,' said Al with a faraway and dreamy countenance. 'Hawkwind, Gong and Bowie all on the same bill, and you paid nowt to get in.'

'Oh Al, you'll never learn will you,' Dominic said, shaking his head. 'All the flowers and the music in 1967 didn't work. The whole scene grew teeth and started getting it together after the Summer of Love.'

Alicia was chomping at the bit to have her say. 'After the Isle of Wight Festival, while you were still sitting around getting stoned and listening to space rock, we were fighting the system with the Angry Brigade. When we saw you at the first Glastonbury Festival, we were trying to raise bread for the cause.' She nodded to Ray. 'The Angry Brigade are still working with the Irish Republican Socialist Movement.'

Ray had been perfectly happy, lost in the musical world of Genesis, until Alicia's comment made him sit up straight. 'My fucking brother was killed in a sectarian ambush; left lying in a ditch somewhere in Antrim, and all because he was in the wrong place at the wrong time!'

Alicia slowly nodded her head, looking at Ray with a look of intense sympathy. 'Were they republicans or loyalists?'

'I don't give a shit! It's not a fucking game you know!'

'Hey, cool it man,' said Dominic.

'Hey, we get it Keats, we just want to rid the world of fascists, okay,' said Alicia, glancing towards Podge. 'We're just dedicated to fighting fascists, especially the Strasserites who seem to be recruiting all the new blood.'

'Sounds about right,' said Podge coolly. 'My fella was well into all that, when he wasn't knocking seven shades of shit out of me.'

'Well, I'm sorry, but that's what you get when you buy into the fascist dogma that's worming its way back into our society.'

'No shit!'

'Oh honestly, you people are so naive.'

At this point, Ray, who had begun to quietly listen to Alicia's argument, erupted. 'Hey, don't you fucking have a go at her. You're the kind of people, eighty years ago, who were telling the working class that they should be out Morris dancing instead of going out to the music halls. Your type are nothing but passive-aggressive fascists; Anarcho-communists my arse. Try reading some of Rousseau's *Social Contract* and you might learn a thing or two about anarchism.'

'He wasn't bad when he was in Aphrodite's Child with Vangelis,' said Al, only half listening to the conversation.

'Well, I'm not going to be spoken to like that by anyone,' said Alicia indignantly. 'Come on, Dom, let's get out of this midden!'

Dom stood up and patted Al on the back. 'It's been nice seeing you again, Al; not so sure about your friends.'

Al, who had remained quiet throughout this robust discussion, decided to have his say. 'Haddaway and shite man; you always were a pair of supercilious, self-righteous bastards. I was there at Grosvenor Square in '68 for the anti-Vietnam riots and I've still got the scars to show it. Me Dad came down to London on the Jarrow March and then got a bullet in his arse, fighting with the International Brigade in Spain. The Summer of Love might have been a naïve dream, but I still believe, man.'

'Well, if that's your final word, Al, I'll just say this—' Alicia piped in, intending to have the last word.

'Good day! You nah where the door is,' said Al with his back to the pair, as he got up and fetched his guitar.

Throughout this exchange, John, Spike and Podge had sat quietly, sniggering at Dominic and Alicia's dressing down. Ray looked over at John, shaking his head. Al settled down with his guitar and began to detune the strings to an altered tuning. He closed his eyes and began to clear his mind of the previous unpleasantness. He began to play an alternating bass pattern with his thumb and then adroitly added an improvised melody with his index and middle finger. The tune had a hypnotic quality, partly blues but also partly Indian. The tune gradually built up in intensity like an Indian Raga. Al seemed to become lost in the deceptively simple variations of the melody. Everyone else was listening serenely, fully relaxed after the exorcism of Dominic and Alicia.

Al continued to play for half an hour. He played in a variety of styles and even played an O'Carolan tune for Ray. After another session with the bong, he declared that he was tired and was going to turn in before the night's work at Wembley.

As the rest of the group left Al's place and began walking down the street, Ray suggested they all go to his house and meet his family. Ray and Spike got into a conversation, while John and Podge walked a few paces behind. John couldn't help feeling attracted to Podge, despite her robbing him.

'You know, if you'd needed money, I would have given it to you.'

Podge blushed, embarrassed that the accusation had finally been served. 'How do you know I took money off you? You might have dropped it somewhere.'

John had to admit to himself that he hadn't thought about this, but he was pretty sure he had the money in his pocket when he took his jeans off.

'Besides,' continued Podge, gaining confidence, 'I think my performance was a bargain at twenty quid. I never said I was doing it for free.'

'Oh, so you know there was twenty quid in my pocket then.'

'Aye, well, you mightn't get a discount next time if you fancy a bit.'

It was John's turn to become flushed with embarrassment now. Podge noted his discomfort and began to feel a little sorry for him.

'Look, I'm sorry for taking the money, I've done a lot of things lately that I'm not proud of. I'll try and pay you back.'

'Easy come, easy go, I always say,' said John, smiling. 'I think I got a bargain anyway.'

Podge smacked John's bottom and then gave it a teasing squeeze. Spike heard them giggling and looked round to see what they were up to. Unaware of their previous assignation, Spike thought that John was on his usual good form at making a hit with the ladies. He remembered that whenever they went out, it was always John who took the initiative whenever they showed interest in a couple of girls.

'You don't really buy into all that National Front bullshit, do you?' John asked Podge.

Podge considered the question, and then said, 'To start with I just started hanging around with skinheads who were more into scooters than anything. Then I started getting into the Oi! scene and followed bands like the Angelic Upstarts and The 4-Skins. Most of those bands were more into socialism and hated fascists. You'd just get people like Fritch creeping around at gigs, looking for anyone vulnerable enough for him to manipulate. I don't think I ever saw more than a handful of black and Asian families round our way. They just kept their heads down and grafted like everyone else.'

'Where I come from, everyone is black when they go down the pit,' said John, and then pointing at Spike added, 'apart from him; he thinks lying in bed and then deciding to have a wank is hard work.'

CHAPTER FIFTEEN

My experience of test cricket was turning into a kind of surreal nightmare. When Alex and I had returned to our seats, Dad had returned to his irascible self-righteous self again. The posh boys who we had run into earlier were waving wads of money about and shouting 'Loadsamoney!' They clearly saw in every spectator at Trent Bridge, a cloth-capped, dole-scrounging northerner. They then continued with a twenty-minute rendition of 'The Eton Boating Song'.

The lunch interval couldn't come quick enough for me. Alex continued drowning his sorrows and Dad was beginning to lose patience with his self-pitying routine. Things hit a massive low point when Alex actually broke down in tears and threw his arms around Dad. Surrounded by gawping onlookers, Dad looked like he wished the earth would open up and swallow him.

An hour went by and Dad fell asleep, while Alex became increasingly drunk and erratic. Alex woke Dad as he budged past him to fetch another drink. Dad had decided to set an example by ceasing to drink any more. He had taken a nap in order to sober up a little for the eventual drive home. The rude awakening had left him in a foul mood, and I just wanted to get away.

A couple of minutes later, a huge cheer erupted around the ground as a streaker came onto the field. Much to my disappointment, my first sighting of this phenomenon was of the male species. He cartwheeled across the field as far as the wicket itself. A worried umpire barred his way from the sacred strip in the centre of the field. The streaker was far from the physical perfection of his youth. A modest beer belly and breasts that could have used a training bra hung from his torso. Balls like the wattles on a rooster swung either side of his flaccid penis. Two policemen and several stewards were strategically trying to corral their prey, spread out like beaters at a grouse hunt.

The crowd was hooting and heckling, some with pleasure, others with disgust and indignation.

'Fuck me pink!' said Dad, waking from another doze. I wasn't surprised that he didn't find the spectacle at all amusing. He would have condoned castration for such a gross act of indecency. Yet, as I looked at the rising expression of anger on his face, it suddenly dawned on me why he was taking the incident to heart. As I watched the two police officers lead the naked man from the field in our direction, I finally got a clear view of his face. There was Alex, as naked as the day he was born; totally resigned to his fate, with a serene expression that showed no signs of his earlier anxiety.

'I'll have to go and sort things out,' said Dad, rising from his seat. 'Will you be alraight making your own way home?'

'Yeah, no problem,' I said, with barely contained joy. I felt like doing naked cartwheels across the pitch at that moment. Before he walked away, Dad put his hand in his pocket and handed me a ten-pound note for the bus fare and a couple of drinks. His anger seemed to have subsided into embarrassment and pity for his friend.

I stayed in my seat for a while, trying to take in the game. All the spectators who had taken an extended lunch had now returned to their seats and the stands all seemed to be full again. The Australian finally returned, still wrapped in his Southern Cross flag. The Old Etonians hadn't yet returned; I was pleased that they hadn't been present to see Alex's Lady Godiva routine.

I finally resolved to leave and undertake my earlier plan to hit the record stores of Nottingham. I remembered I had Myfanwy's phone number in my back pocket. I needed to find a phone box and see if he had got back from Lincoln. I decided to buy one more drink and take a walk round the concourse of the ground for the last time. The Eton boys were drinking at the rear of the Trent Bridge Inn. One of them was doing handstands while another balanced a pint of beer on the sole of his shoe.

I felt a tap on my shoulder as I rounded the corner onto the Radcliffe Road side of the ground. Suddenly, the empty glass that had been the day so far was filled to the brim with the ambrosial gift of the gods. There stood Myfanwy, grinning like a buffoon, with his battered Sid James face.

'I bet I'm the last person you expected to see here,' he chuckled.

'Nothing ever surprises me with you.'

'Why don't you give your old dad a big hug,' he said with outstretched arms. I felt quite emotional as we hugged; Myfanwy had appeared like a *deus ex machina* to revitalise a miserable day.

'So what are you doing here?' he asked. 'I thought you hated cricket.'

'It's a long story, I'll tell you later,' I said, shaking my head. 'I could ask you the same question.'

'It's a long story, I'll tell you later.' He put his arm around me and we began walking. 'Let's get out of this den of iniquity.'

As we exited through the gates, a steward held out a pass card so we could return. We waved him away, adamant that we would under no circumstances return to Trent Bridge that day. We crossed the road and walked down onto the embankment of the Trent. We sat down on some stone steps that led down to the river. A narrowboat was moored near the bank and loud music could be heard from inside. We sat there, taking in the serene summer scene, like figures in a painting by Seurat. A gentle piece of music began to play that complemented the stillness of the river. Then I recognised the opening guitar riff of 'Shine On You Crazy Diamond'. I became mesmerised by the combination of the music of Pink Floyd and the reflections in the water. As the vocals began, I listened to the words. The whole song seemed to have been written for Myfanwy.

I told him all about my day, from the moment Dad dragged me out of bed, to the finale with Alex's streaker routine. My day paled in comparison to the series of adventures that Myfanwy recounted. I had to take some of his stories with a pinch of salt normally, but I had to confess that he'd excelled himself with his exquisite lies on this occasion. The Toy Mistress album *Pseudo-Martyr* began to play on the narrowboat. Coincidently, it was at this point that Myfanwy began to tell me about his meeting with Tip Topley and how they had shared cocaine in a toilet cubicle.

'Yeah, I sat next to Mick Jagger and shared a joint at the cricket today,' I said jovially.

'Straight up!' he said, affronted by my scepticism. 'This Edward bloke introduced him to me; he was totally strung-out so we went for a toot.'

'Edward was the bloke with the eyepatch, right?'

'No, Edward was the QC who wanted to bum me.'

At this point, the owner of the narrowboat emerged from the depths of his lair. He had long gingery blond hair tied in a ponytail and an equally long braided beard. He wore an old pinstriped shirt which hung down over a pair of stripy pyjama trousers. In his hand was a watering can which he used to sprinkle water on some potted sunflowers. The plastic watering can was just like the one I had owned when I was a little boy. It was orange and fashioned like an elephant standing on its hind legs, with its trunk for a spout. He nodded to us as we sat and watched him.

Toy Mistress were belting out 'Velvet Underpants' and I gave him a thumbs-up sign and said, 'You've got excellent taste in music, sir.'

Pleased by the compliment and by having someone to converse with, he came closer, peering down his half-moon spectacles. 'Only the connoisseurs really appreciate *Pseudo-Martyr*, most people only know Toy Mistress for "Piglet's Balloon".'

'I agree totally, I can put *Pseudo-Martyr* on and just lose myself in the album cover.'

'Believe it or not, I designed that cover,' said the sailor.

Myfanwy looked sceptically at me with a 'you can't kid a kidder' expression. Noting the sceptical reception of his comment, the man smile and shrugged his shoulders. He walked away and climbed back down into the interior of his boat.

'So you've snorted coke with Tip Topley, and this bloke designed one of the most iconic album covers of all time, righto.' You had to take a step back and admire his mendacity sometimes.

'Would I lie to you, my dear!' said Myfanwy, doing his best Fagin impression.

'At every conceivable opportunity. Hey, here he comes again!'

The man emerged once again onto the deck of his boat. This time he was clutching some kind of magazine in his hand. He came over to the edge of the boat, flicking through the pages of the magazine. Finding the page he was looking for, he held it out for us to see. 'This is me and Toy Mistress outside Abbey Road Studios.' I took the magazine from him and Myfanwy and I looked at a full-page black and white photo. There were the four members of Toy Mistress, with a tall, thin man with long blond hair, wearing round, tinted spectacles. He was holding the *Pseudo-Martyr* album in his hand. Topley stood next to him in a big kaftan and floppy hat with a scarf tied round it. I looked at the accompanying article on the opposite page.

ROGER WHITSHEAD
PSYCHEDELIC MICHELANGELO

Listening to the new Toy Mistress album becomes a totally sublime experience as you fasten yourself into your seat and escape into the extraordinary cover artwork of Roger Whitshead. After living and working in San Francisco's Haight-Ashbury with the band, Ulysses Lee, this Young Turk is now taking Swinging London by storm. Get ready to have your mind blown by more of Whitshead's artwork.

I looked up at the middle-aged man on the boat and then back at the photo. It was unmistakably the same person. Myfanwy took the magazine and studied the photo. He then held the magazine up for Roger to see, and pointing at Tip Topley, said, 'I've met him today at Trent Bridge.'

Roger nodded his head, impressed. 'Yeah, he came here for breakfast this morning.'

Myfanwy slapped me on the arm. 'I told you I was with him today!'

I was slightly envious that while I was stuck with pater and Alex Godiva, Myfanwy was within spitting distance enjoying the convivial company of Tip Topley.

'Yes, I made him a Full English but he hardly touched a thing,' Roger continued. 'His shrew of a wife kept pecking at him to eat but he didn't take much notice.'

Roger walked to the other side of the boat and began pulling some kind of fishing line from out of the river. 'I've got a jug of excellent Herefordshire scrumpy cooling in the water.' He continued pulling until an earthenware jug appeared at the end of the line. 'Would you care to join me for a drop?'

We accepted this kind offer of hospitality and boarded the boat. We followed Roger down the steps into his inner sanctum. It was cosy inside but surprisingly roomy. Light came in from spherical porthole on each side. There was a small area for cooking, then a settee and a small table. At the far end was a bed which was covered with sheets of paper and drawing material. This area seemed to be where Roger did all his artwork.

Roger poured scrumpy into an assortment of mugs and glasses. He had a pint pot with a handle, while Myfanwy and I had ours in mugs. An ageing greyhound was lying on the settee, which Roger shooed away to make way for his new guests. A mandolin hung on a wall amongst a variety of framed concert posters. They were mostly from venues like the Fillmore West and the Roundhouse. Ornate psychedelic designs advertised concerts featuring the likes of Moby Grape, Spirit and Jefferson Airplane.

'Did you design these?' I asked.

'No, all these are by a friend of mine called Percy Felix.' Roger stood next to me, looking at the poster I was contemplating. 'I don't know what happened to all mine; I think they all got pinched.'

The music from the large portable tape player had stopped. Roger took the cassette out and turned it over. *We're Only in it for the Money* by The Mothers of

Invention began to play. 'Wow, I love Zappa!' I called out excitedly. 'I really struggle to find any decent Zappa stuff where I live.'

Myfanwy was sat on the settee, stroking the dog and enjoying his scrumpy. I stepped over to look at the drawings on the bed. I was thrilled to find that they were all artwork for a comic I read called *Septimus Manktelow: Dystopian Explorer.* The unfinished, black and white comic strip on the bed showed the unmistakable character of Septimus Manktelow. He was dressed in his trademark outfit of slashed leather doublet, trunk-hose and long boots. He was accompanied by his ubiquitous sidekick, Brothelkins the dwarf.

'I don't believe it, you're the actual creator of Septimus Manktelow!'

'It's a living,' said Roger modestly. 'I've been doing comics on and off for twenty years now. I first started doing comic strips when I was in New York in 1967. That's where I first saw the Mothers,' he said, nodding towards the cassette player, 'they were doing a residency at the Garrick Theater. Anyway, I was doing a comic strip for an underground magazine called *Flibbertigibbet.* I used to lampoon different superheroes each week. There was an obscenity trial when I had two superheroes having gay sex in one of the issues. I ended up getting deported after that and that's when I ended up doing all the album covers. I had a spell of writing science fiction novels in the seventies. Then I had a bit of a bad patch which put pay to everything really.'

Roger stared at a photo of a beautiful woman with long black hair and a girl of six or seven with cute Shirley Temple features.

'Is that your wife and daughter?' Myfanwy asked.

'Yes, sadly not with us any more.'

'Oh, I'm sorry,' said Myfanwy regretfully, 'I didn't mean to dredge up bad memories.'

'It's okay, there are no bad memories where those two are concerned; only good ones.' Roger took a drink of his scrumpy then continued, 'They both died in a car crash. It was a few years before I managed to do anything creative again after that. Then I bought this old wreck and started doing the comic stuff again. This place saved my life, really.'

Roger reflected for a few minutes in silence, staring at the ceiling. We continued to drink silently, listening to the music. Amidst the noise of the tape we could hear footsteps above us. The door opened and a pair of legs began to climb down the steps. A pair of cricket flannels held up with an MCC tie came down first, followed by a white shirt that looked more like an old-fashioned nightshirt. On the head of the new arrival was a wide-brimmed straw hat, which fell off as its owner came down the stairs.

'I had to get the fuck out of that place!' said Tip Topley, clearly in a state of panic, 'I had to get away from that harpy for a while.'

'Fancy a drink?' said Roger, holding up the jug.

'Yeah. Oh hello, it's you,' said Tip, surprised to see Myfanwy for a second time that day.

'We must stop meeting like this,' said Myfanwy, looking triumphantly at me.

I remained in dumbstruck silence as one of my heroes sat down to join us for a drink.

'Have you got any coke?' Tip asked Myfanwy.

'No, not on me.'

'What about your chum here?' said Tip, looking at me accusingly.

'No, sorry, I haven't got any drugs,' I said, feeling as though I should be obliged to nip out and fetch some.

'What about you, Rog?' Tip continued. Roger shook his head and I watched Tip, half expecting him to cross-examine the dog next.

As if in anticipation of this, the dog began to bark at Tip.

'Quiet, Bingo!' said Roger.

Tip was so wired. 'Can't you keep that infernal animal under control!'

'You calm down as well, Timothy,' said Roger, picking up a long-stemmed pipe that looked like it was purchased at a tobacconist shop in Middle Earth. Tip slid down to the floor, where he sat huddled, dejectedly. Roger filled the pipe with tobacco from a leather pouch and then lit a match and began to puff contentedly. The familiar, pleasant smell of pipe tobacco began to fill the room as the smoke drifted through the air. Myfanwy and Tip raised their heads and inhaled the smoke like Bisto Kids, desperate for evidence of any illegal substances that might be blended with the tobacco.

'If you've got any glue handy, I'm sure that might do the trick,' Myfanwy suggested helpfully, as if he was contemplating mending a broken vase.

Tip put his head in his hands. 'Oh, for Christ's sake, I couldn't possibly sink that low.'

'Just a suggestion,' said Myfanwy, shrugging.

Tip suddenly looked up at Roger. 'You haven't got any glue have you, Rog?'

Roger slowly shook his head, serenely smoking like a giant hobbit.

After a few minutes, in which he allowed Tip to calm himself down a little, Roger ventured to ask what had caused him to flee from Lucy. 'So, what happened with the old trouble and strife then? I thought you seemed suitably uxorious this morning.'

'Have you heard about this AIDS disease?' Tip looked around for affirmation. 'Maybe you haven't heard of it over here yet, but it's big in the States.'

Myfanwy remained silent, but he had heard all too well about AIDS and the deadly virus that caused it.

'Well, anyway,' continued Tip, 'this friend of mine in LA who's a big porn star, and I mean BIG, well he died from this disease a couple of months back. Then we found out last night that a big name in Hollywood has been diagnosed with AIDS.'

'Who?' asked Myfanwy.

'I can't possibly reveal that at the moment,' said Tip. 'This is an absolute Hollywood legend and a close personal friend of Lucy's family.'

Myfanwy considered the fee he might get from selling the story to the newspapers if he could get Tip to talk.

'So now Lucy is on my back, wanting me to have a blood test for this thing and cross-examining me about who I've been with, how many times, have I been injecting anything. Well, I just had to get out when she started again this afternoon. I just had to get away!'

'You can't keep running away, Tim,' said Roger.

'Well that's rich, coming from you,' said Tip, glancing round the boat.

'Fair comment,' conceded Roger.

Tip looked around for anything to alleviate his craving for cocaine. He walked over to where the mandolin hung on the wall and took it down. Roger glanced across at him, smiling with the half of his mouth not occupied with the pipe. Tip took out the pick from between the strings and strummed the open strings to test the tuning. He adjusted a couple of strings, so each pair was in tune with its twin. Myfanwy and I sat awestruck with anticipation that the legendary Tip Topley might actually perform his magic before our very eyes. I could remember only one track in which he played mandolin on his records. On the *Wicca Manifesto* album, he played sitar, oud and hurdy-gurdy; possibly all at the same time, to judge by the sound.

He sat down cross-legged on the floor and began playing a few runs up and down the tiny fretboard. With the instrument in his hand, he seemed to regain his composure, as if an essential part of him had been returned. He began to play a set of hornpipes, confidently and with the skill and speed of any experienced player from Sligo or Kentucky. First, he played 'Staten Island', then 'Harvest Home' and finally 'The Boys of Bluehill'. Roger nodded his head, his eyes closed and his pipe sending dancing spirals of smoke into the air. Myfanwy and I raised our mugs together in a silent toast.

When Tip finished playing, he examined the mandolin. He seemed to have found solace in music; the one thing that awoke any true spirituality in his soul. Drugs, like most vices, were just a desperate and futile attempt to search for a pinprick hole that might reveal a fragment of the truth of eternal ecstasy.

Sensing the sudden calm in Tip, Bingo came over and lay next to him. As if he had just awakened from a dream, Tip looked up at Myfanwy, remembering the previous events of the day.

'Oh yeah, apparently your sugar daddy is being questioned regarding the body of a young man in his hotel room.'

'Shit!' said Myfanwy, trying to process the news.

'Yeah, and old Freddy is currently at large somewhere with the boys in blue searching for him,' Tip's sardonic smile returned. 'I noticed you got out of there pretty quickly.'

'Yeah, well, I thought they were coming for me about the, err, the coke we did.'

'Yes, I must confess when I saw them come in, the old paranoia began to kick in.' Tip had many bitter memories of heavily publicised drug busts.

Roger had decided to continue his work and was sat on the bed, cross-legged. I had witnessed Tip's legendary musicianship and now watched the great illustrator at work. It seemed to make perfect sense that the magazine had given Roger the epithet of 'Psychedelic Michelangelo'. The muscularity of the figures in Roger's artwork were reminiscent of the work of the great Renaissance master. On a shelf near his bed were several books on the artwork of Michelangelo, Caravaggio and Botticelli. There was also a well-thumbed copy of Vasari's *The Lives of the Most Excellent Painters, Sculptors and Architects*.

Tip began laughing as he recalled something else. 'Oh yeah, and then as soon as we go out to sit on the balcony to watch a bit of cricket, some crazy motherfucker comes cartwheeling onto the pitch stark bollock naked.'

Myfanwy smiled, and was about to tell Tip who the streaker was, when I slapped him on the back and said, 'How about we have a walk into town and see what's happening?'

Tip became animated by this suggestion. 'Hey man, it's years since I've been into Nottingham, why don't I come with you?'

I looked at Tip in disbelief, then spoke to him for the first time. 'Yeah man, come and have a few beers with us,' I said, trying to sound cool.

'And maybe you can find someone who can supply some coke,' Tip said, pointing at Myfanwy. 'Wow, I remember playing at the Boat Club here a few times. We were on the same bill as Hendrix once. I felt like throwing my guitar away after I saw him play. That was the same night that Rod Stewart said he wanted to start a band with me and I told him to fuck off.'

CHAPTER SIXTEEN

Pluto Lockwood would very likely be unfit for the new season. He was lying in a hospital bed with a punctured lung; the result of Rollo's systematic pounding on Pluto's ribs with a sturdy ashplant stick. Strachan was more fortunate with his injuries, a broken nose and collarbone being the worse. His eyes were as black as a panda bear's as a result of the injury to his nose. Strachan could take it as well as he could dish it out.

The news of the attack had reached the ears of Andy 'Cuckoo' Walsh. Walsh was the undisputed leader of the Coocachoo Crew. He had recently been detained in a Belgian prison for his involvement in the Heysel Stadium tragedy. He was released from prison after it was proved that he wasn't actually in the stadium at the time. Cuckoo had been reluctant to part with this information until it became clear to him that he would serve a serious amount of time in prison. His reluctance had initially been due to the fact that he had been in a Brussels brothel during the events at the stadium. He wasn't afraid of facing any of the top football hooligan firms, but drew the line at facing the wrath of his wife.

In Cuckoo's absence, Pluto had played the role of regent; playing the debauchee, like Prince Hal, while Cuckoo played the role of Henry IV. Cuckoo was paying the young pretender and his aide-de-camp a visit. He strutted into the ward in his black Lacoste tracksuit and orange Fila vest, running his hand through his dark, Kevin Keegan perm. His big nose and moustache made him look more like Terry McDermott. Pluto was not available for comment due to his oxygen mask. Strachan, on the other hand, was able to give an honest account of the ambush in the Bridge Tavern.

It had been brought to Cuckoo's attention that a group of rival hooligans from Chesterfield were planning a visit to Mansfield that very evening. Potter had even been polite enough to give Cuckoo a telephone call to announce his intentions. There was no doubt in Cuckoo's mind that Potter's crew had been responsible for the Bridge Tavern attack.

Paul Potter, or 'Pol Pot', was the self-styled 'Don' of the Khmer Blues Crew. With his one A level there was nothing Pol couldn't tell you about Tennyson's 'Charge of the Light Brigade'. He thought that listening to Level 42 was the height of sophistication. He worked at a branch of the Co-operative travel agents and was considered a man of the world by his associates.

Unbeknown to Cuckoo, the Khmer Blues were at that moment boarding the coach after meeting up at the Sun Inn in Chesterfield. Potter had managed to enlist almost a coachload of likely lads, all intent on causing as much mayhem in Mansfield as possible. They were all clad in the finest clothes that Burtons could offer.

'Right then, lads, let's give these scabby Notts bastards a night to remember!' was Potter's rallying cry. It was hardly the stuff of Shakespeare's *Henry V*, but it certainly raised a hearty cheer from the lads from Chesterfield. They were still celebrating the Spireites' promotion to League Division Three after finishing top of the table. A night out in Mansfield to celebrate had been on the cards since the end of the season, after Mansfield had finished in a position of mid-table mediocrity.

Cuckoo, meanwhile, was hastily conscripting any able-bodied hooligan he could find in Mansfield. He was aware that the Khmer Blues could strike again at any time. He was also painfully aware that after the downfall of Pluto, he was now the prime target.

Cuckoo found a payphone in the hospital reception and took a list of numbers from his wallet. It was time to begin calling in a few favours. Once he had made his calls, he walked from the hospital and down the road as far as the Black Bull in Mansfield Woodhouse. The pub was close enough to the town centre to lie low without any danger of bumping into Potter's crew. He put his hand in his trouser pocket and reassured himself that he had his telescopic baton concealed there if he was ambushed. He had arranged to rendezvous at the Black Bull with the supporters that he had successfully conscripted for his counter-attack.

When he entered the games room of the Black Bull, he at once spotted Colin Townroe playing pool. Colin had decided to spend some time there rather than endure another confrontation with Dawn. He decided to lick his wounds and get over the shock of the attack and Jackie's three-timing, before dealing with his domestic problems.

Colin's heart sank when he saw Cuckoo Walsh walk through the door. He instantly made a beeline for the pool table when he saw Colin.

'What are you having?'

'Oh, just a coke mate, I'm on antibiotics so I can't drink,' said Colin, pointing to the wound on his head.

'Don't talk shit. Come on, one won't kill you.'

Colin wasn't in the mood to argue, and accepted a pint of lager. Normally Cuckoo didn't have a lot to say to Colin, who was Pluto's pet. When he returned with the drinks, he told Colin to sit down and give his version of events. The whole thing felt like a cross-examination and Colin gave a fairly accurate account. He told Cuckoo about being hurled through the window, omitting the part about getting up and running away; instead, he said that he had lain unconscious for some time and then dragged himself away before the police arrived.

'Don't worry me owd knacker, we're gonna counter-attack tonight and get revenge,' said Cuckoo enthusiastically, as he slapped Colin hard on his bruised arm.

Colin's heart sunk as Cuckoo told him who else was turning up shortly at the pub. Colin listened to Cuckoo tell him about the phone call he had received from Pol Potter. Colin tried to reason with him that it might have been another firm who had raided the Bridge Tavern.

'No mate, it's gotta be them, they want to rub our noses in it because they got promoted and we're still in Division Four.' He then added, 'They're still pissed off that we wrecked the Barley Mow when we came up there last Boxing Day.'

Colin remembered the day well; he had even smashed a chair himself, unable to find any escape route from the mayhem. He felt like he was once again trapped in a similar position. Even going home to that cheating bitch would have been a better option. He then had an idea to get out of his current predicament.

'Listen, Andy,' he began, reverently using Cuckoo's Christian name, 'a few of my mates are going to be in town in a bit and they can all handle themselves. I reckon I can persuade them all to come and join us. You just tell me where to meet you later.'

Cuckoo pondered this idea for a moment, nodding his head slowly with the effort.

'No, I reckon we all stay together, safety in numbers and that. We can all go together and get some more bodies later.' Cuckoo had made his decision and Colin regretted ever getting involved with the Coocachoo Crew.

Colin's only hope was that the people Cuckoo had called would not turn up. His hopes were quickly shattered when two burly black men walked into the room.

'Now we're talking!' Cuckoo shouted across the room.

Colin recognised the new arrivals as Jay and Carl Letts. The two brothers worked at Warsop Vale colliery, and had worked as bouncers at Harvey's as a source of income during the strike. As Cuckoo got up to shake the hands of Jay and Carl, two more arrivals came through the door. Colin didn't know their names, but he had seen them when the crew had gone on outings to away games in search of trouble.

As Cuckoo briefed his volunteers on the current situation, Colin looked on while the others ignored him. He thought about playing another game of pool but the man he had been playing with had left. He decided that he would have to risk mixing the antibiotics with alcohol, and walked to the bar and ordered a pint of Strongbow and a double vodka.

'Don't get too hammered!' called out Cuckoo, changing his tune. 'We're gonna be feightin' like fuck tonight!'

This raised a cheer from a few of the younger volunteers who had just arrived. They were all decked out in the latest Ellesse and Diadora gear, but would run at the first sign of trouble. Colin was recognised by the youngsters as one of Pluto Lockwood's lieutenants. Keeping their distance from the surly faces that surrounded Cuckoo, they gravitated towards Colin. Pleased to have some company and encouraged by the vodka, he began to regain some of his old swagger.

Cuckoo began to regale his audience with his tales of doing battle with Juventus hooligans in Brussels. The subject then turned to England's remaining qualification games for the 1986 World Cup in Mexico. English clubs had been banned from competing in Europe and some were discussing whether the national team would also be banned. Cuckoo was anxious that England should play in Mexico, if they were allowed to qualify for the finals. It was his hope that a combined English firm should face the Argies and spank them for trying to take the Falklands; beating them on the pitch as well as off it would be cause for double celebration.

Finally satisfied with the numbers he had mustered, Cuckoo told everyone to sup up and move out. He led his band of men up the hill from the Black Bull, that led to the town centre. The first stage of the expedition would be to make camp at the Horse and Jockey. Here they would wait while scouts would search other pubs for signs of the Khmer Blues.

Colin watched Cuckoo earnestly making his preparations. Once inside the Horse and Jockey, all Colin was bothered about was getting another drink. If he was going to take another good hiding, he intended to be too drunk to feel anything.

When Feggy Edwards walked through the door of the Horse and Jockey, the last person he had expected to see was Cuckoo Walsh. He had heard that Walsh was still locked up in Brussels. He was even more alarmed to see Colin Townroe at the bar, which meant that Pluto and Strachan might still be in town. He realised that he would have to concoct a story to explain his absence during the Bridge Tavern massacre.

After a couple of pints in the Reindeer, to calm his nerves, he had walked down the road to Littleworth to see his brother, Eric. He had hung out at Eric's, where they had watched the Live Aid show until it was time for the pubs to open again.

To his surprise, he was given a hero's welcome by Cuckoo Walsh. Cuckoo summarised the day's events. He briefed Feggy on the list of casualties at the Bridge and the plan of action for the rest of the evening. A wave of relief flooded through Feggy, with the realisation that the general wasn't aware of his desertion in the face of the enemy.

Feggy looked over at Colin, who nodded his head in acknowledgement. Feggy didn't recognise any of the burly group that surrounded Cuckoo. He recognised some of the fresh faces of the so-called 'Bash Street Kids'; the cadet branch of the Coocachoo Crew. They were staying clear of Cuckoo's contingent and were clinging to Colin. They greeted Feggy with the respect they always reserved for Pluto and his entourage.

'Rough afternoon, eh,' said Colin, raising his eyebrows.

Feggy clutched his chest and winced. 'Thought I might have broken my ribs, but they're just badly bruised apparently.'

He had intended to claim that he had nipped out for some cigarettes and returned to find the aftermath of the carnage. Now he had a clearer picture of the incident, he concluded that those involved must have been too concerned with self-preservation to note his absence.

'One of them smashed a chair over my head,' said Colin, pointing to his scar.

'I got knocked unconscious,' continued Feggy, elaborating his story. 'I came round when I heard the sound of sirens and did a runner.'

'Yeah, I got thrown through a window,' said Colin proudly. 'I was winded a bit, but when I got up again, I was gonna go back in for another go, but I heard the sirens and decided I'd better go and get my head stitched up instead.'

★ ★ ★ ★ ★

Once we had bid farewell to Roger, we had to navigate the erratic rock star towards the centre of Nottingham. We walked along London Road, past Meadow Lane and then turned left towards the railway station. We stopped at the Bentink Hotel, next to the station. The bar was filled with hardened drinkers who didn't even look up from their drinks to register the presence of a legend. We sat in a corner, near where a television set was showing the Live Aid concert.

U2 were performing and Tip launched into a critical commentary. 'Daltrey and Jagger were doing all that stuff twenty years ago. I met this Bono guy once at an awards bash, and he started giving me all this shit about me playing Sun City. Well, I told him, when he'd been in the business as long as I had, he could start lecturing me, but until then he could just fuck off!'

Tip's voice had gradually become louder as he had become more and more angry with the television. The landlord and his regulars, who were accustomed to trouble, began to glance across at us.

'And that cunt Bowie said, "If Topley doesn't play guitar during my set, I'm not doing it," well that's all the thanks I get for persuading Lou Reed to let him produce *Transformer*.'

I decided to try and calm things down a bit, as I was becoming increasingly nervous that the natives were becoming restless. 'What about Woodstock though, eh Tip? This isn't a patch on Woodstock, is it.'

'Woodstock,' Tip said thoughtfully, 'yes, that was certainly one of a kind.'

The word 'Woodstock' seemed to have acted like a magic spell upon Tip, whose eyes became glazed with emotion. He finished his large brandy, and shoving a ten-pound note into Myfanwy's hand, told him to fetch more drinks.

'We were just about washed up by the time of Woodstock, but it was worth it just to be there.' He took one of Myfanwy's cigarettes and, after lighting it, continued. 'They flew us there in a helicopter. I was already tripping on acid and I remember as we flew over the crowd, it seemed like it stretched on forever; you know, like that scene in *A Matter of Life and Death*.'

I did indeed recall the scene that he referred to: a celestial host, in a heavenly amphitheatre that stretches further and further back to form a galaxy in space.

'Then, when we got off the helicopter, Grace Slick came to greet me, all dressed in white. With her long black hair and white, fringed leather outfit, she became the Moon goddess, Diana. Keith Moon somehow became the Norse god, Loki. I was so out of it when I stood at the edge of the stage and watched The Who perform. Daltrey was swinging his microphone around and then the sun began to rise and he became Apollo himself.'

'What about Pete Townshend?'

'No, he was still a cunt.'

With Tip in a far better mood, we decided to walk to 'Ye Olde' Trip to Jerusalem. The Trip was a pub that sat against Castle Rock, upon which Nottingham Castle stood. Some said that crusading knights used to sup a last pint of ale here before setting off to slaughter Saracens. Tip, after his recollections of Woodstock, liked the pub's name. The building itself was probably built during the Interregnum period of the seventeenth century. The dark interior, with its low ceiling, contrasted with the sunny courtyard outside. As I stood at the bar, looking out at the drinkers in the courtyard, the scene reminded me of the paintings of Pieter de Hootch.

The alcohol seemed to have alleviated Tip's craving for drugs. I had imagined people spotting him and wanting to meet him, but so far we had remained unnoticed. We moved on to the Bell Inn, where William Clarke had been landlord before his fateful move to the Trent Bridge Inn. We walked up Friars Lane towards the pub. Carmelite monks had once established a friary in this area, and the area where the Bell Inn was situated once belonged to the monks. Many argued that the Bell Inn was actually older than the Trip to Jerusalem.

We entered the Bell Inn through a dingy passageway with stone flagstones. At the end of the passageway was a long barroom, where a traditional jazz combo was playing at the far end. As we ordered drinks, the band was playing a vigorous rendition of 'Bourbon Street Parade'. Tip seemed to be really into the music, slapping his hand on the bar, in time with the rhythm.

Myfanwy didn't really get jazz and noted Tip's enthusiasm with disbelief. 'Are you into this sort of thing, then?'

'Yeah, when I was at Oxford, all we listened to for the first couple of years was trad. That all changed when someone played me John Coltrane's *Blue Train*, that was the pivotal moment for me. Once I started getting into Lightnin' Hopkins and Skip James, I started to really get into my guitar playing and lost touch with jazz.'

'It just reminds me of the kind of music they used to play on *The Comedians*,' said Myfanwy.

I had to confess that I was reminded of that same jazz band, dressed in stripy waistcoats and straw boaters, who provided an interlude to comedians like Charlie Williams and Stan Boardman.

Nudging Myfanwy, I said, 'Tip was telling me about his experiences at Woodstock earlier.'

'Oh yeah,' said Myfanwy, 'was it as bad as they say? Didn't that finish Toy Mistress off?'

'Well!' began Tip, raising his eyebrows. 'By the time we finally came on, I was completely out of it. Everything was spiked with acid, water, food, probably even the rain according to some accounts. Everyone had been awake all night, watching The Who and Jefferson Airplane. I think most people were asleep. Someone told me that when we came on, we were all playing different songs for the first twenty minutes. Everyone made a fortune out of the film and records, but we had the recordings of our performance burned.'

The band had taken a break between sets, and the man I recognised as the trombone player came over and tapped Tip on the shoulder. Tip looked round, half expecting a fan to ask for his autograph. At first, he didn't seem to recognise the bald-headed, middle-aged man with the beer belly.

'Hey Timmy, long time no see!' he said. 'It's me, remember, Lardy Macpherson?'

'Well bugger me!' Tip said, finally recognising the name. 'I haven't seen you since we first started playing at the Marquee Club.' Tip slapped Lardy on his paunch. 'You're still wearing the peascod then, eh.'

'It's all bought and paid for,' answered Lardy, rubbing his belly.

'"Bought with a million of repentance", eh?' retorted Tip, with an obscure reference that went over Lardy's head.

'So how's it going, then?' asked Lardy. 'I saw that interview you did on *The Tube*; great to see you're doing a new album.'

'Yeah, I think it might sell a few copies. What have you been up to then, Lardy?'

'Well, it all went downhill after the Marquee days,' said Lardy wistfully. 'I did a stint doing TV stuff in the seventies; *The Comedians*, mainly.'

'Cool,' said Tip, already becoming distracted by the appearance of a couple of young ladies.

'I thought you would be doing this Live Aid thing?' said Lardy.

'No!' Tip replied abruptly.

'Okay Tim, nice to see you again anyway.'

As Lardy walked away, realising he'd put his foot in it, Myfanwy and I glanced at each other in anticipation of another mood swing. Instead, Tip got up and followed Lardy to where the band was getting ready to play again. We watched as Tip spoke to his friend again and the two laughed and shook hands. Lardy then began to introduce Tip to the other members of the band, all of whom shook hands with the star with a sense of awe.

'I thought he was going to go off on one again then,' said Myfanwy, with an expression of relief.

'Who'd have thought we'd be babysitting a big rock star tonight, eh? Nobody will believe us.'

'Like you didn't believe me, you mean.'

'Well, you have been known to stretch the truth on certain occasions,' I said, good humouredly.

The band began to play again, and as we looked round to see what Tip was up to, we were surprised to see him standing at the microphone with a semi-acoustic guitar in his hands. After Lardy and the band had played the introduction, Tip began singing 'Autumn Leaves'. Certain members of the audience were beginning to realise who the guest vocalist was, and Tip soon gained the attention of the entire room. During the song's instrumental break, each band member played a solo and Tip listened intently to every phrase. When his turn came, some of the spectators clapped and cheered. Tip's guitar break complemented the bittersweet nature of the song it accompanied. He was transported into his own world of nostalgia and acceptance of the brevity of life which the autumnal theme evoked in him.

I noted how Myfanwy had been infected with the melancholy of Tip's performance; a tear ran down from his eye, which he tried to conceal from me by turning away.

Putting my arm around him, I asked, 'What's up with you, soft lad?'

'It's that hay fever again,' he said, smiling, 'I need some of Tip's medicine.'

'I think we should start thinking about getting the bus back to Mansfield,' I suggested, 'there's this girl I was hoping to bump into who I met the other week.'

'Do you think he'll be alright let loose on his own in Nottingham?' Myfanwy asked doubtfully.

'I'm sure if he could survive Woodstock on a headful of acid, he can cope with Notts. Besides, he's got Acker Bilk and the boys for company now.'

'Fair enough,' said Myfanwy, 'I need a piss first.'

'I've just been,' said I, 'I'll meet you outside.'

I stood on the street outside the pub, enjoying the summer evening. The bell nicknamed 'Little John' at the Council House chimed nine times. We needed to get to the bus station for the bus at a quarter past nine. I admired the architecture of the Council House, with its statuary which represented commerce, civic law, prosperity and knowledge. The façade on the pediment of the building reminded me of the Parthenon in Athens. I had never seen the domes of Saint Paul's or Santa Maria del Fiore, but the dome of the Council House was good enough for me.

I was reflecting on how much art deco architecture there was in Nottingham when Myfanwy grabbed me and began breaking into a jog.

'Hey, cool it,' I said, 'we've plenty of time.'

'Boz is in there looking for me!' said Myfanwy with a look of terror.

Deciding that he needed to relieve himself in a more thorough manner, Myfanwy had perched himself in the water closet. Whilst regaining his composure from his emotional outburst, he was suddenly distracted by a voice he found familiar. He then heard another voice which he recognised as Nappy Andrews. He shuddered as he heard Boz instruct Nappy to look in the downstairs rooms, while he checked The Belfry restaurant upstairs. Myfanwy quickly made the necessary titivations and then charged up the stairs that led back up to the ground floor. As he came running up the passageway, Nappy came out of the room known as the Tudor Bar and was knocked off his feet as Myfanwy passed him.

We ran as fast as we could up to the Victoria Shopping Centre, which was adjacent to the bus station. The bus was already parked in its allotted bay. We joined the queue of people waiting for the driver to open the doors of the bus.

'I thought you said he'd been arrested,' I said, as I tried to catch my breath.

'Well, he's out again; the sly bastard's probably grassed someone up to get himself out of the shit.'

I looked apprehensively at the entrance to the station and then at the driver, finally relieved as he opened the door to allow passengers on board. Once on the bus we found seats at the rear and silently urged the driver to close the doors and drive us away to safety. The wait seemed like an eternity as more people got on the bus, some with queries and others searching for the correct change.

We breathed a sigh of relief as the bus began to reverse out of its bay. As we looked out of the window as the bus began to turn, we saw Boz and Nappy come running along the platform, waving to our driver. In the tradition of the most pedantic of bus drivers, ours ignored the pleading pair and continued to drive out of the station. We ducked our heads down in the hope that we wouldn't be seen; only daring to raise them when we were safely on our way up Mansfield Road.

CHAPTER SEVENTEEN

After seven hours standing in the heat, it had been a long, gruelling day for Heidi. Frequent announcements had been made for people to move back a few steps to stop spectators at the front of the stage from being crushed; several people had been pulled from the front of the crowd who had succumbed to heatstroke. Heidi thought about Jeanette near the front, but couldn't allow herself the cruel indulgence of imagining her being crushed. When it was time for Spandau Ballet to play, Heidi and Kirstie had been brave enough to make their way as far forward as they could to get a better view. Tony Hadley had worn a long black coat and trousers made from PVC, which must have been stiflingly hot. He looked like a sexy vampire in the outfit. Gary Kemp had looked more summery, with his shades and orange shirt unbuttoned to reveal his naked torso.

They had eaten all the provisions by two o'clock, and by four, both Heidi and Kirstie agreed that they were starving. They had stuffed themselves with hamburgers and hotdogs since then. It was getting a little bit cooler by seven o'clock and everyone was finding renewed enthusiasm as they waited for the headlining acts to perform.

All day long, one act had been shoved out to perform a couple of songs, or three if the schedule allowed. Heidi's favourite moment had been when Noel Edmonds had introduced Sting and Phil Collins; she loved Noel Edmonds. Mel Smith and Griff Rhys Jones came on to introduce Queen. They had come onto the stage dressed as police officers and claimed that they had received a complaint about the noise.

Some of the artists had agreed to perform at the show in the spirit of any charity event. They had come on and sung a couple of songs and then exited stage left, happy to have done their bit for a good cause. Acts like U2 and Queen seemed more aware of their place in rock history, and wanted to pull out all the stops to create an iconic and memorable performance. During U2's set, Bono had climbed down from the stage and grabbed a girl from the front of the crowd and danced with her. Heidi couldn't believe her eyes when she watched this moment on the big screen. She could see Jeanette herself, climbing over the fence to get to the singer.

Heidi hadn't seen Jeanette again until Queen had taken to the stage. For the second time that day, Heidi and Kirstie had ventured nearer to the front of the stage. For the second time that day, Heidi saw Jeanette with a man. This time she was being held by a tall man in a black double-breasted shirt. He looked much older than Jeanette, probably in his mid-twenties. His hair was neatly slicked back and shaved round the sides. Something about the haircut reminded Heidi of a film she'd watched about Nazi Germany during the 1930s. He was standing behind her with his arm round her neck. She looked so young next to this man who held her in such a possessive manner. Heidi shook Kirstie by the arm and pointed towards Jeanette. Kirstie looked around, trying to see what she was meant to be looking at. Heidi pointed again, shouting in Kirstie's ear, 'There, look, Jeanette!' Finally spotting Jeanette and her new man, Kirstie put her hand over her mouth and looked at Heidi with an expression of shock.

After Queen had finished their performance, they both made their way back to where Tom and the others had been stood in the crowd. Kirstie had agreed with Heidi that they should tell Tom about this dodgy-looking man who they had seen with Jeanette. Tom was nowhere to be seen when they arrived in roughly the same place they had stood earlier. Callum was still in the same spot with pimply Paul Hickinbottom. They waited for Tom to return while watching a video link from Philadelphia of Chevy Chase, introducing Bowie and Jagger's video performance of 'Dancing in the Street'. The sister concert at Philadelphia's John F. Kennedy Stadium was taking place simultaneously to the Wembley concert. Between acts at Wembley, the video screens would show performances from Philadelphia, of acts as diverse as The Beach Boys and Black Sabbath, or Joan Baez and Judas Priest. Heidi and Kirstie were watching Simple Minds performed on the video screen when Tom returned with Gareth from a trip for refreshment and the toilet. Tom looked up to heaven in a silent plea for patience after Heidi had explained the situation with Jeanette. He took Gareth with him to see if he could find her amongst the throng, which was massing near the stage to see David Bowie.

David Bowie's performance was, in Heidi's opinion, the best of the day so far. He came out, dressed in an immaculate grey suit, with his hair raised in a stylish bouffant quiff. At the end of his set, he introduced a video that showed the plight of the children in Ethiopia. The video, which was accompanied by 'Drive' by The Cars, showed masses of starving and disease-ridden Ethiopian children. A baby trying to suck its starving mother's breast, which could no longer produce milk. A dead child lay wrapped in a dirty sheet that served as a shroud. The camera focused on a mother holding her starving child. The mother wore a crucifix around her neck and Heidi thought of Jesus crying out 'My God, my God, why have you forsaken me?' Kirstie put her arm around Heidi, wiping tears from her eyes. Looking around, Heidi could see tears of pity and guilt on the faces of many in the crowd. She then turned around to see Callum with a bovine expression on his face, stuffing a hamburger in his mouth and ketchup dribbling down his chin.

★ ★ ★ ★ ★

The plan for everyone to go round to Ray's place was short-lived. John met a friend he had recently made called Spubble, who was on his way to a gig at a pub in Wembley. Spubble wore a tatty mohair jumper with red and black horizontal stripes. He wore black jeans that were faded to a dull grey and basketball boots. His brown hair was long and matted into dreadlocks. Disorder were playing upstairs at a pub called The Wife of Bath. John and Spike grew more interested when Spubble told them that the Scum Dribblers would also be playing there. Spike was thrilled to hear that the band from Mansfield would be playing; he had hitchhiked to several gigs with the band's guitarist, Timmy, several times. Timmy and the vocalist and bass player, Ade, formed the nucleus of this hardcore punk band. Tim and Ade were like a post- nuclear version of Chas and Dave, with several different drummers passing through their ranks.

John suggested to Ray that they meet up again the following day. While they waited for the bus to Wembley with Spubble, Ray continued his walk home. After a short walk, he arrived at his small Edwardian mid-terraced house. When he entered the house, he was surprised at how quiet it was. In the passageway he took off his shoes; in the small kitchen beyond the living room, his wife was making tea. He could hear the kids playing in the back yard as he walked through to where Mary was quietly making tea. He noticed four mugs lined up on the table. Ray was puzzled by Mary's pensive mood. She didn't normally have a problem with him coming in half-cut.

Putting his arm around her, he asked, 'Is everything alright? You're very quiet today.'

'We've got visitors,' she said quietly.

Ray heard a chair scraping on the floor in the front room. He looked at Mary, trying to work out who was visiting that might upset Mary.

'Tamburlaine's found us,' said Mary, a tear now running down her face.

Ray's stomach turned as soon as he heard the name. It had been so long now that he had almost forgotten about the threat of the gangster catching up with them after so many years.

Ray took a deep breath and then walked to the front room. Tamburlaine was looking at Ray's bookshelf; he pulled out a copy of *The Female Eunoch*.

He looked at Ray, and holding the book up, said, 'Is this any good?'

'I don't know, it's one of Mary's,' said Ray, not expecting a discussion about feminist literature.

A cough alerted Ray to the presence of someone else in the room. Sat in an armchair near the window was Tamburlaine's loyal bodyguard, Sweeney McMahon. Tamburlaine wore a cream-coloured linen suit and a blue pinstriped shirt. A blue handkerchief was neatly folded in the breast pocket of his jacket. He had put weight on since Ray had last seen him. His corpulence was emphasised by his diminutive stature, which he had always been sensitive about. His neatly styled brown hair and elegant clothes contrasted with his red face and short, chubby body. Sweeney wore a cobalt blue suit and white shirt; a giant of a man, he still looked like he worked out regularly. He had once made his name as a bare-knuckle fighter. His shoulder-length blond hair gave him a Nordic look. He might have been a descendant from Dublin's Viking ancestry.

'This looks like a bunch of shite to me,' said Tamburlaine, tossing the book onto the floor. 'Is that how you poisoned her against me, teaching her bollocks like that.'

'She's got a mind of her own,' said Ray, defiantly. 'Why have you come here after all this time, you should have moved on by now?'

'The college boy's got quite a pair of balls on him,' said Tamburlaine, addressing Sweeney. 'And who do you suppose you are, telling me what I should or shouldn't do?'

Ray was stalling for time now; he had told Mary to take the kids away, via the alleyway that led along the back of the terraced street.

'Where's that tea, woman?' Tamburlaine called out.

'I'll go and see what's happening,' said Ray.

Ray made the tea and shouted through the back door for Tamburlaine's benefit, telling the now absent kids to play nicely. He recited a few lines of W.B. Yeats in the hope that Tamburlaine and Sweeney might think he was talking to Mary.

'And will you fetch us some biscuits if you have any,' called out Tamburlaine.

Ray returned to the front room with two mugs of tea.

'Ah, now that's a sight for sore eyes,' said Tamburlaine. 'I'm fair parched, so I am.'

Ray stood silently while they drank the tea. It felt like one of those occasions when despised relatives call uninvited.

'That's a grand cup of tea,' said Tamburlaine after a couple of sips. 'I don't suppose Mary and the kids will be joining us, will they?'

Ray thought for a moment for an excuse. 'I'll go and see what they're up to.'

'I don't think that will be necessary, seeing as they're not here, Ray,' said Tamburlaine. 'I do so hate party poopers, what do you say Sweeney?'

'I hate them,' said Sweeney, indulging his boss.

'Ah, he's more of an Ajax than a Ulysses, this one,' said Tamburlaine, gesturing towards Sweeney with his thumb. 'I bet you're surprised I know about them fellas, eh Ray. I know all about Ulysses and Homer and Joyce's Jew.'

'Are you here for a discussion about literature, then?' said Ray sarcastically.

'This bloke thinks I'm an eejit, Sweeney!'

'Shall I kill him now, boss?' said Sweeney hopefully, as he pulled a gun from under his jacket.

'Go and take these cups and make us another cup of tea, while Ray and I have a chat,' said Tamburlaine, without looking at Sweeney.

Sweeney obeyed Tamburlaine with a dejected expression. Tamburlaine then pulled his own gun from a holster under his jacket. He pointed the Walther PPK pistol at Ray and motioned him to sit in the chair vacated by Sweeney.

'Just like James Bond, eh,' said Tamburlaine, nodding at the gun. 'They say Hitler shot himself with one of these, so I guess they can't be all bad.'

Ray watched Tamburlaine silently, content that Mary and the kids had escaped. He sensed that his time was nearly up and was surprised at how calm he felt. He watched his nemesis admiring his gun and listing its merits; it was like the kind of preamble a villain in a film would make before executing someone.

Sweeney came back into the room with two mugs of tea, and handed them to Ray and Tamburlaine.

'Right then, Ajax, take that nice toy that I bought you and stand in that passage and make sure nobody comes in the front or the back.'

Sweeney did as he was told, giving Ray a menacing look as he exited the room.

'Now then, Ray, it seems to me that you and I share something in common at the moment.'

'What's that then?'

'Well, we both seem to be fugitives with people wanting to kill us,' said Tamburlaine jovially. 'First you go off with my woman and go and hide God knows where, and now I've got those Fenian bastards trying to send me to hell; where did you get to, by the way?'

'Ostend, Belgium.'

'Well, maybe I should try Ostend, Belgium myself,' said Tamburlaine, shaking his head. 'You certainly had us scratching our heads there.'

'So what have you done to upset the Provos?'

'Well!' began Tamburlaine, throwing back his head. 'I had a nice little earner, selling arms to the lads. I got into a bit of trouble on account of this with them MI6 fellas. These very nice men said that if I gave them a few names, they wouldn't send me to prison for a very long time.'

'I don't think Ostend will be far enough, if them lads is looking for you.'

'A very shrewd analysis of my current predicament by the learned gentleman,' said Tamburlaine, slapping his leg. 'I have come to the conclusion that this little excursion to London will be my last hurrah. What could be a better way to spend your last days, than catching up with old friends, eh.'

Ray continued to focus his attention on anything but Tamburlaine. He was becoming aware of the fact that these were going to be his final moments of existence. He looked at the plate mounted on the wall, which featured a depiction of Christ's crucifixion. The plate had been a gift from a neighbour to Mary. It was the usual Catholic kitsch that had been commonplace to Ray since his childhood. A far cry from the Renaissance splendour of Michelangelo's *The Last Judgement* or the Baroque exuberance of Bernini's *Ecstasy of Saint Teresa*. Ray had forgone the dogma and rituals of Catholicism as a teenager. He didn't fear the Dantean torments of hell, or the purifying punishments of purgatory. He felt that only an eternity of peaceful oblivion awaited him.

A sudden bump, outside in the passageway, disturbed his meditation. It also caused Tamburlaine to cease his melodramatic swansong. Before Tamburlaine had the chance to enquire what Sweeney was up to, the door burst open. The assassins, who Tamburlaine had been fatalistically awaiting, had finally arrived to deliver retribution. The two men, who had walked up the street dressed in dark suits with name tags on their lapels, looked like a pair of Mormon missionaries. Both of them carried a briefcase which contained a Beretta 92 semi-automatic pistol with a silencer attached to its barrel. They had walked up the alley at the rear of Ray's house and prepared their weapons. The back door had been left open when Mary had fled with the children, making for a swift and silent entrance. It had been easy for the first gunman who entered to simply step to his right and fire through the open kitchen door and beyond the living room, to where Sweeney stood in the front passageway. As Sweeney had fallen to the floor, the gunman had silently moved across the living room and kicked open the door to the front room. It had all happened too quickly for Tamburlaine to react, and he had been shot in the head before he could use his own gun. It had been even more of a shock for Ray, who sat in stunned silence, unaware of what had taken place behind the door. It dawned on him that some kind of gunfire had just taken place. He had heard a noise that he imagined sounded something like a gun firing. The silencer had lessened the noise to some degree, but not to the extent that it was portrayed in movies.

Ray slowly got up from the chair, listening for evidence that someone was still behind the door. There was no sound except for the sound of music coming from the next house. He tentatively walked across the room and glanced round the door. There was no one there but the body of Sweeney with two bloody holes in his chest, and another through his forehead. Ray turned around and saw three almost identical holes in Tamburlaine's chest and forehead. Tamburlaine stared up at Ray from his chair; with his arms spread over the chair's arms and his head leaning back, he looked like a Guy Fawkes effigy. Tamburlaine's gun lay on the floor. Ray considered picking it up and then rejected the idea; he had never touched a gun in his life.

Ray heard the sound of sirens outside and it suddenly occurred to him that Mary might have called the police. Stepping into the passageway, Ray saw that the living room and kitchen were both empty. It suddenly dawned on him that Tamburlaine's pursuers had finally found him and efficiently executed him.

Ray walked to the front door and slowly opened it. Outside were several police cars and an armed response vehicle. Armed response officers were strategically placed with their standard-issue Smith & Wesson revolvers aimed straight at Ray. A stentorian voice ordered him to lie on the floor with his hands behind his head. As he dropped down to the floor, he glimpsed Mary looking through a neighbour's window.

CHAPTER EIGHTEEN

John had to explain to Spike that Wembley was a borough of London and not just the name of a stadium. Spike couldn't get his head around the immensity of the city, and that he was miles away from Big Ben and Buckingham Palace. He felt much more at home when they arrived at the Wife of Bath pub. With its flat roof and surrounded by a big concrete car park, the pub reminded Spike of the Three Lions pub in Meden Vale. The whole area differed from what he had so far seen of London. The pub was surrounded by an estate that looked similar to the ones that surrounded the centre of Mansfield. Outside the pub, several punks were crashed out against a wall. Too much cheap cider had already taken its toll on them.

They passed through a passageway between the saloon bar and taproom to where a stairway led up to the function room. A young man with extremely long, spiky black hair, wearing a plain black T-shirt and a black busman's jacket, sat at a table near the stairs. Here everyone payed their 50p admission and had their hand stamped in case they wanted to leave and return later.

Spike could already hear the noise from upstairs as he sorted through his change for the right amount. He followed Spubble, John and Podge up the narrow staircase. At the top of the stairs was a small area that led to the function room. A couple of goths were passionately kissing and caressing each other against the wall.

The darkness at the back of the function room gave way to the well-lit area where the knee-high platform that served as a stage was situated. On the stage, a band tore through a song that lasted for no more than thirty seconds. The vocalist then introduced another song called 'Weetabix Christmas Dinner'. Three audience members pogoed violently in front of the stage, with their arms around each other in a demented hokey cokey routine. The vocalist, who looked like the inspiration for the character of Vivian from *The Young Ones*, leapt into the middle of the dancers as he performed his song. The bass player had his instrument hanging down to his waist, Sid Vicious style. He abused his Rickenbacker bass guitar like a pirate manhandling a prince. The guitarist wore a green kilt and played a cheap Chinese guitar, more suited to the cacophony than the Rickenbacker. A motley assortment of equipment surrounded the band and more than adequately conveyed a constant, ear-splitting noise. The feedback produced by the amplifiers created a counterpoint that was mostly more pleasing than the musicianship of the band.

Spike was in his element now, and felt completely at home in the anarchic environment of a punk gig. John and Podge seemed to be getting into each other already. Sat at a table at the back of the room, Podge was administering a love bite to John's neck whilst handling his balls.

Spike ripped off his T-shirt, revealing his muscular torso and back. An Oriental dragon design tattoo covered his back. The design lacked any colour, due to Spike awaiting a time when he could afford to have the dragon's majestic body coloured. He leapt onto the now empty area near the stage and proceeded to do a kind of Native American war dance. Round and round he performed a dance worthy enough to bring rain and fertility from the gods. Whoever oversaw the lighting turned on a strobe light that seemed to highlight every individual movement of the dance. John came out and grabbed Spike round the neck, trying to pull him over. They then linked arms and began to do a vigorous polka routine; with his half-shaved head and bare chest, Spike looked like a punk King of Siam.

Whilst this cabaret routine took place, the usual contingent of skinheads had arrived. The old-style, ska-loving skinheads, in Sta-Prest jeans and Ben Sherman shirts, had been superseded by a more sinister breed. The old skinhead haircut seemed long in comparison with the completely shaven heads of the new skinheads; the Sta-Prest and oxblood boots replaced by bleached jeans and black, fourteen-hole Doc Martens. Red braces and T-shirts took over from Ben Sherman. After a few pints, the inevitable round of Nazi salutes and chants of '*Sieg Heil!*' would interrupt the boisterous, good-natured atmosphere of any punk gig.

Things took a turn for the worse when a skinhead in a sleeveless Union Jack T-shirt took a fancy to Podge. Podge began a bit of friendly banter with the gang, who like the look of her in her skinhead gear. Things got ugly when the youth grabbed Podge's breasts. She pushed him away and slapped his face, much to the amusement of his friends. Not wishing to be seen to have backed down, and admiring Podge's feistiness, he grabbed her and tried to kiss her. John and Spike witnessed the altercation and jumped into the fray. Spike had been taught to always take down the ringleader, in such situations. More often than not, most people in such groups are followers, who will disperse when the dominant member has been eliminated. This was not one of those occasions, and John and Spike found themselves beset on all sides by seasoned brawlers.

Spike's assault on the leader worked insofar as to eliminate the most effective fighter. Spike punched his opponent in the face with enough force to send him crashing into a table. He then had to fend off kicks and punches from front and behind.

John was also only managing to avoid being pulled down to the floor, where he would become defenceless prey to his attackers. Fortunately, Podge came to the rescue by hitting one of the opponents over the head with a bottle. With two of the enemy now eliminated, John and Spike both had to contend with two adversaries. Spike managed to plant an elbow in the face of the assailant at his rear. Podge leapt onto the back of one of John's attackers and bit hard into his ear, making him scream out in agony.

The band continued playing during the fight, while the other members of the audience moved to a safe distance to watch the new entertainment. What had become like a barroom brawl in a Western was finally broken up by the landlord and some of his regulars, who came in armed with pool cues.

Once in the car park, the skinheads quickly scattered when a police patrol car coincidentally drove past. John and Spike sat on the pub wall, battered and bruised but in good spirits. Podge stood behind John, stroking and kissing a lump on his head.

A voice called out from behind them and they looked round to see Spubble at the top of a flight of fire stairs. John, Spike and Podge raced up the stairs and through the fire exit that led to the function room. They were greeted by a great cheer from all present.

During a break between bands, someone put on a tape of *It's Time to See Who's Who* by Conflict. John remembered this album fondly and wished he had brought his precious records down to London. He began to read a punk fanzine that was lying on the table where he, Spike and Podge were sat with Tim and Ade. The fanzine was called *Buttock and Twang*. On the cover was a collage that featured the smiling faces of Ronald Reagan and Margaret Thatcher, surrounded by starving Ethiopians.

While John was flicking through the fanzine, Podge had decided to bring Spike's Mohican back to life. She had fetched some soap from the toilets and began to go to work on his hair. At first, he looked like a unicorn when the first column of hair was erected. She massaged a combination of soap and beer into each spike. John began to feel an uncharacteristic sense of jealousy as Podge sat on Spike's knee to do the front of his hair. As the hair was transformed back to its former glory, John's jealousy was replaced by nostalgic memories of their youthful adventures.

When Disorder finally took to the stage, Spike got up and resumed his dancing near the front of the stage. Podge had noticed John reading the fanzine and looking sorry for himself. She snatched the fanzine from his hands and threw it across the room. She then took him by the hand and led him to the fire exit, and back down the stairs they had recently used to gain re-entry to the pub. She led him around the back of the pub to an area where bins and empty barrels were stored. She shoved him against the wall and then, in one agile movement, squatted down before him. As she hastily undid his belt and jeans, he leaned his head against the wall and recalled what Ray had said to him earlier about broadening his horizons.

★ ★ ★ ★ ★

Another crowd had gathered in the Bell Inn, when the news got around that Tip Topley was doing an extempore performance with the resident jazz combo. Lardy kept reminding Tip of all the old blues and jazz songs they used to perform at the Marquee club. Tip had been transported back to his youthful days when he had nothing to lose. The Bell Inn reminded him of a pub in Oxford that used to be the centre of the trad jazz scene; a place where he had discovered the joys of girls, good ale and sweet music.

After several encores, Tip's performance ended and he was mobbed by admirers who insisted on buying him drinks. Potent pints of Theakston's Old Peculiar, chased down with Pusser's rum, might have proved too much for a lesser man; but for a man who has held his own with the likes of Keith Moon and Vivian Stanshall, it was a veritable picnic.

Tip hadn't even noticed the absence of his two young guides. He had no intention of going back to the hotel to be berated by his shrewish spouse. He was enjoying playing Petruchio, and would find a corner of Roger's boat to lay his head when he was ready.

In his ear, he could hear someone telling him how he blew the Stones away at Hyde Park. Tip nodded his head, but was distracted by the two young ladies who had earlier caught his eye, who were standing near the door, giggling at him. They turned away and began walking into the passageway that led to the street. One of them turned towards Tip and winked as she left. She turned away again, flourishing her blond locks with all the panache of the Harmony Hairspray girl.

Tip swallowed his rum in one gulp and followed the girls without a glance at the fan who was still speaking to him. His hero had vanished, and he could hardly believe that the one and only Tip Topley had just been stood at the bar, drinking with him.

Tip rushed towards the pub exit, but was stopped in his tracks by another fan.

'It can't be true!' said the fan excitedly. 'You're Tip Topley!'

Tip forced a smile and patted the fan on the shoulder, trying to push him to one side.

'Can't wait to hear the new album, Tip, can I have an autograph?'

'Look, fuck off will you!' said Tip impatiently and barged past the startled admirer.

He rushed outside and looked one way then the other, then realised that he had missed his chance. He'd spent the last few years in relative obscurity, hardly recognised in the street, then as soon as he found some action, every train spotter in Nottingham wanted his autograph.

He walked up St James's Street, where he was greeted by the heavenly smell of a chip shop. He hadn't eaten anything since the titbits that had passed for lunch at Trent Bridge. He couldn't remember the last time he had enjoyed proper fish and chips. He went into the deserted chippy and ordered a large haddock and chips and a pickled egg. As he waited, he watched Madonna strut around the stage at the JFK Stadium. The burly-looking woman behind the counter glanced contemptuously at the TV.

'Doesn't she think she's it,' said the woman, noticing Tip's visible distaste of the performance.

'Oh, undoubtedly,' said Tip. 'I was having lunch with a record label executive in LA and the manager told us we had to change tables because Madonna liked ours better than the one she'd been offered.'

The woman, who didn't recognise Tip, neither knew nor cared what he was talking about. She took the chips from the fryer and shook the oil from them.

'Yeah, she's no Janice Joplin,' said Tip, 'now, she did know how to party.'

'Do you want salt and vinegar?'

Tip snapped out of his memories of bygone years and nodded his head.

He walked outside and took a bite out of his pickled egg. He hadn't tasted delicacies such as these for twenty years or more. He suddenly remembered the evening as if it were yesterday. He had just done a gig at the Troutbeck Hotel in Ilkly. Toy Mistress played a gig in the Yorkshire spa town, the week after Jimi Hendrix had played at the same venue. Tip remembered queuing with fans at a chip shop across the road from the Troutbeck Hotel afterwards. A police officer had stopped the Hendrix gig after only one song. Twice the venue's capacity had crammed into the Troutbeck to see Hendrix, but the policeman stopped the concert, deeming that the overcrowding breached safety regulations. Despite the premature ending, all anyone could talk about in the chippy that night was how fantastic Hendrix had been a week earlier. This didn't leave Tip with a sour taste in his mouth, as he remembered the best fish and chips he had ever tasted.

He devoured the pickled egg but only managed to eat a few bites of battered fish before he was accosted once again. It wasn't a fan this time, but the dishevelled figure of Freddy, Edward Towton's sponging lover. Lord Freddy was also the second son of the thirteenth Marquess of Straffield. He looked more beggar than lord at that moment. He brushed his floppy auburn fringe away from his eyes, which darted about with an air of paranoia. He was wearing a pair of Jordache jeans and a stripy Pierre Cardin shirt hung half tucked-in around his waist.

Tip might have diagnosed Freddy as being characteristically strung out on cocaine, if he hadn't been aware that something untoward might have taken place earlier in the day.

'Freddy!' said Tip, with his mouth full of food. 'The pigs have arrested Edward.'

'Fucking tell me about it!' began Freddy. 'Last night he bought this boy of about seventeen back to the hotel. He was plying him with anything he had available, including my coke. Anyway, we had a massive row and I stormed out. I marched back in there this morning to have it out with him, but he'd already left. The kid was still there lying in bed. I was there for half an hour rooting through the room to see if the old queen had hidden any cash. It was only when I tried to wake the boy up to ask where Edward was, that I realised he was dead.'

Tip continued masticating thoughtfully, then said after swallowing, 'So, then what did you do?'

'I just totally panicked and got the hell out of the place. I've just been wandering around this godforsaken place all day, trying to figure out what to do.'

Tip tried to offer Freddy a chip, but the young lord declined the offer.

'Don't suppose you've got any coke, have you? It might help me think a bit clearer.'

Tip shook his head and continued eating his fish supper. Nothing was going to come between him and his stomach at this stage in the evening. Freddy sat down on the floor while Tip finished eating, threw the greasy newspaper into a bin and wiped his mouth.

Freddy was growing more frantic and was becoming irritated by Tip's calm demeanour.

'So what do I do, for fuck's sake!' said Freddie with increasing anxiety. 'If this gets in the papers, my family will be ruined!'

'You need to turn yourself in,' said Tip calmly. 'Tell them exactly what happened. Obviously, your fingerprints will be all over the place, where you've rifled through all Edward's stuff. Just tell them you were looking for your ticket for the test match.'

Freddy began sobbing, and not sure what to say next, Tip stared into a shop window. He found himself looking into the window of a second-hand bookshop. Amongst the books on display was the same edition of John Donne's love poems that Tip had read at Oxford. Beside it was the recent autobiography of Waldo Brookes, who Tip had busked with in his university days. Tip had read the book on the plane, coming back to England. There had been no mention of their early musical collaboration. Tip decided it was time for him to settle down and write his own autobiography. He thought about the AIDS test that Lucy wanted him to take and wondered if this might be the last chance for him to write his memoirs.

Freddy had got up off the ground and seemed to have composed himself. He was taking deep breaths, trying to gather his wits for the inevitable police cross-examination. Tip stopped a couple of passers-by and asked them the way to the police station. After being pointed in the right direction, Tip put his arm round Freddy and led him to his fate. He thought that Freddy was a spoilt Little Lord Fauntleroy, but he also saw something of himself in the young man.

They walked up Market Street and past the slender Corinthian columns of the Theatre Royal. Tip looked at Freddy, who looked like a man being led to his execution. He smiled as he imagined them being driven to the station on a tumbril, surrounded by jeering Parisian *sans-culottes*.

'I'll try and get my lawyer to come as quickly as possible,' said Tip, as he led Freddy through the doors of the central police station.

Freddy looked terrified, but Tip thought the place looked serene compared with the police station in New York he had once been locked up in. He decided it wouldn't do his profile any good being seen inside such a place with a crime suspect. He made a hasty exit when he saw Freddy approach the counter to hand himself in.

Once outside in the fresh air again, he began searching for a suitable watering hole. He walked back down to the market square, feeling more alive than he had in years. He decided that he needed to get away from all the bullshit of the music business; maybe find a nice quiet bolthole like Roger. He could settle down somewhere quiet and write his autobiography. He thought about the production on his new album and was reminded of the saying about putting lipstick on a pig. He decided that what he really needed to do was get back to his roots. He had enjoyed playing with Lardy and the boys, and decided that those were the kind of people he needed for his next project. He was about to go back into the Bell Inn to see if Lardy was still there when he was suddenly distracted by the Harmony Hairspray girl sashaying past with her friend. As she walked past, she looked round at him and blew him a kiss. He stood in the doorway of the pub, torn between discussing music with Lardy and experiencing his lost weekend with the girl of his dreams. She looked his way again and as he began to casually follow her. He decided that music would always be there waiting for him.

CHAPTER NINETEEN

I remember passing the cemetery on Mansfield Road, and then the next thing I knew, we were arriving at the bus station in Mansfield. I had missed the twilight beauty of the trip from Nottingham to Mansfield. Through the sylvan splendour of the Nottinghamshire landscape, we had found a brief interlude from our adventures. We had passed the ancestral home of Lord Byron, where that evening, an open-air performance of *A Midsummer Night's Dream* was taking place. I remembered the line from that play which seemed most fitting to me and my companions that day:

'The lunatic, the lover, and the poet are of imagination all compact.'

We walked down Stockwell Gate, where it was becoming quiet now that the Saturday night revellers had mostly gravitated to the Swan on Church Street or the Horse and Jockey on Leeming Street. We were in need of food and made our way across the market square to Chan's Garden on Leeming Street. It wasn't yet busy in the Chinese takeaway. Most of the custom would come after the pubs called last orders.

Inside, the young man we called Chan was watching the Live Aid concert on the television set on the wall. People treated Chan with the same degree of contempt and amusement commonplace in Chinese takeaways. He was probably just helping out his family while he studied to be a doctor.

The finale of the London show was taking place on the television. Pete Townshend and Paul McCartney were carrying Bob Geldof on their shoulders, to the centre of the stage. Geldof looked exhausted, as the artists who had performed throughout the day joined him in a final rendition of 'Do They Know It's Christmas?'. We ordered curry and chips and watched the end of the historic show that I had seen very little of. My abiding memory of the event would be sitting in a pub and listening to a rock legend rant and rave because he hadn't been asked to

154

perform. Of course, Tip wouldn't admit that his vanity made him envious of those that had been chosen for the concert.

We sat near the window and ate our supper while Chan told us that people had been saying that The Beatles were going to perform with Julian Lennon. Only Paul McCartney had appeared, playing 'Let It Be' with a malfunctioning microphone that made it difficult for anyone to hear him.

★ ★ ★ ★ ★

Myfanwy hadn't slept at all during the bus ride. He had been enjoying the views that he had missed so much in prison. The fragrance from the fields and woods that wafted through the open windows was more potent than any of the drugs he had consumed in his short life. After Tip had brought up the subject of the virus that caused the disease called AIDS, Myfanwy had wanted to discuss the subject with Dean, but they had been distracted by other events and then Dean had slept all the way to Mansfield.

When Myfanwy had volunteered to take part in clinical research whilst in prison, he'd first had to give a blood sample. Several weeks later, he had been told to visit the prison's doctor. He had been given the news that he had contracted a virus that left the body's immune system vulnerable to the disease called Acquired Immunodeficiency Syndrome. It had taken him a while to get his head around the difficult name, and it had been a while before he heard it referred to by the simpler acronym of AIDS.

It was unclear how Myfanwy had contracted the virus, but sharing hypodermic needles and bodily fluids with other inmates had been one of his favourite pastimes in jail. The doctor had asked him to write down a list of the people he had shared needles or had sexual contact with, so they could be tested for the virus. This had been no easy task, as the number had been quite large.

Since the news, Myfanwy had felt that his body was like a ticking time bomb. Every ache and pain or sniffle seemed to be a harbinger of the full-blown disease that awaited him. He just wanted to tell Dean to make the most of every precious moment of his life; Myfanwy had never put much value on his own life until the doctor had given him what seemed to be a death sentence.

We continued eating our chips as we walked over to the White Hart pub where my brother worked. A local alcoholic down-and-out called Albert Black was hanging about on the street outside the White Hart. He grinned at us, shrouded in his long black overcoat, and muttered something about prostitutes. We gave him the remainder of our chips, which he wolfed down gratefully.

We found my brother behind the bar of the taproom of the White Hart. It was fairly quiet, apart from a couple of people playing pool in the games room. Most of the action was taking place upstairs in the function room; here, a weekly disco took place where the local gay community could meet in a discreet and friendly environment. The gay scene in Mansfield was still emerging tentatively from the world it inhabited before the Sexual Offences Act of 1967 decriminalised homosexuality.

My brother bid us welcome and poured us two pints of the Ayingerbrau lager. I always like the beer pump's emblem, of the jolly old man dressed in Alpine garb. I imagined that the brew would be a great disappointment to the lederhosen-clad man, if he tried to quaff it from his stein.

From time to time, people would emerge from or ascend to the club upstairs. I recognised a middle-aged man, wearing a matching blazer and tie as the treasurer of the club that I had worked in. It had been his companion who had been assaulted with a beer glass, in a vicious and unprovoked homophobic attack. A man in a yellow vest and red shorts, with a thick moustache, who I recognised as a regular at the pub, came down the stairs. He always reminded me of the people I had seen in an episode of *Whicker's World*, which had explored the lives of the gay community in San Francisco. A woman with a blond flattop and a Guana Batz T-shirt, who was into scooters, went upstairs to the club. The pulsating rhythm of Hi-NRG music filtered through the ceiling.

My brother was pleased to see me, but displayed some sibling concern about my shambolic appearance.

'You know, you've really let yourself go recently,' he said. 'It's no wonder you can't get a girlfriend.'

'Thanks,' I said, feeling hurt, 'you sound just like Dad.'

Being compared with Dad made Ian realise that doing your own thing, and allowing other people to do theirs, was the best option.

'Fair enough,' Ian conceded, 'I just worry that you're not happy, when I see you with your hair long and wearing clothes that look too big on you. I know you're rebelling against Dad and I can understand that more than anyone; but I think you hide yourself under those long shirts because he belittles you so much, you've got little self-esteem.'

'Okay, well thanks, Sigmund Freud,' I said, feeling totally overwhelmed by this evaluation of my psyche.

Myfanwy was standing near the cigarette machine talking to an emaciated-looking character in sunglasses and a black Harrington jacket. His jaw looked shrunken, like an old man; his greasy blond hair was tied in a ponytail behind his bald pate. I watched him hobble to the toilets as Myfanwy bought some cigarettes from the machine. Myfanwy then proceeded to go to the toilet. I gathered from this cloak and dagger performance that some kind of drug deal was taking place. Myfanwy had always dabbled with drugs, but I had noticed that something more sinister had gradually ground him down and enthralled him over the past twelve months.

'So how is pater?' asked Ian, with an undercurrent of contempt.

I gave him the full story of how Dad had decided that he wanted to be buddies and go to the cricket. Ian stood, mouth open in shock and disbelief, as I described the streaking incident.

'Apart from that,' I said, 'basically, we rarely speak to each other. He still walks in the front room and turns over the telly when I'm in the middle of watching something.'

'I'd invite you to stay with me, but there isn't really enough space for two,' said Ian sympathetically.

'Oh yeah, I forgot,' I said, clicking my fingers, 'Mum was bladdered first thing this morning, but she sends her regards.'

'Ah, bless her.'

'So how's the installation progressing?' I asked, eager to change the subject.

'Yeah, brilliant!' replied Ian enthusiastically. 'The college let me have a room to work in and I'm hoping to be able to have it ready for display in a few weeks' time.'

'Excellent!' I said, genuinely excited that his artistic ambition was finally becoming reality. 'Remind me, what's it all about again?'

'I've got all these toilet bowls and in each one is a dish of haute cuisine food. I call it *Pretentious Shit*. It's a statement about Western decadence. If I can make any money out of displaying it, I'm going to donate it all to the Ethiopian famine relief.'

'You should try to get Bob Geldof on board,' I suggested.

'When it goes on public display, you'll be able to bring Dad to see it,' Ian said cynically.

'Hey, you never know,' I said, 'just keep Mum off the bubbly and the whole thing could be a triumph. Get Dad talking to Brian Sewell and I'm sure they'll get on like a house on fire.'

The conversation was terminated when Myfanwy came out of the toilet, looking sheepishly at Ian. It was time to move on around the corner to the Sherwood Rooms to dance.

★ ★ ★ ★ ★

The concern about Jeanette's wellbeing had taken the edge off any further enjoyment of the concert. Tom had hesitated to get the police involved, suggesting that they wait till the end of the show before raising alarm bells. It was true that the fickle Jeanette would probably tire of her new playmate and return unscathed. Heidi felt that Tom's procrastination was motivated by him not wanting to appear to be losing control.

Once the final rendition of 'Do They Know It's Christmas?' had concluded, Tom and the others began to slowly make their way out of the stadium. Tom was eager to get back to the minibus, in the hope that Jeanette would soon appear again. Gareth, as ever, clung onto Tom like a limpet. He had gone down in Heidi's estimation throughout the day. His toadying to Tom and incessant flirting with anything in a skirt had put her right off him.

In their haste to get to the exits, Tom and Gareth had pushed their way through so many people that they had become totally separated from the rest of the group. As they approached the exits, it was Callum who tapped Heidi on the shoulder and pointed out Jeanette. She was still with the man in black, who seemed to be hurrying her along, with his hand held tightly round her arm. The iconic towers of Wembley had now taken on a menacing presence, like turrets in a Gothic horror story. For once, Jeanette's blasé confidence seemed to have evaporated into an expression of fear.

'Where are we going, Fritch?' she asked him. 'I need to be getting back to my friends now; they might call the police if I don't get back to them.'

'I thought we were having a good time,' said Fritch. 'We're just going for a ride. Have you ever done it in the back of a Ford Capri?'

Fritch, the neo-Nazi and sexual predator, had travelled down to London to find Podge and Suze and hand out retribution for their betrayal. He had already found Suze, who he had shoved into the back of his car and beaten about the face until she was dead. He had just intended to ruin her pretty face, but in the savage frenzy of his attack, he had beaten her until her pleas for mercy had been replaced with silence. He had driven down to a remote location on the South Downs and buried her. Now he had killed once, it only seemed fair that Podge should face the same punishment.

He had been searching for her in north London for the past week, after he had been given information that she had been sighted in the Primrose Hill area. He booked into a bed and breakfast in Camden Town, and it was there that he read in a newspaper about the Live Aid concert. His warped mind became enraged by the project that had been dreamed up by an Irish bogtrotter, and the Jew, Goldsmith. *All this*, he thought, *for a bunch of niggers in Africa.* He decided that he would attend the concert and leave a body outside Wembley Stadium, wearing a 'Feed the World' T-shirt.

Heidi and Kirstie tried to keep them both in their sights, pushing past people to get close. As they entered the concourse that led to the main exits, the crowd spilled out, giving them more space to pursue Jeanette. Once through the main gates, they ran down the steps that led from outside the stadium towards the car park. They still had Jeanette and Fritch in their sights. He continued to hurry her along with his arm around her. Heidi saw Jeanette looking round desperately for help, and the man whispering something in her ear and putting his hand in his trouser pocket, as if some weapon were concealed there.

'Kirstie, go and fetch Tom!' Heidi shouted, taking control. 'Callum, you stay with me.'

Callum obediently nodded his head and Kirstie began to run towards where the minibus had been parked.

They continued their pursuit down Wembley Way towards Wembley Park tube station. Heidi and Callum were gaining ground on them when Fritch suddenly turned right onto Fulton Road. Heidi grabbed Callum's hand to try to hurry him along. He was beginning to falter already.

'You need to cut down on all that crap you eat,' said Heidi, realising that it was a totally inappropriate time to be giving advice about dieting.

They were close enough to hear Jeanette sobbing when they rounded the corner. Fritch pushed her towards the passenger side of his black Ford Capri and began to open the door. As he shoved Jeanette into the front passenger seat, he produced a stiletto knife from his trouser pocket. He pressed the spring-assisted switch and the bayonet blade sprang out inches from Jeanette's face.

Heidi cried out, 'Hey, leave her alone!'

Fritch turned round, momentarily startled by the sudden intrusion. After a brief inspection of his pursuers, he grinned sardonically.

'What the fuck are you gonna do, like?' he said, pointing the blade towards Heidi.

'The police are on their way, so you'd better let her go!' said Heidi, with barely concealed terror in her voice.

Fritch locked the passenger door and marched round to the driver's side. Callum had stood silently during this time, catching his breath. He had harboured a secret crush on Jeanette, ever since he had first met her at the Baptist youth group. Even though she was openly hostile towards him, he still adored her. Mustering courage inside himself that he scarcely believed he possessed, he realised his time had come. He remembered all those miserable, cold afternoons on the rugby pitch, with the PE teacher bullying him into participating. He charged at Fritch with as much momentum as he could muster. He flung himself at him, driving his shoulder into Fritch's thigh and wrapping his arms round him; just as the PE teacher had made him do, over and over again. Callum brought Fritch tumbling to the ground and the knife went spinning down the pavement.

Stunned by Callum's sudden heroic actions, Heidi almost forgot Jeannette. She ran to the passenger door, which Jeanette was already frantically trying to unlock. Jeannette finally found the latch to unlock the door and almost fell out of the car in her haste to escape. Heidi grabbed her hand and they ran as fast as they could, back onto the road to the stadium. Tom and Gareth were already running down the road; Kirstie was behind them, trying to keep up.

'He's still got Callum!' screeched Heidi, pointing toward Fulton Road.

Fritch cursed and tried to extricate himself from the limpet-like clutches of Callum. Part of him wanted to get the knife and bleed the boy like a pig. He also knew that he needed to get in the car and get away, before the police arrived. He tried hopelessly to drag himself away, but Callum wanted to hold him until the girls were safely out of harm's way. Fritch began to throw punches at Callum's head, finding it hard to get a decent punch, due to his incapacity of movement. Callum thought about the success of his rugby tackle and once more saw clearly the face of that PE teacher who had made his life such a misery. With his head resting below the crotch of Fritch's trousers, Callum closed his eyes, took a deep breath and sunk his teeth into Fritch's testicles. He really did hate that PE teacher.

People were still streaming down the road from Wembley, oblivious to what was taking place around the corner. As Tom came running down the road, someone could be heard crying out in pain.

'Oh my God, he's stabbed him!' Heidi shrieked.

A moment later, Callum came running round the corner with the momentum of an Olympic sprint runner. He charged past Tom without recognising him, almost knocking him over as he passed. He only stopped when he reached Heidi and Jeanette.

'I bit the bastard's balls!' Callum announced triumphantly.

'My hero!' said Jeanette, flinging her arms around him.

She then turned around and flung herself at Kirstie. 'I'm so sorry!' she said, sobbing.

Kirstie looked over Jeanette's shoulder towards Heidi, rolling her eyes.

CHAPTER TWENTY

We went through the back door of the White Hart with the sound of Hi-NRG music coming out of a window upstairs. With the towering viaduct above us, we walked up White Hart Street to where the car park of the Swan was situated. The car park led to the rear of the Swan pub and the entrance to the Sherwood Rooms. There was no queue when we got there, just the usual doormen, dressed in the obligatory black suits and bow ties. Myfanwy nodded to Gladstone Roberts, who nodded back with an amused expression on his face. Harry, the manager, looked on, ringing his hands and calculating how long the nightclub might remain economically viable. We paid our entrance fee to Miss Mansfield of 1960 and Myfanwy left his jacket in the cloakroom.

The interior of the Sherwood Rooms was dominated by the large dance floor at its centre. The dance floor was surrounded by long tables that gave the place the formal appearance of a wedding reception. The bar was situated in a raised balustrade area in the corner. One could lean on the wooden railings here and safely view the inevitable brawling that would take place at the end of the evening.

We walked across the packed club to the three-deep queue at the bar. One of Myfanwy's mod friends was preparing to be served and consented to order our drinks as well. The mod, who was known as Speed, wore a dapper, three-button jacket of grey and black pinstripes, matching trousers and Chelsea boots. He had the kind of layered hairstyle that reminded me of the Small Faces, circa 1966. Speed stood out from all the other mods and had the elegance of a latter-day Beau Brummell. I was also drawn to his musical tastes, which went beyond the standard tastes of the other mod revivalists.

We quickly supped our ale and ordered more. Last orders were at twelve, so we only had an hour to fill our boots. Our drinking was interrupted when the

DJ began to play a sequence of soul records. 'The Champion' by Willie Mitchell began and people began to get up and do the basic Northern Soul shuffle. A couple of more adventurous types attempted a more vigorous, shuffle and stomp routine.

Myfanwy enjoyed the freedom of being able to move his feet on a dance floor again. The hypnotic rhythm, complimented by the robust horn section, danced you like a puppet. I thought about asking the disc jockey if he had 'Jump and Dance' by The Carnaby. This was Myfanwy's favourite record, so I decided to make a request to commemorate his freedom. The disc jockey just shook his head in his usual taciturn manner.

After a brief rest to continue our carousing, it was time for the 'alternative' dance. 'Should I Stay or Should I Go?' began and a few goths and psychobilly types got up and began warming up, with a few gentle flailing motions with their arms. The psychobilly boys, with their mutated pompadour hairstyles, revved up the dance with 'Wrecking Crew' by The Meteors.

I noticed my work colleagues, Mo, Harry and Zoot, sat at a table in a corner and led Myfanwy across to meet them. A young man in a wheelchair sat at the end of the table, sucking a pint of lager through a straw. Mo introduced him as his brother Steve, the notorious piss artist and novelist. After the introductions, Mo shouted in my ear that he'd been to the sex shop and had bought some poppers. He produced a small brown bottle, and after passing it round, asked me if I wanted to try some. I took the bottle and read the label, which said 'Liquid Gold'. I had heard all about amyl nitrate, or 'Poppers' as it was also known. I inhaled the chemical-smelling liquid and passed the bottle back to Mo. Harry and Zoot already had big grins on their faces, which had become flushed. All of a sudden, the disco lights and the music became a blur of colour and noise. I began to feel my face become hot and flushed. The sensation abated after only a few seconds, and I'd had my first experience with this instant nervous breakdown in a bottle.

There seemed to be a more aggressive atmosphere in the place than normal. A group of youths, lined up along the edge of the dance floor, began singing 'Chesterfield, la la la' to the tune of the *Banana Splits* theme. The singing took me straight back to my days on the terraces at Saltergate. I knew that there was trouble brewing if Spireites were in the house, goading their rivals in one of their own bastions. They then began chanting 'Scabs!' which began to get things warmed up with the locals. A couple of the youths from Chesterfield wore the kind of designer sports gear, characteristic of the football casuals that rampaged across the terraces of

Europe. It seemed to me that the casuals were the new mods, with their passion for European designer fashion and violence.

Someone tapped me on the shoulder and I was pleasantly surprised when I turned around to find Sarah Figg standing there, looking lovely. Sarah was a classmate of mine from school. She was one of the smarter kids at school and I got to know her in history classes; the only subject that I studied in the top set. It was the first time I had ever seen her wearing anything but her school uniform. That wasn't entirely true; I remembered seeing a photo of her, dressed as a nun in a school production of *The Sound of Music*. She wore her red hair in a shoulder-length bob. She looked very summery in her short denim dungarees and stripy blue and white T-shirt. Instead of her usual spectacles she wore at school, she was trying out contact lenses. I always thought the glasses really suited her.

I had almost forgotten about the girl called Heidi; I seemed to have thought of little else for the preceding week. She had said that she might be coming to the Sherwood Rooms, but she was nowhere to be seen. Nor did I recognise her silly blond friend, who seemed to find me amusing. I had seen her friend in the Sherwood Rooms several times, always clinging on to a different man at the end of each evening.

Sarah was celebrating the end of term and was returning to school after the summer holidays as a sixth former. I told her what I had been up to since leaving school, which she seemed to think was really exciting. I felt insecure about telling her about me leaving school with no qualifications, for a dead-end job in a factory. She seemed to think it was cool that I had left school and found work, while she still had another two years at the Meden ahead of her.

I lit a cigarette and offered her one. She awkwardly held it in her hand and more awkwardly attempted to light it. She said she didn't normally smoke, but liked one with a drink. I guessed that this wasn't very often, but thought that her incongruous attempt to appear grown up made her seem even more lovely.

Some playground shoving around began to take place between some of the Spireite boys and a few locals. One of them, with his back to Sarah, fell backwards, knocking Sarah off her balance. I grabbed hold of her and she held on to me. I suggested we get out of the way, and led her to the balustrade where we watched the dancing. 'Oops Up Side Your Head' came on and people began to sit in a line with their legs spread around the person in front. They then began to rhythmically sway from side to side, then back and forth like a funky rowing boat.

★ ★ ★ ★ ★

Pol and his Khmer Blues crew had travelled to Mansfield in easy stages. First, they had stopped at the Young Vanish pub in Glapwell. They had then made a stop at the Plough in Pleasley, and then the Pheasant on Chesterfield Road. Pol wanted Cuckoo to spend all evening searching round the pubs in the town centre. Pol's excursion around the pubs on the outskirts of Mansfield finally ended when the coach arrived in the Swan car park at ten thirty. Rather than drawing too much attention to themselves, they had merely remained tolerably rambunctious.

Once inside the Sherwood Rooms, Pol began to encourage more mischief from his crew. After half an hour, there was still no sign of Cuckoo or Pluto. He began to wonder if the rival firm had bottled out of a confrontation. He decided it was still too early to become complacent. An ambush outside the club was still a possibility. Pol had to imagine every possible outcome. He tried to remember what he had learned from reading *The Art of War*; if only he had brought a copy with him, he thought to himself.

Cuckoo and the remainder of the Coocachoo Crew had gone from pub to pub, looking for the Khmer Blues. He had expected some kind of ambush waiting for him at every turn. He felt safer when he was outdoors, with room to manoeuvre. The last thing he wanted was to be pinned down inside a pub in the same fashion as Pluto. Potter's crew had already scored a major victory in the Bridge Tavern. Maybe they were already back in Chesterfield, celebrating.

The bouncers at Harvey's nightclub knew Potter by sight and had been warned in advance about his presence in Mansfield. If he couldn't gain entry to Harvey's, that only left the Sherwood Rooms for a final showdown. Cuckoo knew he had to approach the Swan with stealth. Entering the car park which led to the Sherwood Rooms via either White Hart Street or Market Street carried risk of ambush. He decided that walking across the market square and up Market Street gave him more of a chance to fight on open ground.

The Letts brothers had now left Cuckoo's ranks depleted, making the excuse that they had to catch the last bus home to Shirebrook. Several of the youngsters in the group had deserted the ranks after they had got chatting to a couple of girls in the King's Head.

Cuckoo noted that Colin Townroe seemed to be the only one in the group who still had any swagger left. He had already tried to start a fight in the Wheatsheaf.

Cuckoo had been forced to restrain him before he jeopardised the whole mission by getting everyone arrested. Cuckoo decided that as Townroe was feeling confident, that he would send him into the Sherwood Rooms ahead of everyone else to see if Potter was inside. He told Colin to stay in the club if Potter was there, and come straight out if not. He decided that if Townroe didn't emerge from the Sherwood Rooms, they would wait in ambush; splitting into two groups, one on White Hart Street and the other near the Market Street entrance.

Cuckoo had put Feggy in charge of the group that waited on White Hart Street. He was still wearing his old PE shorts, which had been a source of amusement for everyone who saw him walk into a pub that evening. His brother had disappeared hours ago, after claiming he was going to the toilet. Feggy knew he was more afraid of paying for a round than being involved in a fight. Early on in the evening, Feggy himself had been looking for an opportunity to escape. Cuckoo had massaged his ego all night, telling him how well he had done when they had visited Bradford for a Freight Rover cup tie.

Feggy remembered the day well and still had nightmares about it. They had been caught in an ambush in a subway, assailed from both exits by Bradford's hooligan firm, known as 'The Ointment'. Feggy had been at the rear of the group when the ambush had taken place. Due to the lack of room in the subway, there had been little room for the Bradford firm to take advantage of the ambush. For Cuckoo and Pluto, it had been like the Spartans holding out at Thermopylae. Feggy had done a Muhammad Ali rope-a-dope routine long enough for the police to intervene.

Cuckoo had slapped Feggy on the shoulder and told him that he was now his right-hand man, since Pluto and Strachan had been taken out of the game. The general's superlatives had succeeded in buttering up Feggy for the coming confrontation. He stood on White Hart Street, eagerly awaiting his chance to shine.

Colin was happy to be asked to go into the Sherwood Rooms without Cuckoo on his back. He was having the time of his life after what had been the day from hell. Cuckoo had been strutting around like Napoleon all evening. One minute he was telling someone to drink less, then ordering someone else to get a couple of drinks down their necks. He had been trying to press anyone he vaguely recognised into joining him for his reckoning with Potter. He would keep providing everyone with psychological insights into Potter's mind:

'What you need to realise about Pol, is that he's a lot more intelligent than your average football hooligan.'

Cuckoo would emphasise each point by holding up his thumb and index finger, forming an 'O' shape that seemed to subliminally suggest that he was an arsehole.

'You need to get into his mind-set,' Cuckoo continued. 'He needs to be taken down by stealth, just like in the Rumpo films.'

'You mean Rambo?' interrupted Colin.

'No, not like Bambi, you twat!' said Cuckoo, irritated that someone had interrupted his flow.

Once Colin got inside the club, he was almost relieved to discover that Pol and his crew were assembled within. He had a full hour to enjoy himself while Cuckoo and the others played cowboys and Indians outside. He was just getting warmed up with a blond, who looked like one of the girls from the Human League, when he suddenly felt ill. The sudden wave of nausea sent him rushing to the toilets, where he was violently sick. He sat in a cubicle, leaning against the toilet bowl, his head spinning. He remembered what he had been told about mixing the antibiotics with alcohol. He tried to think about the girl he had left on the dance floor, but another bout of nausea forced him to throw up again. He curled up on the floor, his entire world spinning round. He heard someone knocking on the door, but he was too ill to move. He began to panic that he might be going through some kind of drug overdose due to his misuse of the antibiotics. After vomiting a third time, his nausea began to subside. The back of his shirt was soaking wet with sweat, which was beginning to cool him down from his feverish state. He slowed his breathing down and after a few minutes he began to fall asleep.

★ ★ ★ ★ ★

Meanwhile, inside the club, Pol Potter had found a distraction in the shape of Gladstone Roberts' sister, Moira. Some of the other Khmer Blues had followed his example and paired off with girls. Those that hadn't found a mate had become so inebriated as to forget about creating havoc. One of them had his arm around a youth from the Ladybrook estate, who he had been fighting with earlier. Another sat alone and dejected as he enviously watched the fortunate few who had found a girl to dance with.

At twelve o'clock, Cuckoo began to rally his crew for the attack on the Khmer Blues. Colin Townroe had not emerged and Cuckoo had waited patiently for his moment. The first of the revellers were beginning to leave the Sherwood Rooms. Cuckoo recognised the DJ's signature record that he always signed off with each evening. He waved to the other group stationed on White Hart Street, led by Feggy Edwards. They would come running as soon as they saw Cuckoo commence the attack.

Cuckoo had waited what seemed like an eternity, itching for his moment to advance across the concrete battlefield, like Agamemnon and his Greeks on the plains of Troy. He had lost Pluto, his Achilles, who now lay injured in hospital. His Ajax, the pugnacious Strachan, was similarly incapacitated. Colin Townroe, a mere Thersites, had been relied upon to ascertain the enemy's position.

More people began to stream out into the car park now, and a couple of squaddies from Clipstone, who were on leave, came staggering towards where Cuckoo was waiting. One of them barged past Cuckoo, who was barring their way towards Market Street.

'Watch where you're going, twat!' said Cuckoo, impatiently trying to keep an eye out for Pol.

'That's feighting talk where I come from!' said one of the squaddies, pushing Cuckoo. Momentarily surprised by the push, Cuckoo staggered backwards. He fiddled in his trouser pocket like a dirty old pervert for his telescopic baton.

'Look, I haven't got time for this shit!' Cuckoo shouted, trying to shove his assailant to one side.

The other squaddie then sprang to his pal's aid, punching Cuckoo squarely on the jaw. Cuckoo went down like a felled tree and his comrades retaliated. A gang of youths from Clipstone appeared from the club and, recognising the squaddies, rushed to support them.

Meanwhile, Feggy and his group still awaited the moment for their chance to reinforce Cuckoo's attack. The coach driver who had brought the Khmer Blues into Mansfield had just filled up with fuel and was returning through the White Hart Street entrance. At the moment the coach came through the entrance, Pol and the Khmer Blues appeared from within the Sherwood Rooms. By the time that those stationed on White Hart Street had a clear view, Pol's group had already become obscured by the coach. At the other end of the car park, Cuckoo lay on the ground, out cold, while the rest of his contingent fought a running battle into the market square.

CHAPTER TWENTY-ONE

At the far end of the car park was an abandoned garage. The garage had no doors and was awaiting demolition. It served as a place for randy couples from the Sherwood Rooms and a Parisian-style Vespasian urinal. On this particular night, the garage was a refuge in which Myfanwy could cook up some heroin and inject it into his veins.

He had dabbled with the brown powder for a year now. He had resisted the compulsion to become hopelessly enthralled by the drug for many months. The novelty of freedom, alcohol and adventure had all kept his mind occupied throughout the day. Seeing the junkie known as Johnny Jesus had instantly drawn Myfanwy back into the orbit of heroin.

He had made the arrangements when he had seen Johnny in the White Hart, to rendezvous at the garage at midnight. Johnny had gone through the cloak and dagger routine of procuring the drug. Myfanwy sat and watched Johnny cooking up the brown powder, using all the essential paraphernalia. He watched in fascination, as the heroin liquefied and bubbled up on the tablespoon that Johnny heated with a lighter. He then drew the liquid into the hypodermic and tapped the tip of the needle, to remove any air bubbles. Myfanwy was impressed by the clinical precision with which this ritual was carried out.

Myfanwy was surprised when Johnny undid his jeans and pulled them down to his knees. He then realised that Johnny's addiction was so advanced, that the veins in his arms had probably collapsed. This meant that he would have to find veins elsewhere to shoot up with. Myfanwy had the sudden horrible thought that Johnny might inject into his groin. He was relieved when Johnny began tapping his thigh to make a vein visible. Once this was done, Johnny pierced the vein with the needle and began to inject the heroin. Johnny leaned his head back against the wall with the expression of someone who is receiving gratifying fellatio.

While Johnny retreated into his heroin-induced trance, Myfanwy began to perform the same process of preparation to get high. When it came to the point where he was ready to inject, he needed to take off his belt to use as a tourniquet around his arm. Nobody likes a gatecrasher, and Myfanwy was startled when he saw Boz standing before him. In his sudden haste to score heroin, he had forgotten all about Boz. Myfanwy had no intention of discontinuing his current task after the song and dance of finding a vein and prepared to inject.

Boz approached, illuminated by the lights from the street. In his hand was a building brick.

'I'm going to smash your head in with this,' he said matter-of-factly, holding up the brick.

Myfanwy continued to let the heroin flow into his body and removed the needle. As Boz held up the brick, ready to smash it down on his enemy's face, Myfanwy jabbed the needle into Boz's leg.

'Ah, you bastard, you'll be sorry for that!' hissed Boz, bending down to pull out the needle.

He lifted the brick up again but was interrupted a second time as Myfanwy's body began to violently convulse. His eyes rolled back behind his eyelids and he began to foam at the mouth. Boz had never seen someone overdose before and he watched with fascination and pleasure. He watched until Myfanwy's seizure began to abate. Boz walked to the side of Myfanwy and pushed him over with his foot. Myfanwy lay with his eyes staring ahead of him. His face was grey and his lips had turned blue. During this time, Boz hadn't even given Johnny a second glance. He was blissfully oblivious of the man standing over him with a building brick, or Myfanwy's overdose. Boz was certain that Myfanwy was dead, and was about to urinate on him when a commotion in the pub car park changed his mind. As he walked down Market Street, he felt the pain in his leg where the needle had been jabbed into him. He realised that the needle had snapped and the end of it was still embedded in his flesh. He would need to go to the casualty department and get it removed. He decided that this was a small price to pay for the satisfaction of seeing Myfanwy in his death throes.

Nappy Andrews watched Boz walk away towards the market square. He crouched in the doorway of a shop that sold collectable stamps and coins. He had spotted Myfanwy and his buddy on the back of the bus from Nottingham, both trying to duck their heads to avoid being spotted. He and Boz had waited an hour for the next bus to Mansfield, where he had led Boz round the likely spots that Myfanwy might be found.

Their first port of call was the Blue Boar, one of the few pubs where Nappy could be guaranteed not to be turned away. They sat in the pool room where two of Nappy's juvenile friends were in the middle of a game. They were both bickering about the legality of a shot that had just been played. One argued that the shot was legitimate, as laid down by the laws of the old rules. His opponent argued that they were playing by the new rules.

Though it was one of the hottest days of the year, both of the boys wore mod parkas. One wore his with beer mats sewed on its back. He was the spitting image of Pogo Patterson from *Grange Hill*. The other parka had a variety of patches denoting various scooter clubs. The cherubic youth, with his pageboy haircut, looked as though he might still own a child's scooter.

Nappy recognised Dog and Sammy sat in a corner; neither of them seemed to have a drink. Nappy nodded to them in acknowledgement. He was about to get his cigarettes out but decided to wait till later. The two punks would no doubt pounce on him and begin pestering him to give them one.

While Nappy occupied himself with his mod chums, Boz was acquainting himself with a snaggle-toothed whore who was showing off the fishnet stockings that she wore under a red dress. She led Boz down a corridor to where the toilets were situated. Beyond the toilets, a door led to an alleyway at the rear of the pub.

Nappy's friends had heard that Myfanwy was coming out of prison, but they hadn't yet seen him. They were sure that he would be either at the White Hart or the Sherwood Rooms. Both were wary of meeting Myfanwy again. One of them had tried glue the last time he had been with Myfanwy, causing him to see nightmarish visions. The other's parents had forbidden him to associate with Myfanwy again after he had been caught shoplifting at the Warsop Costcutter.

Boz re-emerged, a few minutes after he had disappeared into the alley. The prostitute looked more satisfied than Boz as she came out wiping her mouth. She cleansed her palate with the glass of mild that she had left at the bar and resumed watching the Philadelphia leg of the Live Aid concerts.

Nappy and Boz had better luck when they arrived at the White Hart. Johnny Jesus was stooped over a fruit machine when Boz and Nappy walked through the door. When Johnny burgled to pay for his next fix, he brought his stolen wares to a mutual fence of Nappy. Johnny told Nappy that he had earlier seen Myfanwy, who was looking to score. Nappy told him that Boz was new in town and was also in need of a fix. Once the time and location of the rendezvous had been ascertained, it was simply a matter of killing time until Boz had his chance for revenge.

Boz had told Nappy that he wanted to be alone to enjoy his reunion with Myfanwy. He had been relieved that he wouldn't have to witness whatever Boz had in store for Myfanwy. Since his mentor had been in prison, Nappy had been at a loss for the companionship of a guttersnipe of the same calibre of Myfanwy. Nappy had met Boz in Nottingham whilst on a shoplifting spree. Boz had recognised his talent for thieving and taken him under his wing. He had soon discovered that Boz wasn't the avuncular figure that Myfanwy had been. Nappy was in the thrall of a man who he now showed loyalty through fear. He had recently earned a beating after Boz discovered that he had kept back some stolen money for himself, after they had broken into a house.

Nappy shrunk back into the doorway as he watched Boz walk away from the garage. He was horrified by the thought of what Boz might have done to Myfanwy, and terrified of what he might do to him if he tried to help his friend. Now Boz was in Mansfield, there no longer seemed to be anywhere to hide.

There seemed to be a disturbance taking place at the back of the Swan car park. Nappy watched two groups of youths begin a running battle into the market square. The fighting seemed to distract him from his fears long enough to focus his mind on helping Myfanwy. He ran across the road to the garage where Boz had emerged a few minutes before. He could just make out Johnny Jesus in the darkness, clearly as high as a kite. As he became accustomed to the darkness, he saw Myfanwy slumped on the floor. He rushed over to him, not sure what kind of state he would be in. There didn't seem to be any evidence of facial injuries, but he feared that Myfanwy was dead. He lifted Myfanwy's head and tried slapping his face and desperately calling his name. He heard a gurgling noise in Myfanwy's throat and then he began choking. Fluid began dribbling from his mouth. He suddenly became aware that Boz might return and decided that he would have to hurry. He remembered attending the Saint John's Ambulance Brigade sessions with his auntie Jane. He did his best to put Myfanwy in the recovery position. He gave Myfanwy's back a few slaps, which forced him to begin coughing up vomit. He finally remembered to tilt Myfanwy's head back and lifted his chin to keep open the airway. He then ran as fast as his legs would carry him, to the phone box on Queen's Street.

★ ★ ★ ★ ★

Making their way from the Wife of Bath, Spike, John and Podge shared the first part of their journey mingling with people leaving the Live Aid concert. They got talking to some people who had been to see Dire Straits at Wembley Arena. The band had already done a slot at the Live Aid concert before their gig at the arena. Spike wasn't aware that the arena was a separate entity to the stadium, and it took John a while to explain that Dire Straits had played at two separate venues. John thought about Al and Jean Louis, who would be beginning the big clear-up at Wembley Stadium. Until that evening, John had been fairly reliable, but he was aware that he might not be picked for future jobs if he didn't turn up regularly. The casual nature of the job meant that he didn't know when the next day's work was coming anyway, so he concluded that it wasn't worth the worry. With his arm around Podge and his best friend by his side, finding gainful employment could wait till another day.

'I still reckon we should go off travelling,' said Spike. 'Yugoslavia is supposed to be dead cheap and they love punk there.'

'Well, there's fuck all here,' said John, 'and even fucker all in Mansfield.'

'I'm going off the idea of going on the road with the convoy, after meeting those two clowns today,' said Spike, shuddering at the thought of Alicia's sour face.

'Well, I heard from Al that they live in a nice Victorian terrace in Islington and just pack up and join the travellers at the weekends,' said John, with a wry smile.

Podge felt a slight pang of envy as she observed the almost brotherly bond that John and Spike shared.

'I bet you two were a right pair of tearaways when you were kids,' she said affectionately.

'Oh mate, too right!' Spike said with a gleam in his eye. 'Remember that time when the gala was on and we nicked them bottles of cider from that shed outside Elkesley House?'

'Yeah,' remembered John, 'we must have only been about nine and we were hammered. I got sent straight to bed when I got home.'

'Yeah, and your dad came round our house and started on my old man, about me being a bad influence,' said Spike, pushing John playfully.

'Well, I got a thick lip when that bloke came round that time and told me dad that he had seen us playing near the slurry ponds,' said John, with a hint of bitterness.

They were walking through Willesden when a black Ford Capri drove past, unnoticed by the happy trio. Fritch had gone to ground for an hour after his failed attempt to abduct Jeannette. He went back to the bed and breakfast and collected his belongings. When he came down the stairs with his holdall, the owner was hovering about the hallway, anxious that Fritch might be trying to leave without paying. The owner was in his late middle age, with thinning hair and National Health spectacles perched on a hook nose. He wore a threadbare cardigan and walked with a stoop. He stood ringing his hands as Fritch counted out the money. Fritch watched him, staring at the money. He reminded Fritch of the Jews he had seen in the old Nazi propaganda films. He was certain the man must be a Jew, though he had never actually met one yet. It was the same with the Pakistanis who owned the newsagents where he lived. He had tried to intimidate them into leaving for months before he learned that they were from Bangladesh. He just couldn't tell who was who anymore.

Fritch toyed with the idea of killing the B&B owner as he watched him carefully count the banknotes. He decided that the sensible thing to do was to find out if he was a Jew.

'Can you tell me where I might find the nearest synagogue?' asked Fritch.

The owner looked up as he put the money into the drawer of an old-fashioned, wooden cash register. 'I think the nearest one is on Belsize Square,' he said thoughtfully. 'This is North London, there are synagogues everywhere.'

'Oh, which one would you recommend?' Fritch asked; *They're a wily bunch, these Jews*, he thought.

'I couldn't tell you, I'm Church of England myself.'

Fritch looked the man in the eye, trying to judge if he were Jew or Gentile.

'You'll find a lot of Jews in Golders Green; maybe they can help you,' said the man helpfully.

Fritch bid the man good day, satisfied that he wasn't a Jew. He decided that he would go to Golders Green and set an example, to undermine Goldsmith and Geldof's Zionist propaganda exercise.

Fritch was pretty sure that it was Suze who had poisoned Podge against him. Someone had mentioned to him that Susannah was a Jewish name, and Fritch had become convinced that Suze had been used by the Zionists to infiltrate and undermine his neo-Nazi organisation. All his followers had deserted him, one by one, after Suze had appeared on the scene. Once he had caught up with her in London, she had paid a heavy price for her Jewish friends.

He wasn't sure how to find Golders Green, so he stopped and asked a man for directions. The bearded man wore a round, fur-lined hat and a big black coat; Fritch thought he must be a Russian. The man was very helpful, but Fritch thought the curly locks of hair that hung down either side of his face rather strange. He didn't mind Russians because he had watched a programme which claimed that Stalin had killed more Jews than Hitler. He knew the Russians didn't get on with the Yanks either, who everyone knew were financed by Jewish bankers.

After he had been driving some time, he began to wonder if he might have made a wrong turn. For a moment he couldn't believe his eyes as he passed three people walking towards a pub. Two of them were young men in scruffy punk gear. The third was a slim young girl, dressed like a skinhead. He slammed the brakes on, after his mind had processed that he had finally found Podge. He began to beat his fists against the steering wheel and howled with rage. He turned the car around and began speeding towards where Podge was standing. She was cupping her hands, as one of the men lit a match to light her cigarette. They were stood in front of a brick wall that provided the boundary to a pub car park. Fritch mounted the pavement and sped towards her as she raised her head and inhaled her cigarette. As it finally dawned on the three that the car was coming straight for them, Spike leapt over the wall. Podge stood mesmerised like a rabbit as she saw the face of Fritch speeding towards her. At the last moment, John leapt across the front of the car and knocked Podge out of the way. He hit the left side of the car's bonnet and was sent flying into the road. The car carried on straight into the side of the brick wall, adjacent to the car park entrance. Fritch was catapulted through his windscreen, and the last thing that he saw was the grey concrete of the car park. He had finally got the *Kristallnacht* that he had dreamed of for so long.

CHAPTER TWENTY-TWO

A hammering on the toilet door woke Colin from a deep sleep. He had no idea how long he had been asleep, and as he got up his body ached due to the awkward position he had lain in. He opened the door to see a large bouncer glaring down at him.

'What time is it?' asked Colin, rubbing his eyes like someone who had just received an alarm call.

'Time to go home. Come on, fuck off!'

Staggering into the foyer, Colin recognised some of the bar staff getting ready to go home.

He walked across the market square and looked at the time on the town hall clock. It was twelve thirty. He suddenly realised that he must have slept through the entire confrontation between the Coocachoo Crew and the Khmer Blues. Part of him felt relieved that he had avoided another potential hiding. He was also painfully aware that if Cuckoo had noticed his absence, there might be consequences. He decided that in future he would give the football crowd a wide berth. He concluded that he was a lover not a fighter.

It took him half an hour to walk from the town centre to Blake Street in Mansfield Woodhouse. He was dehydrated and desperate for a drink of water. He coughed, and tried to hack up the acid taste of vomit in his throat. He spat and ended up with saliva dribbling onto his shirt. The lights were still on when he arrived home, which meant that Dawn would be waiting for him for another argument. He saw the cellophane taped to the rear windscreen of his car and felt renewed anger about the cost of replacing it.

Dawn wasn't waiting up for him; she lay on the sofa, asleep. On the coffee table sat a two-litre bottle of Kwik Save Lambrusco, that now held maybe a quarter of a litre. Phil Collins was singing 'Against All Odds' on the television. She had watched the final few hours of the London concert and then continued watching the Philadelphia show. She had fallen asleep at some point during Neil Young's set. After she had put the kids to bed, it had been bliss to put her feet up with a drink and finally watch the Live Aid concert.

The front door slammed shut and Dawn looked up, rubbing her eyes. Colin strode past her to the kitchen without speaking. She heard the sound of cupboards opening and slamming shut and then the sound of running water. She then heard the fridge door open and slam shut. *He must be hungry,* she thought; *good, let him eat shit.* She was fucked if she was going to make him anything. She looked at the time, and then at Phil Collins on the television. Surely he'd already been on once at Wembley.

Colin sulkily walked into the living room and threw himself down on an easy chair.

'I see there's fuck all to eat again,' he said, staring at Phil Collins.

'Well, if you'd been here at teatime, I might have had something ready for you,' said Dawn, ready for battle. 'Have they introduced all-day drinking now, then? The last I heard, they stop serving at three, so you can go home for a couple of hours.'

Colin got up and turned off the television set; he knew that he was going to have to face the music, sooner or later. He sat down again, suddenly feeling lightheaded after getting up so quickly. He felt like he had the worst hangover he had ever suffered and now he had to face a cross-examination from his wife.

'I got hit on the back of the head and had to go to casualty and get stitches,' he said, pointing to the wound on his head.

'Oh right!' said Dawn, raising her voice. 'So you've been out fighting again?'

'A bunch of blokes in ski masks came in the Bridge, tooled up, and gave everyone a good hiding.'

'Oh brilliant, and who did you upset to earn that, then.'

Colin lost his patience and snapped, 'Look, just fuck off, I've had enough for one day!'

'Watch your mouth, there's two kids asleep upstairs,' she hissed.

Colin sat with his head in his hands, groaning. He tried to change tack in a vain attempt to elicit some sympathy. Dawn went into the kitchen and filled the kettle. He could whistle if he thought she was making him a drink. She still found it too much of a coincidence that Tony should have an accident involving Colin's car, immediately after he had left her bed.

She poured herself a mug of tea and went back into the living room. Colin was sat with his head in his hands; Dawn recognised this as one of his cowardly ploys to avoid confrontation.

'I've had to go to hospital today,' she said. 'Gran's got a bladder infection and she doesn't know what day of the week it is.'

'What's new,' said Colin with a sardonic grin.

'Well, it will be me who has to go round and keep an eye on her, so don't you worry yersen.'

Remembering seeing her holding hands with the man in the hospital bed, Colin decided to broach the subject.

'So you went to see Gran, did you; did you see anyone else in there?'

Dawn saw him look her straight in the eye with an accusing look. She then realised that if Colin had visited the hospital, then he might have seen her with Tony. She hesitated long enough before answering to reveal her guilt.

'I was fetching something from the shop for Gran when I saw someone I know from work, and thought I'd drop in and pay a visit.'

Colin had played this game too many times himself and Dawn could see the look of triumph in his eyes.

'Good mate, is he?' he snapped. 'Because you looked cosy enough, holding hands with him'.

Dawn had made her mind up that something had to give, earlier in the day. There seemed no way of avoiding the inevitable, and this seemed as good a time as any to have things out.

'Alreight, he's fucking me,' she said, shrugging her shoulders. 'There, is that what you wanted to hear?'

Colin had always been so absorbed in his own affairs that it had never occurred to him before that day that Dawn might be doing the same herself.

'Well, he must be hard up then,' he said, 'is he fucking blind or what?'

'He might be, but his cock is definitely in full working order,' she said spitefully.

Colin got up and went into the kitchen to get another glass of water. He could hardly contain his rage, but he didn't want Dawn to see the tears that were welling up in his eyes. As he stood leaning against the sink, Dawn walked into the kitchen.

'What were you doing on Bath Lane this morning?' she asked him, knowingly.

He looked around, pretending ignorance. 'Bath Lane, don't even know where that is.'

'Don't gimme that bullshit!' she said, losing her temper now. 'What were you up to this morning?'

'The same as you, by the sounds of it!' he shouted back.

'Oh, so you were up to your old tricks again then!'

'Yeah, well, can you blame me,' he said, looking her up and down, 'look at the state of you.'

Dawn was nearly in tears now and was determined to find out if Colin had in fact had anything to do with Tony's accident.

'So tell me exactly,' she demanded, 'what happened with that bloke this morning?' Suddenly it all became clear to Colin why she was so concerned about his whereabouts the previous morning.

'Oh, I get it!' he said, slamming his hand on the dining table. 'Lover boy was on his way home from giving you your fill and ended up in the back of my car!'

Tears began to run down Dawn's face as Colin stood grinning at her. Anger welled inside her that she should be made to feel shame after everything that Colin had put her through. He looked at her with an expression of triumphant self-righteousness, as if he was absolved from the guilt of his previous infidelities. He then walked back into the living room.

Dawn followed after him, then took a deep breath and announced, 'I don't want to be with you any more, I want a divorce.'

Colin forced a laugh of contempt and then replied, 'You're going to shack up with your boyfriend then, are you?'

'No,' said Dawn, 'I won't be seeing him any more, I'm done with men and I want you out.'

Colin let the information sink into his mind, and then said, 'Listen, you fat bitch, I'm not going anywhere and you needn't think you'll be taking the kids with you.'

Dawn began to shake, and her resolve was crumbling as Colin's contempt began to get the better off her.

'And another thing,' he said, jabbing his finger at her, 'I was with someone else this morning; knocking a fucking hole in her I was, and she fucking loved it.'

Dawn suddenly couldn't stand to hear any more and slapped Colin across the face.

'You fucking bitch,' he said, clutching his cheek. Colin had never hurt Dawn physically before, only psychologically; indulging in affairs, the putdowns about her looks and her weight. He pulled back his left arm and swung a punch into Dawn's face, sending her reeling onto the settee. Colin stood looking at her in a state of shock. She clutched her face, more in disbelief than feeling any pain. She composed herself and then stood up again.

Once Colin's shock had subdued, he suddenly felt a sense of power, almost sexual.

'Now get to bed, unless you want another one!' he said, feeling like he had the upper hand for the first time all day.

Dawn stood facing him, her hands shaking. She looked at him and all the disdain she had harboured for him began to boil over in her mind. He looked her up and down scornfully. He had made her feel worthless for so long and suddenly something snapped inside her. She put her hands on his shoulders as if she was about to beg forgiveness. She looked him squarely in the eyes and threw her head back and then butted him; her forehead hitting him hard in his nose. He staggered backwards, legs apart, in a reverse John Wayne pose. As he staggered back, Dawn kicked him hard between the legs. He let out a high-pitched cry as he sank down to the ground, clutching his testicles. He then retched and vomited on the carpet. Dawn grabbed him by the hair and dragged him on all fours to the front door. She opened the door and shoved him outside like a dog.

Dawn marched up the stairs and went into her bedroom. She took the suitcase from the top of the wardrobe. They had shared that big blue suitcase since they had bought it for their honeymoon.

She remembered, fondly, the week they had spent in Malta. It had been the first and the last time Dawn or Colin had ever been abroad. She remembered the clear blue sea and the endless sunshine. She remembered being able to wear a bathing costume without feeling self-conscious. Colin had made her feel like she was the only woman alive, or so it seemed. She still had the agility to wrap her legs around his waist back then.

She threw the suitcase on the bed and began opening drawers and pulling out Colin's socks and pants. As she threw them into the suitcase, she realised that she would no longer have to wash his filthy underwear; the semen stains and God knows what else that he had brought back from his whoring sessions. She opened the wardrobe and pulled out his shirts and trousers. She crammed them into the suitcase and fastened it. He would need to learn how to iron his own clothes for when he started playing the field again.

She pulled the case down the stairs, trying not to wake the children. She opened the front door and threw the case outside. She could hear Colin blubbing beside the door. She shut the door and leaned against it, taking a deep breath and closing her eyes. For a few moments, she began to pity her husband. He was a pathetic character really, she concluded; so desperately insecure that he constantly needed to prove his virility. He didn't have the intelligence to express himself in any other way.

Before she had the chance to change her mind, she heard the sound of a car starting. She looked through the curtains and saw Colin drive away. It was too late to turn back now. She switched the TV back on and poured herself a glass of wine. Led Zeppelin were on the stage in Philadelphia, with the ubiquitous Phil Collins in place of John Bonham.

★ ★ ★ ★ ★

The Nottingham central police station was situated on Shakespeare Street. Standing outside the station, taking some fresh air, Norman was taking in the Gothic splendour of the Arkwright Building. He wasn't familiar with the city centre and thought that the university building was a cathedral. It was getting very late and Norman had been waiting for his friend Alex to be released. It was a warm night, and the city centre was still alive with the sights and sounds of Saturday night carousers.

He had partly gone outside because the station was growing lively with drunks and prostitutes. A prostitute had seated herself next to Norman and complained endlessly about how one of her fillings had come out. He wasn't sure whether she thought she might be at the dentists. An Australian cricket fan had been brought in after a pub brawl. The Australian, draped in his nation's flag, got himself into further trouble when he unzipped his flies and began to urinate against the counter. He was so completely drunk as to believe that he was still in the gents lavatory of the last pub he had visited.

Norman had tried to plead with the duty sergeant about the state of Alex's mental health, but his pleas had fallen on deaf ears. After nine hours, Norman finally managed to speak to the duty sergeant who had the misfortune of overseeing the Saturday night shift; overwhelmed with drunken cricket fans and prostitutes with toothache, the duty sergeant finally decided to release Alex, after administering him with a caution. Fortunately for Alex, this police officer had seen it all, but reminded him that a man of his age should know better.

It had been lucky for Alex that Norman had managed to retrieve his clothes, which a steward had found at the back of the Parr Stand. He faced the ignominy of being treated as though he were partly responsible for the streaking; an act which the steward found utterly disgusting.

During the interminable waiting, Norman had had plenty of time to doze off and imbibe numerous cups of coffee. As they began the drive back to Mansfield, he felt that he was at least refreshed and sober enough for the journey. Alex sat in silence, utterly broken and filled with shame for his earlier display. Norman couldn't help feeling that the whole debacle had been his fault. In hindsight, he realised that he should have let Alex get things off his chest and then get some rest. Instead, he had dragged him to a test match and plied him with alcohol. Norman knew that the problem was due to the fact that he didn't know how to deal with another man's emotions, and he had simply tried to evade the serious matter of Alex's fragile mental state.

Dean had clearly not enjoyed the test match, and had been forced to witness the embarrassing antics of a man who was practically an uncle to him. Norman realised that he had made another grand gesture to try to paper over cracks in his fractured relationship with his son. Maybe if the two of them had gone to the football together, like old times, they might have been able to talk and even drink a pint or two.

It wasn't long before Alex fell asleep and Norman was happy to let his friend rest. Apart from anything, he was finding it hard to think of anything to say. He wondered whether he should stay with Alex till the morning, fearing he might attempt to take his own life again. Norman had never once spent a night apart from Ann and he was already in the doghouse.

'What did you mean about holding something over Mick Cooper?' asked Alex.

Norman was surprised by the sudden question, unaware that his friend was awake. He didn't answer immediately, but then decided that it probably wouldn't make any difference if he told him.

'Don't say anything to him, because he won't have any reason to stay quiet about his car,' said Norman confidentially.

'Fair enough,' said Alex, 'I'm listening.'

Norman took a deep breath and began: 'You know Mick's got a son, don't you?'

Alex had to think a moment and then said, 'Yeah, Mark, he's in the marines or something; Mick's always bragging about how well he's doing.'

'Yeah, that's right. Well, before he went into the marines, he used to come round and see a lot of our Ian. Anyway, one day they were up in Ian's bedroom and after about an hour it had gone really quiet. Well, I was planning on wallpapering Ian's room and I wanted to do some measurements to see how many rolls I would need. It had been quiet up there for so long that I thought they had gone out. Anyway, I went in there with this tape measure in my hand and they were both lying next to each other on the bed, wanking each other off.'

Alex suddenly burst into uncontrollable laughter.

'It's not fucking funny!' said Norman angrily.

'I'm sorry!' said Alex, wiping tears from his eyes. 'I just can't get over you walking in there with a tape measure and them two lying there with their cocks out.'

Norman shook his head and had to stifle a laugh. 'Yeah, well, I dragged Mark back to Mick's house and told him what I'd seen. He tried to defend Mark and said they must have just been messing about. I didn't speak to him for a few months after that, and then all of a sudden he starts being all pally-pally with me. Obviously he had found out the truth about Mark and he wanted me to keep it a secret about what I'd seen. By this time, Ian had left home and rumours were going round about him being queer. Mark had just joined the marines and Mick knew that he would get a dishonourable discharge if it was made known that he was gay.'

'You should have said something,' said Alex, with a sour expression, 'wipe the smile off that smug bastard's face.'

'I was trying to keep it quiet about Ian at the time. I was more worried about people at work taking the piss out of me. It's common knowledge now, so only Mick and his son have anything to lose.'

When they arrived at Alex's house, they noticed Maggie's car outside and the living room light switched on. Norman was quite relieved that someone was waiting at home for Alex. He decided that it would be best if he left the two of them to talk about whatever it was they needed to talk about. Alex tried to persuade him to stay a while, but Norman was anxious to get home. Ann would have been expecting him home since early evening and would be beside herself with worry.

Alex hoped that Maggie hadn't brought Mick with her. He could only imagine that the reason for her visit would be to sound him out about Mick's car. He was relieved once he had entered the house, to find that she was alone. Maggie had an anxious expression on her face that transported Alex back to the time when they had heard the news about Kevin's death.

'Where've you been!' she shouted, more with concern than anger. 'First, I hear that you've smashed into Mick's car; and then he told me this afternoon that he'd spotted you on TV, streaking.'

Alex sat down and put his hands over his face. He began sobbing; everything had unravelled throughout the day and he could no longer seem to control his emotions.

He hadn't expected sympathy, and was surprised when Maggie sat next to him and put her arm around him.

'I came around here because I was worried about you. We've both been through a lot these past few years and we both shut each other out. I thought I could move on with someone else, and you've bottled everything up and got yourself into a proper mess.'

Alex took a few deep breaths, trying to control the panic that was taking control of him.

'That's it, take a few deep breaths, because you're going to need to be strong,' said Maggie, finding a clean tissue in her bag and handing it to him.

'What do you mean?' Alex said, beginning to panic again. 'It's John, isn't it? No, please, not John as well.'

Maggie put her arm round him again, shushing him like a child. 'He's going to be alright, his mate Spike rang just now and said he's been in some kind of accident.'

'What sort of accident?' said Alex anxiously.

'He's injured his leg in some kind of collision with a car, but it doesn't sound serious.'

Alex felt a sudden wave of relief pass through him, and for the first time that day he began to clear his mind and take control of himself.

'Come on,' said Maggie, 'our son needs us.'

CHAPTER TWENTY-THREE

Norman drove back through the deserted streets of the village. He was finally succumbing to the emotional and physical exhaustion of a turbulent day. He remembered driving through the same streets, the previous morning. He could have earned some easy money and kept the peace with Ann. He could have dozed off in the afternoon, accompanied by the reassuring sounds of the test match.

As he pulled into the drive, he noticed that the living room curtains were still open. Ann would never go to bed without closing the curtains, so he assumed that she must have gone to bed early after her drinking binge. He was beginning to wish that he had stayed with Alex. The last thing he needed at that stage was an argument.

He tried to unlock and open the front door as quietly as possible. If Ann didn't wake up, then there was the chance that things might be easier in the morning, with the distraction of the Sunday newspapers. He surreptitiously opened the living room door and peaked in. Ann wasn't asleep on the settee, so he consoled himself that she had at least found her way to bed.

He sat down in the living room for a few minutes, listening for any signs that Ann was still awake. He wondered if he might be better off sleeping on the settee, but concluded that Ann would misinterpret this as an act of defiance. He finally plucked up the courage to go to bed, too tired for any more nonsense. If Ann wanted to cross-examine him about his whereabouts till the early hours, she could do so in the morning.

He got up and marched defiantly up the stairs, like Sydney Carton going to the guillotine. As he looked up the stairs, he noticed that the bathroom light was switched on. He stopped midway up the stairs and listened for the sound of Ann moving around in the bathroom. After a few moments he concluded that she must have accidentally left the light on.

Once at the top of the stairs, he could see his and Ann's bedroom door open. He walked in and saw that the curtains were still open, but the bedclothes were unmade. He turned round and went to the bathroom door and knocked.

'Ann, are you alright?'

No reply came, so he opened the door. He was so utterly horrified by what he saw that he fell down on his knees in shock. Before him in the bath, lay his wife. Her left arm hung limply over the edge of the bath. On the floor lay his carpet knife. He took her hand in his and he saw a deep vertical incision on her wrist. He got up and held her face and began calling her name. He began slapping her cheeks, but she just stared lifelessly back at him. She had draped a blanket over the bath in an attempt to protect her modesty. With the cover over her, she looked like Jaques-Louis David's painting, *The Death of Marat*. Norman finally pulled up the blanket to reveal the blood-drenched bath. He suddenly felt overwhelmingly ill, and quickly moved over to the sink and was violently sick. His hands were shaking and his mind couldn't process what he was seeing.

After a few moments, he realised that there might be a faint hope that Ann was still alive. He ran downstairs and out through the front door. He ran across the lawn and leapt over the fence into the next garden. His neighbour, Mrs McGinney, had a telephone and had always allowed him to use it in emergencies. He began banging on her front door. He grew impatient as he waited and continued banging on the door. The elderly Mrs McGinney took some time to put on her dressing gown and come downstairs, but eventually Norman saw the landing light come on. He could see her shuffle towards the door through the frosted glass in the front door. She opened the door and he began rambling apologies and explanations. Mrs McGinney told him to calm down, and picked up the phone herself and rang the emergency services number. As soon as a voice answered, she handed the phone to Norman who began stuttering the situation.

While he waited for the ambulance, Mrs McGinney came with him and made him a cup of tea. He sat in the kitchen, his mind a whirlwind of confusion and shock. The reality of the situation began to sink in as he sat waiting for the ambulance. When the ambulance finally arrived, he was informed that his wife was dead. Rigor mortis had set in her body, which meant that Ann could have taken her life any time in the preceding six hours.

Mrs McGinney tried her best to comfort him in his inconsolable grief. He was not normally prone to such displays of emotion, but found a cathartic release from his tears, which left him feeling strangely calm. He began to ruminate on whether he could have done something to help Ann. He knew she had always been susceptible to depression and anxiety. She spent most of her life alone when he or the kids were not present. He thought that if only he had gone to work that morning, things wouldn't have turned out this way. He thought about how he had driven Ian away. He hadn't considered how his bigoted bullying had affected Ann, who made no secret of her special fondness for her eldest boy. She had always been proud of his artistic talent, which Norman had always displayed ambivalence towards.

He wondered when Dean was going to come home. He began to grow irritated by his son's absence and his old prejudices began to return. If Ian hadn't started messing around with other men, things would have been alright. Norman began to blame Ian and his selfish self-indulgence for the destruction of Ann. She had always had a special relationship with her eldest son, and Norman concluded that it must have been the revelation that he was gay that tipped her over the edge.

Norman walked over to the mirror on the wall and looked at himself. He remembered when Ann had decided to take a job as a sewing machinist at the Meritina factory. He had practically laughed in her face when she mentioned the job. He remembered telling her she wouldn't last five minutes with the other factory women and would soon come home crying. Ann never brought up the subject again after that. He wondered whether he should have encouraged her, though he was sure she would have found it hard. He looked at the face in the mirror and realised that it was he who had failed Ann. He felt like butting his head against the mirror, but turned away and sank to his knees and began to cry once again.

He curled up on the floor and lay there for a while, and a soothing calmness eventually enveloped him. He got up and decided to go to the kitchen and make a cup of tea. As he filled the kettle, the memory of filling Alex's kettle the previous morning popped into his head. The events of the whole day suddenly unfolded in his mind. The entire day seemed like a strange dream: Alex streaking across Trent Bridge, and then Ann... He tried to remove the image of his wife lying dead in the bath. It suddenly occurred to him that he would have to contact Ian. He began to wonder how he would get in touch, not having a phone number or address to contact. He was sure that Dean would know how to get in touch with his brother. He had remained loyal to Ian after discovering that he was gay and had been very supportive. Norman then realised that it was Dean who had been the man in the family, when he himself had behaved like an immature bigot.

He heard the sound of a car outside and walked through the hallway and opened the front door to see if Dean had finally come home. Norman was relieved to see his youngest son walking down the drive. He needed Dean to be strong for him now, like he had never done before.

* * * * *

Sarah and I danced together to 'See the Day' by Dee C. Lee. It was the first time that I had ever had a partner to join me in the slow, romantic dancing that ended each evening in the Sherwood Rooms. The bittersweet lyrics and melody seemed to foreshadow heartbreak rather than the joy of a new relationship. While others on the dance floor groped their partner's buttocks, I held Sarah chastely round the waist. We gazed at each other, smiling like a newly married couple during their first dance. We finally kissed each other's mouths; eager tongues barging into each other's mouths with the haste that is characteristic of all inexperienced lovers. I closed my eyes as we kissed and when I opened them to gaze at her, her eyes were staring right back at me.

It was an uncharacteristically peaceful end to the evening's entertainment at the Sherwood Rooms. The rambunctiousness of the Spireite lads had been replaced with amorousness; they had all been seduced by the charms of the local beauties of Mansfield. Outside, the car park wasn't being employed as a battlefield, but an ambulance had arrived as we walked out onto Market Street.

Neither of us wanted the night to end yet, so we decided to go for a walk down to Titchfield Park. The sultry heat of the day had been replaced with a more agreeable warmth. We walked past the viaduct and along Victoria Street to where the park was situated nearby. We both knew that the park would probably be deserted, and an unspoken anticipation of undisturbed intimacy began to make us tremble with excitement. As we walked through the deserted subway that ran under the ring road, we gave each other a knowing look and then grabbed each other and tried kissing once again.

We hurried on towards the park, our hearts racing. We could feel each other's hands trembling. The park was deserted as we entered, passing the tennis courts and bowling green. We walked with the river on one side and the flower beds on the other, to where a little bridge crossed over to a playground.

Sarah sat on a swing and I gently pushed her.

'I remember my grandma pushing me on the swings when I was little,' said Sarah, nostalgically. 'I used to say "Push Nana, push!"'

I kissed her head adoringly. 'I always liked the bobby's helmet best.'

'Did you ever go in the paddling pool on the Carrs?'

'Oh yeah,' I said, recalling a distant memory, 'I remember when I was a little boy, I fell over into it.'

Sarah got up off the swing with an exaggerated look of sympathy and sadness. She hugged me and kissed me on the forehead. We then gazed into each other's eyes and then kissed again with renewed passion.

I took her by the hand and led her to a large concrete pipe on the edge of the playground. Once we were huddled together inside, we began to kiss with more urgency. Our passion was quickly extinguished when we heard someone sing, 'We know what you're doing'. A group of people who were heading home towards Nottingham Road had spotted us. Both of us felt too embarrassed and self-conscious to continue, so we decided to walk back into the town centre.

We sat on an empty stall in the marketplace and talked for a while. I looked at the clock and saw that it was already half past one. The previous couple of hours had gone so quickly; this time that I didn't want to end was slipping away like sand in a faulty hourglass. Surely time moved at different speeds; at work, the hours could drag like purgatory, yet moments like these seemed to pass in an instant.

'I was thinking of going to see *Back to the Future*,' said Sarah, 'don't suppose you fancy going to see it as well.'

My heart danced for joy at hearing these words. I was being asked out a second time.

'Yeah, why not,' I said, trying not to sound too eager. 'I'm not doing anything tomorrow, if that's convenient for you.'

'You mean today?' she said, smiling and glancing at her wristwatch.

'Okay then, would you like to go to the cinema, later on today, Sunday the fourteenth of July, the year of our Lord, nineteen hundred and eighty-five.'

'Yes,' she said, bowing her head gracefully, 'that would be most agreeable, and would you like to meet me at the Hare and Hounds at twelve noon, to partake of refreshment before catching the bus.'

'Aye, methinks this would suit me passing well.'

We walked up Regent Street to the taxi rank. I was relieved to see several taxis parked at the deserted taxi rank. There were often huge queues of rowdy drunks waiting for taxis home. We got into the back of the first of the taxis, greeted by a cheerful driver. He was a tall, dark-haired and thickset man, wearing a pair of spectacles with big black frames; his teeth protruded from his mouth and his overall appearance reminded me of Bingo from the *Banana Splits*. He kept looking at us through his rear-view mirror, first asking us were we had been and then asking if we'd been watching the Live Aid concert.

'I don't normally rate Queen, but they knocked the rest into a cocked hat,' he said excitedly. 'I reckon they ought to give that Bob Geldof a knighthood for getting all that lot together.'

'I agree entirely,' agreed Sarah.

'I'd like to have seen Tip Topley doing his stuff, though,' I said, omitting that I had spent the afternoon with him. I hadn't even told Sarah about our day with the illustrious rock star; I didn't want her to think I was a complete fantasist.

'Now you're talking!' said the driver, pricking up his ears at the very mention of the name. 'I don't care what they say about him, he would have played a blinder if he'd been there.'

We had been riding along to the soothing late-night sounds of Radio 2. Herb Alpert began to sing 'This Guy's in Love with You' and Sarah and I gazed at each other. The driver continued to talk, oblivious to our billing and cooing. The two o'clock news followed Herb Alpert and the driver turned up the radio to listen. Initial reports claimed that the Live Aid concerts had so far raised an estimated £50 million. Sectarian-related executions had taken place in Kilburn, North London. A man had tried to abduct a girl at the concert at Wembley Stadium. Items had been found in his car which linked him to the murder of a young woman, whose body had been recently discovered on the South Downs.

'The usual cheerful stuff, eh,' said the driver, switching off the radio. 'It makes you glad you live a quiet, boring life in Mansfield.'

He pushed a cassette into the tape player and the unmistakable guitar introduction to 'Everybody Wants to Rule the World' by Tears For Fears began to play. The notes of the opening arpeggio sequence fell like raindrops, soon to be replaced by the sunny rhythm of the song.

As I once again passed the golf club, I was reminded that I would be soon passing in the opposite direction again. Just like Sisyphus, eternally condemned to roll his huge boulder up a hill, only to start again once he had got to the top. Zeus had conceived this punishment for Sisyphus, and I wondered what I and countless others had done to deserve a similar fate.

My boulder would already be slowly rolling down the hill and be waiting outside my front door on Monday. Another would be waiting for Dad to break himself against. From the moment my mother awoke, hers would be rattling around her head. She would whittle away the day, pushing it up the endless Escher stairways of her mind.

I had been provided with a sweet interlude from my labours, in the form of Sarah. I held her close to me and she nestled her head against my chest. She had a serene smile on her face, but she was clearly fighting to stay awake. She was still unused to keeping such hours, for pleasure or work. I sincerely hoped she would never be forced to experience soul-destroying night shifts as I had done after leaving school. She had worked hard at school, and would continue until she had completed her A levels. She would then go to university, where she would have the space and freedom to develop her mind. Her parents probably understood the benefits of a good education and the value of nurturing talents in their daughter. I always remembered her at school, lugging a cello around in its big black case. I regretted missing out on the opportunity to learn an instrument at school. When I had recently obtained a cheap Chinese electric guitar, Dad had taken one look at it and said, 'It's a pity you can't learn to play it.'

As we approached Warsop, I became aware that it was almost time for Sarah and I to part. I reminded her of our arrangement to meet at lunchtime, afraid that she might already have changed her mind. She kissed me gently on the lips and assured me that she would be waiting for me. We dropped her off outside a detached dormer bungalow, not far from the school. We bid farewell, blowing kisses to each other as Sarah stood on her drive, watching the taxi drive away.

The taxi continued down the country lane where I used to walk home from school. A little wood stood on one side, hiding the river. Open fields and a railway track that transported coal were on the opposite side. I passed the little farm with ducks in its garden and over the bridge that crossed the river.

I began to wonder if Dad had arrived home, and whether Alex had been free to join him. Thinking back, the cricket hadn't been so bad after all. There was something romantic about Trent Bridge that made me want to return again one day. Dad had tried to repair bridges with me and repair whatever psychological damage was ailing Alex. He needed to come to terms with Ian's sexuality before he lost his eldest son altogether.

In hindsight, he hadn't done a bad job at raising us. Maybe he had tried too hard to toughen us up instead of accepting us as we were. I couldn't agree with Larkin's verse, which pointed the finger at parents for being responsible for their children's failures in life. We can all fuck ourselves up without any help from our mums and dads. Freud took the argument even further, by saying that our adult lives are shaped when we are learning to use a potty or by how our mothers respond when we need the nourishment of their breasts.

It was all quiet on the summit of the pit tip. No moon buggies patrolled the lunar landscape. No lunatics howled at the moon from its peaks. Only poachers and perverts would be creeping about the ducal estates that surrounded the village. A few lights were still on as the taxi made its way around Egmanton Road. Some of them might even have stayed awake to watch the final hour of the global jukebox. As we approached my house, I observed that one of those lights was shining in our living room. I would have been surprised to find either Mum or Dad staying awake to see the finale of the Philadelphia show. I realised that Dad must have only just got Alex back from the police station.

I walked down the drive, enjoying the early morning fragrance. My head was spinning from the euphoria that accompanies the meeting of a new sweetheart. I knew that I would fall head over heels in love and would most probably end up with a broken heart. Nothing could take away the memories I would treasure of such a special day. I don't think I had ever felt so happy as I did at that moment.